CRISIS DELUXE

CRISIS
DELUXE

CHRIS COFFMAN

ODYSSEUS PRESS

Published by
Odysseus Press
Springtown, Pennsylvania

Crisis Deluxe
Copyright 2021 Christopher Coffman

ISBN: 978-1-7367391-0-5

To contact the author, email to: OdysseusPress@protonmail.com
Cover design: by Virtually Possible Design
Book design Russel Davis, Gray Dog Press

Printed in the United States of America

Publisher's Cataloging-in-Publication data

Names: Coffman, Christopher W., author. | Knight, Eric S., audiobook narrator.
Title: Crisis deluxe / Chris Coffman ; audiobook narrated by Eric Knight.
Description: Springtown, PA: Odysseus Press, 2021.
Identifiers: LCCN: 2021906517 | ISBN: 978-1-7367391-0-5 (paperback) | 978-1-7367391-2-9 (paperback) | 978-1-7367391-1-2 (Kindle) | 978-1-7367391-3-6 (audio)
Subjects: LCSH Financial crises--Fiction. | Bankers–Fiction. | Banks and banking, International–Fiction. | Family–Fiction. | Hong Kong (China)–Fiction. | Thrillers (Fiction) | Love stories. | BISAC FICTION / Thrillers / General | FICTION / Romance / Suspense
Classification: LCC PS3603.O44 C75 2021 | DDC 813.6--dc23

AUTHOR'S NOTE
Crisis Deluxe is a work of fiction. The characters, conversations, and events in the novel are the products of my imagination, and with the exception of the person on whom the character Jacqueline is modeled, and only in a general way as she is depicted in this story as an adolescent, no resemblance to the actual conduct of real-life persons, or to actual events, is intended.

Although, for the sake of verisimilitude, the characters participate in situations that may be analogous to situations in which public figures may have been involved, I have imagined those situations without the knowledge or cooperation of any public figure or living person; all the interactions between my characters are completely invented and are wholly my creation.

No aspect of this novel is intended to be understood as a description of real events or to reflect negatively upon any public figures or persons living or dead, or to suggest anybody in real life has ever acted in any way as depicted in this story.

"For the past, thanks;
To the future—Yes."

Dag Hammarskjöld, *Markings*

CRISIS
DELUXE

Chapter One

The call came through as I was finishing my first cup of coffee on a hot morning at the beginning of January over twenty years ago. I could already feel the heat coming through the big windows of my hotel room and see the glare shining around the buildings to the east as the sun rose over the great gulf of the Río de la Plata. It was not yet six thirty in the morning.

I assumed the call—an inconsiderate, too early call—was from London or from one of our offices in Europe where it was early afternoon. Anyone could have called my mobile phone, not necessarily realizing where in the world I was, but not that many people had the number of my hotel.

But it was the voice of Jim Walmsley on the phone, calling from New York. That surprised me because it was just before four thirty in the morning for him.

"Hi, Jim. What can I do for you?" I said.

"You can get on the next plane to Hong Kong," he said. "We'll talk about what else you can do when you get there and tell me what you see."

I sighed. "What's up?"

"Things are starting to go badly, very badly, in the Asian markets."

I had just finished the merger of two companies into what was now the largest petroleum company in Latin America not owned by a government. I had flown the eleven hours from Buenos Aires to New York in order to spend two days with my family over Christmas, and then flown back to finish up the deal.

"Yeah, I know," I said. "I've been watching the markets get choppier over the last few days as I brought the Petróleos Argentinos deal in for a landing. I don't know why emerging markets traders in New York and London always start dumping Argentine stocks and bonds whenever there's a whisper of trouble anywhere in the world. Pisses me off."

"Put that deal behind you, Dusty, we've got much bigger problems to worry about," said Walmsley.

I was staring at the oily film collecting on the surface of my cup of coffee as it started to go cold in my hand. Lovely swirling greens, blues and reds against the black. "I know you wouldn't be calling me at four thirty in the morning if this wasn't important, but—"

"Look, Dusty," he interrupted. "I know what I'm asking. The markets have just closed in Hong Kong."

"Down another ten percent?" I asked.

"Ten percent, my ass. The bottom fell out. I need you there now."

"What is this all about—the Transco deal, whatever it's called—is that it?" I set the cup of coffee on the nightstand and lay back on my bed, my head propped on the pillows. Our firm had been negotiating for almost a year to acquire a big investment bank based in Hong Kong as part of a strategic expansion into the Asian markets. At that moment, I just couldn't remember the name of the firm.

"TransPac. Yeah, we've got big trouble with the TransPac deal," Walmsley said. "But that's not half of it. The market has been expecting us to close on that deal for the last two months."

"I thought everything was agreed," I said. "At the weekly partners' video conference before Christmas you said you were expecting financial close any day."

"I was," said Walmsley. "All we had to do was sign."

"So cut the price by twenty-five percent and sign," I said. "In these markets, there's nothing they can do about it."

"The situation's worse than that."

"Okay, cut the price in half. Cram it down their throats. Look, Jim, I've been working for six months straight on this Petróleos deal. I've seen my wife and kids for a total of ten days, including Christmas, since June. I feel like I've been rode hard and put away wet. I just can't—"

"Dusty, I've just spent an hour on the phone with our guys in Hong Kong," Walmsley said. "The losses of the last few weeks are turning into an avalanche, and it's spreading across Asia and starting to infect the European and US markets. Panic is setting in. Traders have been looking to the TransPac deal as a sign smart money is still willing to invest in Asia. We're heading toward the biggest market crash in a generation out there. If we cut TransPac loose, traders are going to sell everything they can get their hands on—stocks, bonds, currency. It might cause a total collapse in places like Indonesia, the Philippines, and Korea. You've got to figure out whether or not we can salvage the deal."

"Right."

"What have you got left to do in Buenos Aires?"

A gala banquet had been scheduled for that evening to sign the closing documents and celebrate the successful completion of the merger: the Ministers of Resources, Mining and Petroleum were going to attend, along with the boards of directors and chief executive officers of both companies. Bottles of champagne, whiskey, and French and Argentine wines worth thousands of dollars each were going to be served. Mountains of caviar, prawns, and aged Argentine steaks would be offered. The usual fountain pens made in France and Germany would be handed out, engraved with the date and the name of the new company, Petróleos Argentinos.

"Nothing," I said. "Peter and Ricky can cover for me."

"Tell me which way you're headed and I'll arrange to get you all the data at one of your layovers," he said.

I called the concierge and asked him to check out the flight options while I took a shower, shaved, dressed, and packed.

There turned out to be little difference between Miami-San Francisco-Hong Kong, Santiago de Chile-Auckland-Hong Kong, or London-Hong Kong, but I thought I might as well relax and get some sleep. I chose to fly into the night.

The flight for London was leaving in a couple of hours. By the time I was packed and ready to leave for the airport, it was a decent time in

New York and I could call my wife, Samantha, and explain that I wasn't coming home the next day as expected.

I'd been dreading having to make the call ever since I got off the phone with Walmsley. It had been a terrible year for my family and me. I had missed my daughter Stephanie's entire basketball season, and the second half of my son Timothy's Little League season, including the championship in which he had pitched. He told me on the phone that if I had been there in the bleachers watching him, he could have hung in there through the bottom of the ninth inning when his team was up by only one run. Everyone wants to shift the blame for a loss onto somebody else, anybody else, but I believed Timmy. I had let him down.

Going to Hong Kong would mean missing the rest of Christmas vacation with the kids. Samantha had already rescheduled the two-week skiing vacation in Wyoming we had planned to a one-week skiing vacation in Vermont, but that was going to go out the window too. Unless she took the kids herself and they went up without me. Samantha had already warned me that the kids' grades were starting to suffer.

When I told her, she was silent on the other end, not making it easy.

"Darling, if I had a choice, I wouldn't be doing this," I said.

"How much longer *are* you going to do this?" she asked.

"I'll be thinking about it all the way to Hong Kong."

"The kids and I can't stand another year of this."

"Do you want to put Steffie and Timmy on the phone?" I said. "I can try and explain."

"That will make it worse."

I was feeling defeated as I dropped my suit bag into the boot of the big black car that had come to take me to the airport. The driver executed a quick U-turn as we pulled away from the hotel, taking a right a block from the hotel and gliding down the hill past the high walls of La Recoleta cemetery, the district of the dead that gave its name to the most fashionable area in Buenos Aires. The Argentines joke that the walls of La Recoleta are the most irrelevant in the world—those who are outside don't want to get in, and those who are inside can't get out.

La Recoleta is a busy district of Buenos Aires for its tombs are tended carefully by the families who own them. They come by the scores during the week, and by the hundreds on the weekends. The elegant crowds have a content air as they make their way to change the flowers at their family tomb, polish the brass door handles or plaques, or perhaps to tip the keepers.

Parents with their children walk thoughtfully down the raked gravel paths, under the clipped and expertly pruned foliage, reading and re-reading the inscriptions of prominent departed Porteños, calibrating their achievements against those of their own ancestors. Elderly widows make their way to pay respect at the lasting resting place of their husbands and family members, the stately tomb shining in the sun as it awaits them.

The deluxe ambience of La Recoleta has little in common with the tumble-down sepulchres, weed-overgrown paths, and melancholy air of the Parisian necropolis Père Lachaise. Buenos Aires has always aspired to be Paris, but Père Lachaise ought to emulate La Recoleta.

The car drove me through the vast parklands along the banks of the Río del la Plata on the way to their airport, and as I idly watched the morning joggers and the soccer players darting under the huge fig trees, I thought about Samantha and the children.

Samantha was an Australian, and even after ten years she had not gotten used to the cold and darkness of winter in the northern hemi-sphere. She and the children might want me to be home with them, but the big five-bedroom house in Scarsdale didn't come cheap.

I had grown up in enough locations in the world where you can't drink the water and can hardly breathe the air to appreciate what America, and specifically what Westchester County, could offer, but I was spending most of my time back in those kinds of places, while my family was experiencing everything I had ever wanted as a child.

A couple of years ago, I might have asked Sam whether she wanted me to quit my job and spend more time with her and the kids. I knew what the answer would be. But there had been more dark winters since then, and another two years of raising the children almost single-handedly.

Now I was afraid to ask her because I was beginning to suspect that the answer might be different, and I wasn't ready to accept it.

I went through passport control at Ezeiza, handing my chunky passport with the two inserts of additional pages to the clerk in the booth. When I first came to New York, I was told not to trust a man with a tan: a tan meant that he was either lazy and took too much vacation, or that he was vain and went to tanning salons. Somebody else told me, about the same time, that if a man had a single digit golf handicap, he was playing too much golf. Nobody had warned me not to let my passport collect too many visas.

Waiting for me at the airport in London were two big envelopes of information and several disks that contained the financial valuation model and other data. The material was a detailed description and analysis of the proposed acquisition of the Asian investment bank. I was tired after the flight from Buenos Aires, and I still had fourteen hours of flying ahead. I was tempted to call Walmsley from Heathrow and tell him that the deal just looked too hard. He wouldn't have liked to hear that, but there wasn't that much he could have done about it. I could then fly back to my family in New York. But I didn't.

After the plane lifted off for Hong Kong, I waved away the wine that was being offered in the first-class cabin and loaded the TransPac disks onto my laptop. The model glowed eerily onto the screen, a virtual, miniature version of a huge investment bank that employed thousands of people and was capable of influencing the prices of currencies and other financial instruments across Asia.

A financial model is based upon thousands of detailed, highly accurate pieces of information. An investment banking team collects this information, breaks it down into numerical values, and then loads them into a model that is specifically designed to replicate the company. The financial model has the same relationship to a real company that those CAD-CAM programs that represent objects in webs of fine lines have to a human body. Another way of thinking about what a financial model represents is to think of what you can learn about a city by looking at it in the distance from a great height. You don't see the humans who built the city and who live there, but you can see how and where they live. A financial model can also tell you about the city's transportation systems and its power and water systems, about the population density, and the occupational and demographic segments of the city's population. It can tell you a great deal, but it can't tell you everything.

The purpose of a financial model is to act as a guide to the future, to help an acquiring company predict how profitable its acquisition will be in the years ahead. A model is often used to project twenty years into the future. It's a lousy tool for that purpose, but it's the best one that anyone has invented so far.

When I landed in Hong Kong, I made my way right to the Peninsula where I showered and changed clothes. I'm not a good traveler and have to be very careful about negotiating when I've just gotten off a plane. On the surface, the TransPac acquisition looked like a good deal. During the final hours of the flight from London, however, I decided that I was just too exhausted to completely turn around a situation that had been irretrievably caught in crashing markets. If the people working on it before I arrived had completely screwed it up, I didn't have anything left with which to put Humpty Dumpty back together again. I was also going to make damn sure the TransPac guys didn't stick me with the blame for the deal falling apart. I had been in bad situations before, and I had seen guys go feral: punching out their own advisors and colleagues. And I had seen guys get hysterical: breaking down and weeping uncontrollably.

I was just too tired to put up with that shit this time. If just one of the bastards running the target company crossed me in the slightest way, I would call Walmsley and tell him to kill the deal, and then go home.

In the car on the way to the offices of TransPac, I was too numb to look out the windows for any sign of change since the handover to China.

"I'm here to see Mr. Entrekin," I said at the sumptuous reception desk.

"Yes, sir," said the beautiful receptionist. "And your name, please?"

"Street, Alexander Street, from Coldstream Holdings, New York."

Simon Entrekin came from around his desk to greet me as I was ushered into his office. "Mr. Street," he said. "What a pleasure to meet you. James said you would be coming to help us establish our partnership. He said you were an expert at completing transactions in difficult markets. I'm sure you won't find Hong Kong particularly strains your talents."

"You're very kind," I said. "But of course one never knows."

I wasted a couple of hours with Entrekin as he described how he had built TransPac into the first major Asian investment bank capable of competing with US investment banks and English merchant banks. Entrekin's management were principally Brits who had reached the status of Old Asia Hands, which meant they had lived on this side of the Pacific all their adult lives, and no longer had anywhere else to go home to.

"I thought we might have lunch at my club," Entrekin said. "I've arranged for a private room and invited along key members of our senior management, whom I expect you'll be seeing much more of in the future."

Five old guys were ushered in and introduced.

Landing in Hong Kong had put some reality around the TransPac deal. What Walmsley had told me about the threat to the financial markets and the stability of Asian economies if the TransPac deal fell apart had only crushed me with a sense of the enormous task ahead of me; it hadn't whet my appetite for the deal. It just made me feel more bone-tired and demoralized about what was happening in my family, and if they couldn't find some other guy, it would have been easy for me to kill the deal from Buenos Aires or when I first reviewed the transaction documents at Heathrow.

But now that I was actually in Hong Kong, I could sense all the elements of a great deal: panic and fear in the markets producing irrationally low prices; a mediocre management team who had been on the right side of history accidentally, but could be gotten rid of as we implemented a plan to supercharge the value of TransPac; and a great franchise in a huge new market that would give us a head start by years on our competitors.

I already knew what the problems were. I was trained to screen out the consequences of failure: tight rope walkers don't think about how high the rope is or how many eyes are watching them; demolition experts don't think about how many kilotons of explosive are on the other side of the thin steel skin of the bomb they are defusing. The idea that the collapse of the TransPac deal might trigger a market rout that could end up causing misery to billions of people living in Asia was a factor I acknowledged and had then put at the back of my mind where it wouldn't affect my ability to do my job.

Now I was feeling a little hope: it was impossible to avoid the thought that TransPac just might be the right deal. Maybe even the best deal of my career.

Chapter Two

That was what I told myself, and that was the reason I went to lunch and wasted another three hours of consciousness even though Entrekin had not invited Sebastian Nin to the lunch. If I had been convinced I was going to pull the plug, I would have refused to go to lunch with Entrekin and his mates until he produced Nin. The valuation model and the notes on the negotiations all pointed to Nin and his bond-trading operation as the key to the value of TransPac.

After lunch we returned to Entrekin's office. Entrekin favored me with his charming, worldly smile. "Well, what do you think? How can we help you progress your analysis?"

We were alone.

"Simon," I said, "in one hour I am going to ring Jim Walmsley in New York to give him a briefing. If I don't speak to Sebastian Nin before that telephone call, I am going to recommend we immediately cease further work on this acquisition."

Sebastian Nin was slightly built, but muscular, and he moved with a guarded assertiveness that made me think of a demigod and a hoodlum at the same time. He wore his hair very short, and the taut skin, stretched across his high cheekbones, and the bags under his eyes gave conflicting impressions of vitality and decay.

"Alexander Street, I said. "Coldstream New York."

"Sebastian Nin," he said briefly.

We shook hands.

He spoke English with an American accent, but despite that familiar touch there was a sense of otherness about him that made me decide to proceed carefully. We sat down in a conference room rich with tropical hardwoods.

"So, you've just come out from New York?" he asked.

"Yes," I said. It was true enough.

He nodded and waited silently.

"We've almost got a deal here," I said.

Nin looked at me silently.

"I'm sure you've been heavily involved in putting this deal together, and it's right at the line, almost done," I said. "You feel good about that?"

Nin's mouth pulled down dismissively, and something behind his eyes almost made them sparkle. "It's the right deal. It should get done."

"Your operation is the single biggest generator of revenues and profits at TransPac," I began. "We wouldn't want to proceed with this transaction, even this late in the game, unless you were completely behind it. How do you feel about Coldstream as a prospective acquirer?"

"I strongly support the transaction; Simon knows that."

"Why?"

Nin was good. He leaned forward, and his posture and gestures remained under tight but inconspicuous control as he laid out the strategic benefits of the union. There are lots of kinds of bond salesmen. There are plenty of successful dumb ones, who speak the language of sports and ply their accounts with booze and whores. But there are some very smart salesmen, who know just enough about a host of topics to sound as if their minds range as widely as did Napoleon's.

"Sebastian," I said at last when he had finished, "I think this firm is gutshot and I need to find out quickly if it can be saved and, if so, how much it'll cost. Coldstream Holdings isn't going to let itself get sucked into a bottomless pit. If you think TransPac can be saved, you have to help me. Because otherwise I'm going to walk."

"Why should I help you?"

"You said you believed in the acquisition."

"That's not what I asked. I asked why I should help *you*."

"Because if you don't, your ass is going to be out on the street along with everybody else who works here."

He looked at me contemptuously. "If you think these markets have changed the value of TransPac to Coldstream Holdings or any other international financial player, you've just failed the stupid test. What's going on in the markets is all noise. To the extent my fellow TransPac partners are dumb bunnies, and most of them are, they can be pressured into selling out to Coldstream for less than they should because of what's happening in the markets right now. But that's it.

"Acquiring us would be the greatest deal of your career. Why should I hand it over to you when the same information will bring in another buyer?"

It sounded good. But as a simple matter of fact, what Nin had just said wasn't true. An investment bank's assets are the stocks and bonds and other trading positions it holds. TransPac was unfortunately not a Trans-Pacific investment bank, despite its name. Its assets originated exclusively on one side of the Pacific: Hong Kong, Indonesia, Malaysia, Thailand, the Philippines, and Korea. And those markets were down by fifty percent in the last three months. There was no way the value of TransPac itself could have stayed that much higher than the value of the assets it held.

"Point me to any value that's left in this place after yesterday's meltdown in the markets, and I will ensure that value is reflected in our offer. I give you my word," I said.

"Ha," he said.

"If you've got another acquirer in mind," I said slowly, "perhaps you should make the phone call, but explain to Simon why I went home. On my way out I'll tell him to ask you about it."

"Fine," he said.

I got up and walked toward the door. He sat tightly coiled at the table, watching me. At the door I turned.

"I've got a strange feeling you have something against me," I said, "and I can't imagine what it is. You don't even know me."

"I do, though," he said.

"From where?"

"Just to make absolutely sure," he said, and I could see his face redden and his voice trembled slightly, "did you by any chance ever used to call yourself 'Dusty?'"

"My friends still call me Dusty," I said.

"Ok, Dusty—not that I want to cause any confusion—you used to go out with my sister Jacqueline right here in Hong Kong twenty years ago."

I was too exhausted to stand any longer. I haltingly walked to the table and collapsed into a chair.

"Forgive me," I said. "I've been awake for over forty hours." I covered my eyes.

When I looked up Sebastian Nin was staring at me coldly, almost murderously.

"You're Jacqueline's little brother," I said. "Stevie Nin."

"That was a family nickname. I go by my real name these days."

I leaned over the table and extended my hand with a smile. "It's a pleasure, Sebastian. Sorry I didn't recognize you. How's Jacqueline and your parents?"

Sebastian shook my hand and settled back into his seat. "Mom and Dad are great. Dad's retired now."

"Still living in that beautiful spot up on the Peak?"

"Yes, Dad keeps saying he's going to sell it but he never will," Sebastian said. "Someday, after Dad and Mom are gone, it'll go to Jacqueline and me—or to the Communists."

"The mainland seems to be behaving itself since it regained control of Hong Kong," I said. "At least that's the way it looks from New York. What do you think?"

"We Chinese are long-term thinkers," he said, then shrugged. "But the Communists aren't stupid. It might be okay."

"And Jacqueline?"

Sebastian looked at me. "Jacqueline married an American and is living in Marin County. Her husband is the head of oncology at one of the big hospitals in San Francisco."

"Which one?"

Sebastian shrugged indifferently. "I can't remember."

Typical, I thought.

"They have a little girl, my niece, Anaïs."

"That's great," I said. "I'm happy to hear everyone is doing so well."

Sebastian chuckled. "Yes, it's kind of amazing, isn't it?"

I laughed, too. I wasn't sure why.

"You were going out with my sister all those years ago, and now here you and I are. Who could have predicted that?"

I smiled.

"We had some fun back then, didn't we?" Sebastian was continuing to laugh softly. "Remember that time you called me a bastard on the playground of King George V? God, that was funny!"

"You took a chip out of my head with a cricket bat that day," I smiled. "You and your friends, when you jumped me after school."

"That was the funny part," Sebastian said, wiping tears from his eyes as he continued to chuckle. "And, as far as I was concerned, I missed with that bat. I barely nicked you."

"Oh, don't sell yourself short," I smiled. I pointed blindly toward my forehead, feeling with the tip of my finger for the outer edge of my left eyebrow. "Do you see that scar? That's where you connected; I got eight stitches."

Sebastian nodded his head. "Those were the days. And do you remember—you never did admit you called me that." He observed me, still laughing softly.

It didn't seem that funny.

"You told Jacqueline I was a liar," Sebastian said, "and you never admitted you really had called me a bastard. For a year, you told my family I was a liar, and you left Hong Kong without ever admitting the truth."

We looked at each other.

"What a memory you have," I said. "I haven't thought about that in years."

Sebastian smiled. "That's the great advantage of coming to Hong Kong for only two years and then moving on. You don't have to live with the mess you make."

"That was all just silly schoolboy stuff," I said.

"Absolutely," Sebastian said. "Long forgotten. Meaningless. It was just a shock to see you when I walked into this room, that's all."

"We've got a job to do," I said.

"That's right," Sebastian said.

I got up. "Take me by the trading floor. I want to know where the markets closed today before I go back to the hotel."

We took the elevator to the trading floor and Nin called the senior currency trader over for a debriefing. The man's face was gray with strain. The currencies of Indonesia, Malaysia, Thailand, and the Philippines had hit new record lows. Both the Tokyo and the Hong Kong stock markets had fallen.

I looked at Nin. "We'll have to work together, and work hard, to have any chance of getting this deal done. See you tomorrow."

I found Entrekin and told him I wanted to meet with everybody at 9.00 a.m. the next morning. Entrekin offered to get me a car, but I thanked him and refused. I wanted to make a telephone call on the way back to the hotel and I didn't want his guy listening. I went out, caught a cab, and called Walmsley on the mobile. I told him that I'd arrived just in time to go over the waterfall—Asian markets down again and not looking good for the rest of the week. I said I'd call him back in twenty-four hours. Then I called my wife, talked to her for a few minutes, and as she was calling the kids to the phone, I passed out. The bellhop shook me awake when the taxi pulled up to the Peninsula.

Chapter Three

I WOKE UP IN MY SUITE at the Peninsula the next morning out of a dreamless sleep, ordered breakfast, and started going through the two hundred-odd emails waiting for me, but my mind wandered.

My twelfth birthday had disappeared into a fold of time as my family flew across the International Date Line from San Francisco to Hong Kong one year in the late 1960s, lifting off on the 28th of July, and landing in Hong Kong on the 30th of July.

Sebastian Nin's sister Jacqueline was two days older than me. She celebrated her twelfth birthday that year unaware of my existence, although we might have met once before, far away from Hong Kong. Her father was Chinese, a doctor who had received his degree at the Sorbonne. Her mother was French, from a once-wealthy family who had become refugees when Shanghai was sacked. Jacqueline was born in the Hôpital Américain in the posh Parisian suburb of Neuilly, where her father was doing his residency. At that time, the Hôpital Américain was considered the finest natal hospital in Paris, and to this day, many members of the Parisian *haute bourgeoisie* possess birth certificates signed there.

My parents were living in Rotterdam at the time I was born, but although my mother was heavily pregnant, my father insisted on going to the South of France for their annual summer holiday. On the way back, my mother went into labor with me in the automobile just to the south of Paris. It was a difficult breach birth, and after an initial stop in the emergency room of a public hospital, we were sent on to the Hôpital Américain, where I was born. So it is possible that Jacqueline and I had already met before I arrived in Hong Kong.

One of my emails was from my eleven-year-old daughter Stephanie, who was trying out the new computer that Samantha and I had given her for Christmas not quite two weeks before. I found an image of the Peninsula on the hotel intranet, copied it into my email, told her which window was mine, said that I'd see her and Tim in a week, and sent it, love, Dad.

Stephanie was only two years younger than Jacqueline and I were when we first met. It was hard to believe that a life-changing year was only two years away for Stephanie—but that's what happened to me and Jacqueline.

My school, King George V in Kowloon, had been admitting girls for some years by the time I started there, and it was in the halls and on the playing fields of King George V that I first became aware of Jacqueline Nin, who from the instant I saw her was more than a mere human to me. The nymphs Kalypso and Thetis had unforgettable forms and features and limbs; they were immortals who were loved by men and bore their sons. Jacqueline had a high forehead and a delicately arched nose that revealed her Gallic heritage, and the elegant cheekbones and lustrous black hair of her father's genes. Her lips were full and set in a strong, aristocratic chin, and she was tall and slender, athletic but voluptuous, and her long legs had the slightly awkward stride of a horsewoman.

By the time we were fourteen, we had several classes together and Jacqueline and I, in the borderland between childhood and becoming a man and a woman, became friends. It was a more innocent time and place, at least in the upper reaches of the Hong Kong mercantile class to which our families belonged.

Jacqueline, who was two days older than me, might have been two years older; prepared by her family and forewarned to defend herself against importunate boys, she was poised and sure of herself long before I had even decided to be importunate. While Jacqueline had already had the game explained and been briefed on the major lines of attack and defense, I was simply communing with my own indistinct feelings and urges, unsure of what I was becoming and reluctant to bring them into contact with a person I respected and admired as much as I did Jacqueline.

It was a beautiful, tense relationship. We talked for thousands of hours and never touched. I could have idealized Jacqueline and matured into a gay man without revising my memories in any way. As it happened, I went on to other women and finally married Samantha. For many years I wondered whether, perhaps, I had loved Jacqueline.

Jacqueline's brother Stevie, as I knew him then, was two years younger than me, and a student of the lower school that was a part of the complex of King George V. One morning shortly after Jacqueline and I had become friends, I encountered Stevie on the playground of the lower school.

"Hi! How're you doing?" I smiled, bestowing my affection for his sister on the schoolboy.

"Fine," he said, watching me.

"So what are you up to?"

"Nothing."

"Going into class soon?"

"Yeah."

"Well, see ya later, ya little bastard," I said affectionately, smiled, and walked away.

In retrospect, it's hard to recollect the companionship offered with the bad language, but Stevie saw things differently anyway. That afternoon after school, Stevie and half a dozen of his friends attacked me. Stevie had a cricket bat, and he landed a few glancing blows on me until the howls of his friends, whom he had accidentally struck while swinging the bat at me, convinced Stevie to drop his bat and dive onto the pile of struggling bodies that had enveloped me. Sheer weight was in their favor until things got too confused, and I was able to crawl out from underneath the pile and start kicking and wrenching the boys apart. Stevie had landed one good crack just over my eye with the bat before I went down, and as I pulled them apart and his friends got a look at me, my face covered in blood, they ran away. When I got home, my mom took me to the doctor, who closed the split in my eyebrow. I was left with the stitches and a few bruises.

When I returned from the doctor, I telephoned Jacqueline to explain what had happened. Sebastian had been virtually untouched, but to his family he pointed out the frayed knees in the trousers of his school uniform and a scraped elbow he had acquired while rolling around on the ground with me and his gang. I mentioned the cut in my eyebrow briefly. Jacqueline was upset, of course, but as I finished my explanation, I could tell that there was something else wrong.

"Did you call Stevie a bastard?" she asked. Her voice was quiet, strained.

"What do you mean?" I asked.

"Stevie said that the reason the fight started was because you insulted him on the playground this morning. He said that you called him a bastard. I said I couldn't imagine you saying something like that."

The word, the scene, and the time were correct. How could I admit to them while explaining my friendly intentions? I was only beginning to get to know Jacqueline and I had only met her parents briefly. Because of a ridiculous misunderstanding my exclusive friendship with the most beautiful girl at King George V was suddenly in jeopardy. Reviewing the alternatives as hastily as I could, I chose the unimaginative, wrong route.

"No, of course I didn't call him a bastard," I said. "Why would he say such a thing?"

"I don't know," said Jacqueline, "but Mother was very upset. She thought you were so polite when you were here."

There was a silence.

"Why did the fight start?" she asked.

"I don't know," I said weakly.

Sebastian and I cordially loathed one another from that moment. We were to see each other daily during the school week for a year and often on weekends when I began spending time with Jacqueline at the Nin family home. He knew I had lied, and I knew he had tried to turn Jacqueline against me. I doubt that either of us understood the other's intentions. I know I didn't even understand my own.

Chapter Four

I DIDN'T KNOW HOW LONG I had been staring my computer screen. I needed to get focused.

It was six o'clock in the evening in New York the day before, and I hurriedly scanned the websites of the *Wall Street Journal*, the *New York Times*, and the *Washington Post* to check out the latest news from the day, before going to the Coldstream Holdings intranet and looking at internal data on how the European and US markets had closed.

My breakfast arrived and I tipped milk from the miniature bottles of the Hong Kong Trappist Dairy, with their red letters and crucifix, over my cereal and the fresh raspberries, kiwis and banana slices that covered it.

Next, I called the heads of the various bond desks at Coldstream to get their read on where the markets were going. I got some of them on their mobiles on the way home. What they had to say was interesting. Then I called an old friend at the State Department and ran a couple of the rumors by him. He didn't sound happy to hear that I knew as much as I did.

"Jesus, Dusty," he said. "How can you expect us to get anything done with you guys sniffing around like a pack of jackals? Indonesia isn't dead yet."

"I don't want it dead," I said.

"Oh, so you're on the other side of the trade," he said sarcastically. He had litigated securities cases for the SEC years before.

"I'm trying to restore order," I said.

A bitter laugh came down the phone.

"You want to restore order? Is that what you're trying to do? Jesus Christ, what a relief! Then why don't you and your friends just not pick up the phone today? Huh? And don't answer it! And don't sell any more fucking rupiah! How about letting me restore fucking order, okay? Leave it to the United States Government. Is that okay with you, god damn it?"

I listened to the sound of his breathing slow down. Then I said, "I'm trying to keep a bank from going down the tubes, Terry. Just trying to bring her into harbor before the hurricane sinks her."

"Aw, Dusty," he said. "Shit. Look, I'm having a bad week. I mean, shit—I know you're not a currency speculator. Jesus Christ."

"We're all currency speculators," I said. "Don't kid yourself."

The phone was silent.

"Is there anything else?" he said.

"No, thanks," I said.

He had told me all I needed to know.

By the time I got to TransPac, it was a little after nine in the morning. A cold misty rain was falling, and Hong Kong was gray and indistinct around me except for the eerily clear noises of traffic: mournful car horns and the swish of tires through water. I stepped quickly from the taxi into the building.

Entrekin was seated at the board table with Nin. Eight or nine TransPac directors were seated between them. Ted McKee, who was running the due diligence team for Coldstream Holdings, was standing at the window smoking a cigarette.

"Good morning, Ted," I said, walking over and shaking his hand.

McKee looked sheepishly at his cigarette. "Can't do this in New York anymore."

"Yeah," I said. "That's the great thing about doing a deal in a five-thousand-year-old civilization."

We were not alone; executives from TransPac were waiting on the other side of the big conference table.

"Good morning, gentlemen," I said, shaking the hands of each of the TransPac people as they walked up to me; I had met most of them at lunch the day before. Nin remained where he was at the table, watching, his face expressionless.

Tea and coffee were served as we sat down. "Well, gentlemen, we're all going to be part of the same team if everything goes well," I said, by way of introduction. "I suggest we begin acting like it from here forward."

Entrekin and some of the TransPac directors nodded. Nin and McKee said nothing.

"The reason I am in Hong Kong is because Coldstream Holdings wants to complete the transaction we set out almost a year ago to do," I said. "When we started our negotiations, your shareholders' equity was worth almost one billion US dollars. Today, it's worth less than half that, isn't that right?" I looked at McKee.

"At most," McKee said.

Men stirred in their seats.

"Nobody's happy about it," I said. "But it is what it is. The partners of TransPac sitting around this table own the majority of the shares. Simon, I understand you have the power to vote on behalf of the shareholders who represent the rest of the shares?"

"Yes, I do," said Entrekin, grinning crookedly. "I certainly do."

"I would like to sign on the dotted line by this time tomorrow, but I don't think that's realistic," I said.

"Not at the price you've just mentioned, it's not," someone muttered.

"Yes, that's correct," Entrekin said with an indignant look. "Alexander, we understood that you were going to put a creative proposal to us. I would hardly describe a drastic reduction in price as a creative proposal. I thought that we had an agreed deal."

"The captain of the Titanic thought he had an unsinkable ship," I said.

Entrekin said nothing, but his face became very red.

"Okay, I'm not here to get everybody upset," I said. "I just want to make sure that everyone understands the situation so that we can work together while there's still time. I might as well put on the table this morning one simple fact. The markets are moving against the deal. And it looks like they're going to continue to do so."

I looked around the table at each person. "The only investment Coldstream Holdings is willing to make will further cut the value of the equity around this table well below the half a billion I just mentioned. You're going to get less than you were hoping to get. A great deal less."

There was silence.

"Do you have a figure in mind?" Entrekin said.

"Not yet," I said. "That's what we need to spend the next couple of days deciding."

"Excuse me," said a fleshy man with wavy gray hair brushed back from his forehead. I could distinctly see five deep wrinkles etched horizontally in his forehead from across the table. "I'm Pelham, Head of Corporate Finance. If I may say so, the next two days isn't going to make a farthing's difference in my department. My shares, according to you, are worth eighteen million at the moment, and I don't see why they're going to be worth any less on Friday quite frankly."

"That's quite right," said the bald man sitting next to him. He had two gray tufts that looked like caterpillars above his eyes, and the pouches under his eyes gave him a deeply outraged look as he glanced around the table and then leveled his gaze at me. "The fact of the matter is that my equity origination department isn't going to do marvelously, by the looks of it, for the next quarter or two, but I can tell you right now that I am not going to be voting for an investment that dilutes my twenty-five million in TransPac shares. That's the bulk of my personal wealth—I don't mind saying so—and I've worked for over thirty years to accumulate it. You are not going to leave me to retire on tuppence, sir."

Murmuring rumbled around the table. Men began to lean forward and glance up the table at Entrekin.

Entrekin was sitting quietly in his seat, running a finger under the bracelet of his gold watch, back and forth between the metal and the skin of his wrist. "Yes, well, I must say, the valuation of the firm is really the heart of it, isn't it?" he said. He looked around the table. "We've all worked very hard to build up the firm, most of us for well over fifteen years."

The man with the caterpillar eyebrows broke in. "Not just fifteen years—when I joined this firm, I purchased my partnership with capital

I had built up over almost twenty years. My TransPac shares represent the labor of an entire career!"

Entrekin nodded. "It certainly isn't the intention to throw that all away, Grahame. On the contrary, I think we all see the alliance with Coldstream as an exciting new stage in the future of TransPac."

He looked at me, smiled, and nodded cordially. "Alexander has brought a distressing bit of news, but at the end of the day, he has assured us that he and Edward are here to determine a mutually agreeable price for the investment," Entrekin said, gesturing at us with his knobby, prematurely aged mottled hand. "If recent market developments have damaged parts of the firm, of course, we will have to work with Coldstream to make the necessary adjustments."

A large thin man with iron-gray hair cleared his throat abruptly and stared sternly at me. "I'm Llewellyn Jones, Alexander," he said gruffly, looking at me. "I run Asset Management. No problems in my department. I'm damned if I'm going to let some spivvy punk in the bond department expropriate the value of my shares. To hell with that!"

A tumult broke over the table. Middle-aged men twisted around in the chairs, nodding their heads vigorously, and chattered all at once. They slapped the table with their palms, and tapped the table with the tips of their fountain pens as their fury rose.

"Damn right!"

"Quite so."

"Hear, hear!"

Nin watched the proceedings with folded arms, a small bitter smile on his face.

"Gentlemen, gentlemen," Entrekin said, holding up his hands, palms up, as if patting forward suddenly thickened air in front of him. "Please."

When there was silence, he said, "Now, Alexander quite rightly began our meeting with the observation that we need to all act as part of the same team. We are on the same team. And if some of us need to make sacrifices for the good of all, in order to get a fair deal done with Coldstream—"

Nin leaned forward. "Fuck you, Simon." He turned to his colleagues. "And fuck you, Ralph. And fuck you, Grahame, and you, too, Lew. You were perfectly happy to take your bonuses out of the general pool that I put eighty percent of the profit into. You're not going to fuck me over now. Bastards."

He stood up abruptly and pointed his finger around the table. "Don't kid yourselves, you double-crossing bastards. TransPac stands or falls on my bond-trading operation, and this deal is going to stand or fall on my bond-trading operation. So the rest of you can just go fuck yourselves. Meanwhile I'm going to the trading floor, where I have business to do."

He started to stalk toward the door.

Entrekin twisted in his chair. "Sebastian? Sebastian!"

Nin disappeared and slammed the heavy door of the boardroom.

There was silence around the table.

McKee leaned toward me and murmured, "He's right."

CHAPTER FIVE

THERE WAS MUCH CLEARING OF THROATS and shifting around in seats from Entrekin and his remaining team after the door slammed shut on Nin's exit.

I struggled to keep a small smile to myself, thinking how little Sebastian had changed from the hot-headed boy I once knew. The result of our first clash twenty years before had seemed initially like a clear win for Sebastian: the blow from his cricket bat required stitches above my eye; enough of the incident was discovered by school authorities to earn me a month of Saturday detentions at King George V, and a pall was cast over my already indifferent career there; and, at least at first, it looked like Sebastian had succeeded in making me *persona non grata* in the Nin family.

But, as it turned out, Sebastian's life became intertwined with mine. The key part of our daily routine was the twenty-minute trip on the Star Ferry from Hong Kong Island to Kowloon, where King George V is located. The Nins, sister and brother, descended most mornings in their family's chauffeured car to the Star Ferry terminal, and it was there I would await their arrival. When it pulled up, Sebastian would dart out of the car with a quick scowl, grabbing his book bag and heading toward the ramp, and Jacqueline and I would board the ferry together. In the afternoons, the three of us returned together as well, but somehow the afternoons were more loosely organized, affected by the events of the day, and the passage back on the ferry was more spontaneous, more casual, and there were more possibilities.

In the morning, Sebastian seemed to feel a cold fury about seeing me, and while he dashed away as soon as he could, on the ferry he haunted us, whether we sat together talking or going through last minute homework questions together, and I always felt his shadowy presence when we walked the decks on the sides or on the prow. Sometimes I would look back and see him observing us with a grim look on his face, or if we were on the main deck, I might glance up to the upper deck and see him peering down a gangway, glowering at me.

So, while Sebastian won the first fight, he couldn't disengage either himself or his beloved sister from me. While Jacqueline and I slowly developed a relationship that was less than romantic but increasingly unique as a friendship, Sebastian and I were trapped in a bitter and protracted competition. A competition for Jacqueline's affection.

I never really understood the relationship between Jacqueline and Sebastian. She rarely referred to him, and she seemed to ignore him when she and I were together. Over time, I realized that there was a tremendous unseen depth to her feelings for him, but she maintained separate relationships with the two of us in a way that made her feelings for Sebastian a mystery to me. It would have been difficult for her to say as little about me in her family as she said to me about Sebastian. There was no reason for Jacqueline and me to talk about Sebastian, but her parents obviously wanted to understand from Jacqueline how she and I were getting along, so I must have been an ever more constant presence for Sebastian that year than he was for me.

My Saturday detention at King George V ended about the time the stitches were removed from my head, and a few weeks afterwards, Jacqueline invited me to come by her house on a Saturday. I had been restored into the confidence of her parents. Sebastian counterattacked by using his schoolboy network to collect gossip about me. Like everyone else, my friends and I explored all over Kowloon, and Jacqueline was supplied with wild rumors about my adventures. She asked me whether I had smoked cigarettes in King's Park; skulked through Tsim Sha Tsui trying to buy explosives, ninja throwing stars or pornography; had tasted rice beer; or browsed the lingerie shop that was located beneath the cricket ground of King George V.

I was able to convincingly deny these accusations and so continued to be invited up to the Nin's home on Saturdays. When I knocked on the door of their house and was ushered in, Mrs. Nin would rest her icy gray eyes on me, smile faintly, and say "Hello, Dusty." She pronounced it "Doosty."

As a matter of fact, Sebastian's greatest victory in his campaign of petty harassment was a blind accident. He set the clock in the gazebo in the Nin's garden back an hour, and as a result, I was an hour late returning home for the lunch I was required to attend every Saturday. This had serious consequences.

I was the oldest of four children. My father was Dutch and my mother was Swedish, and their northern European mix seemed to give the family sufficient strength to block out all of the warm, human influences of the many places in which we lived. Neither of them spoke the other's native language either, so in our household we spoke English, sometimes German, and depending on what year it was and where we were living, a smattering of the language of the servants with an occasional word of Dutch or Swedish that referred, in baby language, to body parts or functions.

At the time, I didn't know the details of my birth, but I sensed as I grew out of childhood that my mother had feelings about me that were, at best, ambivalent. Her blonde hair was brushed back from her forehead and held tightly against her neck, setting off her long elegant neck and her lithe athletic body.

She would level her blue eyes at me, a shadow of disapproval in them, and give me my orders for the day. As the oldest, I was expected to assist my mother and the *maman*, the nanny-housekeeper, with my sisters and little brother. Until about the time we moved to Hong Kong, when she embraced me she would press her hands between my shoulder blades and draw me to her, where my head would be positioned on her hip bone, or later, as I grew taller, against the bones of her lower rib cage. By the time we lived in our Hong Kong apartment high above Conduit Street, she no longer embraced me.

But my mother's lack of physical affection did not mean she stinted her attention on me. I gradually realized she listened in on the extension in her bedroom when I made phone calls, she read my diary until I ceased making entries, she stripped my bed personally and carried the sheets to the wash, absolving *maman* of that part of her chores. She would ask seemingly simple questions of me when I came home from school, and only slowly did I realize the one or two questions she had asked were like the corner of an unseen room that she had already designed like an architect from a series of inquiries and reports from my siblings and from her extensive contacts in the tiny expatriate community of that era in Hong Kong. The question she put to me was either an attempt to calibrate my truthfulness against the information she had already acquired, or perhaps it was the keystone of a moment of voyeuristic pleasure she extracted from the encounter. Whatever her motives, I never sensed they were founded on any sense of concern for my happiness or well-being.

What I remember was the impossibility of having a conversation with my mother. When I would speak to her, she contracted her eyebrows and pursed her thin, elegantly shaped lips, and as soon as she thought she understood the direction of my sentence, she would cut me off with an "Ah!" or a "Naturally not!"

I remember seeing my father very rarely. He worked in the shipping industry all his career, and although he didn't seem to do too much traveling during our years in Hong Kong, he would leave for his office before I woke up, and in the evening would generally return only long enough to shower and shave and change into dinner clothes before he and my mother went out for the night.

I have since learned that people tend to behave the way they are expected to behave. Treat someone with trust, and they will act in a trustworthy manner. Treat someone with suspicion, and they will confirm your suspicions.

For my part, I had actually resisted the temptations of Kowloon in my first year at King George V, but as the oppressive net of my mother's surveillance closed around me, I began to concentrate on devising ways to embark on forbidden expeditions without getting caught by her network of informants. To do so I had first to cultivate a small set of friends who could be united in hermetic secrecy, and once I succeeded in doing so, all Hong Kong became open to me. One of these friends, a Chinese boy named Richie, who is now one of the wealthiest men in Hong Kong, knew the most amazing things about the underbelly of the city in which we lived.

Together we tracked down the location of the secret warehouses where raw opium resin was converted to heroin, we haunted the back alleys where the prostitutes would start to appear in mid-afternoon after sleeping to go on ordinary errands to buy food, and under Richie's guidance, I was to acquire a taste for the race track that almost ruined me. His father was a member of the Hong Kong Jockey Club, and until my parents found out where I was going when I went to visit Richie, I experienced one of the most exciting racing traditions in the world. Except for the race track, these expeditions were pursued in the spirit of daredevilry, without any desire to directly participate in the wickedness we so triumphantly ferreted out.

It was the irony of that time that my mother, unaware of my secret explorations of Kowloon or of my speculations at the great old race track in Happy Valley, focused her obsessive attentions on my entirely innocent relationship with Jacqueline Nin.

When I was invited to Jacqueline's house on Saturday morning, I would arrive promptly at nine o'clock, knowing I had to be home, at all costs, by twelve noon on the dot, when our family lunch was served. The excuse for this requirement was that as my parents led such active social lives, Saturday lunch was the only meal we could be guaranteed to eat as a family. The real reason was my mother wanted to prevent me from spending too much time with Jacqueline. I was severely punished for being even one minute late for lunch.

I was to learn many years later, in a chance remark by one of my sisters, that the reason why my parents permitted me to spend Saturday mornings with Jacqueline Nin at all was because my mother feared that, denied any outlet, I would be driven to seek satisfaction in the arms of the Kowloon prostitutes. If only she had known with what dread, what appalled curiosity, and what awe I regarded those tired young women, devoid of makeup, whom my friends and I would see lugging plastic bags of groceries in the middle of the afternoon!

The Vietnam War was being fought to the southwest of Hong Kong in those days, and my parents were great believers in domino theories and salami tactics. For some reason, they saw nothing absurd about applying strategies the Americans and the Chinese Communists accused one another of using in Asia to the social activities of their fourteen-year-old son.

The idea was if they permitted me to be one minute late, I would become routinely five minutes late, and if that were tolerated, I would become fifteen minutes late, and then eventually I wouldn't appear for lunch at all. As if I were some teenage Vietcong terrorist, my parents assumed my rebellion would then spiral into an out-of-wedlock pregnancy, an elopement with Jacqueline, and a decision by the two of us to drop out of King George V, probably to reappear in some park in a city in the United States as hippies, living in a sleeping bag high on drugs and protesting against the Vietnam War. The war must have made a lot of bourgeois Westerners very nervous if my parents were any example.

In any case, one of my few memories of my father from the time was being slapped up and down the dining room table for being one minute late for our family lunch. He had initially landed one hard slap on my cheek before I understood what was going on, but as he continued to flail at me, I put up my hands in front of my face, forcing him to flail at my head and arms, backing me up against and overturning chairs until he had beaten me down to the carpet. The ordeal ended as I lay among the overturned chairs, covering my head in my arms, listening to my father breathe heavily until his voice pronounced, "Stand up and get out. Don't come out of your room until you are told to do so."

When Sebastian set the clock back in the Nins' gazebo, he tricked me into being fifty-seven minutes late. The consequences when I presented myself at home, still unaware of my crime, were a beating with a belt and home detention for three months. The result was that I saw Jacqueline outside of our shared classes only on the morning and afternoon ferries, and the atmosphere between Sebastian and me became irredeemably poisonous.

Perhaps it is not surprising some of the best memories of my life come back to the Star Ferry. It was on the Star Ferry that the three of us shuttled between two worlds, the special world of Hong Kong Island and Kowloon, where the great hidden mass of China meets the South China Sea. As we went back and forth, we were sailing farther away from childhood and closer toward becoming adults. It was on the afternoon Star Ferry I had first suggested to Jacqueline we go to a movie together, a warm, misty afternoon when the sun above the clouds made them opalescent to the west, swirling gray and tinged with blue in the fading light to the east. It was on the Star Ferry that the three of us, Jacqueline and I, with Sebastian in some cunning orbit somewhere nearby, repeatedly crossed over from Hong Kong Island to Kowloon and back, seemingly going nowhere but getting older and learning a little more about each other every day on every trip.

Hong Kong Harbour is one of the most magnificent harbors in the world, and the buildings of Hong Kong rise like fretwork and filigree on the mighty slumbering rock of Hong Kong mountain with all the beauty and the tragic impermanence of a dream. The Peak seems to point toward a special cleft in the heavens, as if Hong Kong is at the center of some eternal order, and yet there is something fragile and splendid about the city, which is hinted at in only the faintest possible way by the sea, the sky, and rock amidst which it is cradled.

Years later, when I saw San Francisco for the first time, the San Francisco Bay failed to capture my imagination. I already knew Hong Kong. Only Sydney Harbour, with its long elegant lines of sandstone and the sparkling blue water surrounded by perimeters precisely the perfect distance apart, can match the drama and beauty of Hong Kong, although Sydney reclines around its waters like a woman lying on a chaise longue, while Hong Kong rears up on the breathtaking and somehow fateful rock of Hong Kong Island.

It was against the backdrop of the Peak I remember Jacqueline Nin most clearly—her cotton school uniform fluttering and snapping against her body in the wind off the harbor; her perfect legs rising out of clumsy school shoes; a strand of hair blown free across her forehead; her clear brown eyes, grave and intelligent, leveled at me as if it were necessary to inspect me daily in case I needed to be somehow recalibrated. She was beautiful, and she was in complete control.

The only spontaneity I remember was when the ferry would plow into one of the deceptively powerful wakes carved into the harbor by a heavily loaded freighter. The bow would snap up in a fan of sea spray, and Jacqueline would clench her seat with a quick hand and laugh nervously, balancing with her hips as her crossed legs swayed with the heave of the ferry.

Perhaps many boys would have become impatient, or felt deprived of affection, or been bored by her perfect restraint, but Jacqueline listened to me, and she smiled when she saw me standing waiting for her in the morning, and she was friendly to me. I was growing to love her, and she was gentle and kind to me.

In those years, homeless people still lived in boxes along the side of the Star Ferry terminal on Hong Kong Island. The smell of the coal fires and the odors of the markets that swirled around the terminal would suddenly lift in the stiff breeze off the harbor as the ferry pulled away from its berth, until ten minutes later we would start to be enveloped by the exotic but familiar odor of China as the ferry berthed at Kowloon. It was a stirring and dramatic daily passage, and there was something secret and significant about it, as if we were participating in a ritual we would have to experience more, much more, of life to possibly hope to understand.

Chapter Six

The meeting of TransPac directors concluded rapidly after Sebastian left. McKee and I excused ourselves, and he took me to the War Room where our team was working.

McKee was a precise, unimaginative man. He was completely honest, and he reported only what he could document, scrupulously editing away the slightest additional inference, assumption, or opinion from his work. He did not believe in God.

His job was to come as close as possible to an appraisal of a deal in the absence of an idea, a strategy or a ploy that could wring truly extraordinary profits from an acquisition. His assessment was the basis for the price we offered. It was my job to come up with the idea that would make the acquisition produce returns, something so creative that the seller—who intimately knew the company—hadn't thought of it himself, and therefore hadn't priced into his offer.

I had done it before, time and again. It was one of the reasons Coldstream Holdings was the most sought-after advisor for international mergers and acquisitions. It was like breathing spirit into a cold body.

The War Room was full of the evidence of a big deal that had been in the works for a long time. Shelves jammed with durable three-ring binders, their contents clamped tightly and their spines carefully marked, lined the windowless walls. Two high locked filing cabinets, which I knew would be full, stood on either side of the door. A row of coffee mugs were lined on top of a microwave oven, its insides spattered and irradiated dark brown. Two long conference tables stood at either end, and in the middle were four cubicles containing high-end computers and a big linked printer. On the other side of one of the filing cabinets was a high-speed copy machine. It was all here: the acquisition factory.

Like an Afghan gunsmith shop or a Mexican amphetamine lab. But it was too neat, too orderly. The air was neutral and air-conditioned, only a bit stale; it didn't have that close odor of bodies, and dry mouths, and over-worked shoes and suits. This was a War Room that looked like its deal was completed. The only remaining step was to get the guys from the security storage company to haul all the stuff away.

McKee closed the door after me and I sat down with the team who had been pouring over the books of TransPac and, most importantly, marking to market the bond positions.

McKee introduced me to the two young analysts from our Hong Kong office, Fai and Peter, who had been running the due diligence under his supervision.

"How's it going, guys?" McKee asked.

Fai watched politely as Peter rolled his eyes. "Not another good day in the markets from what we hear," he said. "We're going to have to knock down all these prices in the model again."

"Don't do anything until the end of the day on that," said McKee.

Fai nodded. "We'll just get the download from Bloomberg directly into the computer when the market has closed," he said quietly.

McKee looked at me. "What did you make of this morning's session?"

"The lads are running low on brotherly love," I said.

"They're a bunch of snakes," McKee said sourly. "They've been coming to me behind one another's backs for months, trying to argue that their parts of the firm are worth more than the others' departments, and that therefore, they deserve a bigger cut of the price. Each one of them has come on the sly to make the same case for themselves."

"You could think of it as funny."

"I've been too busy trying not to throw up," he said.

"For the most part they seem like FILTH," I said, a cynical acronym meaning Failed in London, try Hong Kong. "Except Nin."

"Except Nin," McKee agreed.

"What's the assessment on the total value of the firm, Ted?"

The expression on McKee's face was unemotional, but in his eyes I could see contempt. "Well, Dusty, these guys have a balance sheet of about five billion US, about a billion in equity and four billion in debt funding their assets."

"Not bad."

"No, it isn't," McKee conceded, "assuming the quality of the assets held up to scrutiny. By and large the quality did stack up—they've got all the usual stocks and bonds, mostly government securities, on their balance sheet. A lot of short-term commercial paper. That stuff's okay. Right guys?"

Fai and Peter nodded. "Minor losses," said Peter. "A few hundred million."

"Now, by the way," said McKee, "keep in mind that these guys at TransPac aren't stars, not by a long shot. The stuff isn't underwater, but it isn't making that much money either. Our Hong Kong trading desks kick these guys' asses in all the straight stuff. Right guys?"

Fai nodded. "They are approximately fifteen percent as profitable as our operations, on an equivalent basis."

"Why don't we buy all of TransPac and just wind down all that stuff," I said. "Just keep what we want."

"Exactly," said McKee. "At least, that's what we were thinking until this week."

"Okay," I said. I looked at him intently.

"Well—here's where it gets fun," said McKee. "The relatively good stuff is part of TransPac's treasury assets. We'd never do the deal for that stuff, but it wouldn't stop us either. The rest of it, billions of it, supports Nin's bond-trading operations. It's a bunch of bonds issued by corporations, banks, and some second- and third-tier government entities, you know—states and cities, not national governments. And it's denominated in a bunch of currencies: some US dollar and yen, Hong Kong dollar, but also lots of rupiah, ringgit, won and all that shit."

"What's it worth?" I said. "Make my day."

His assessment was brief.

"We can value about a billion and half of it, Dusty, and that stuff's all worth about seventy percent of what it's held on the books at. The rest of it is really anyone's guess. Right now it's probably worth fifty cents on the dollar at most."

"Next week it might be worth ten cents on the dollar—or nothing," I said.

"Yeah," he said.

"Or it might be back above book value," I said. "Maybe in six months."

"I guess," McKee said. The look in his eye suggested he was not impressed.

"I can see why the boys were getting hysterical this morning," I said. "That level of losses will wipe out almost all the equity in the firm."

"Yeah, if we're lucky," said McKee. "If we're not lucky, the losses will burn through all of the equity—and more—and bankrupt TransPac."

"That's why I'm here," I said. "To see whether there's anything left to acquire."

"Better move fast," said McKee.

"I'm worried, but I'm not too worried," I said. "Coldstream would never have bothered talking to TransPac at all if the only thing to TransPac were the businesses run by those also-rans around the table this morning," I said slowly. "What we want is Nin and his operation."

"Yeah, and what's scaring the shit out of me right now is that we might get him," said McKee.

I laughed. "Give me a likely downside estimate—what is TransPac worth?"

McKee looked at his guys. "What's the latest?"

Fai looked at Peter and cleared his throat quietly. "Every day we keep redefining downward the limits of our worst-case scenario," he said. "Right now, our worst-case scenario says the firm is worth less than a couple of hundred million US."

I thought about it. "If it's that bad, we're close to disaster," I said. "The real problem—"

McKee nodded his head vigorously.

I stopped. "Go ahead, Ted."

"You're exactly right, Dusty. We're getting to the point where the price doesn't matter. The way these markets are ripping up the value of TransPac's bond portfolio, we're starting to worry about the nuclear winter scenario—"

I interrupted. "The banks pull their funding lines to TransPac, suck the oxygen out of its trading operations, and TransPac goes into a liquidity crisis and bankruptcy."

Cash is an asset to you and me, but to banks it's a liability. If you invest a million dollars in securities issued by an investment bank, they have to find a way to invest that million in a place that earns more interest than they agreed to pay you. Banks lend to each other through interbank funding lines, which turn the cash that's sitting as a liability on their books into an asset earning interest from another bank. The international banking community had extended billions of bank funding lines to TransPac.

"That's it," said McKee.

"In the model it looks like they're rolling over about a hundred million a week," I said. "Until the end of the month, when they have to repay about four hundred and twenty-five million." It was just over three weeks away.

"Yeah, they're repaying a five-year bond."

"Are the banks continuing to roll over their funding lines?"

"So far."

"Because they're expecting Coldstream Holdings to acquire TransPac," I said.

"Right."

What this meant was Coldstream Holdings was up for not just the purchase price of TransPac, say five hundred million, but the cost of repaying any bank lines or maturing bonds that had to be repaid over the next several months and couldn't be refinanced through normal market operations. The model said the funding requirement to keep TransPac afloat if banks cut off their funding lines could be another seven hundred million to a billion dollars. It was an insane price to pay for Sebastian Nin and his operation.

I casually walked to one end of the War Room and McKee followed me. I sat down on one of the tables, and across the room could just see the tops of the analysts' heads in the cubicles. "Sentiment is not good out there," I said in a low voice. "I was talking to our boys in New York this morning, and people aren't just worried, they're letting fear take over. Walmsley sent me out here because he and the Executive Committee think if TransPac goes down the tubes, it might trigger a general collapse in Asian markets. That could infect the rest of the global markets. We might have a depression on our hands."

"And to think I came out here a few months ago just trying to make a few bucks for Coldstream," McKee said. "I don't want to save the world. I just want to get out of here with my ass in one piece."

"Too late," I grinned, punching him on the shoulder. "You'll be lucky if you've got enough left to sit on when this is all over."

"I'm serious, Dusty," Ted said, looking down. "I don't want to be anywhere near this shitty deal anymore. I gave it my best shot. It should have gone to financial close last month."

"Don't worry about that. Let's just do what we do best. I can't say how this is going to turn out yet, but it's too early to panic. As long as the market knows we're showing up at TransPac every morning they'll keep rolling over those bank lines—it's only a hundred million a week—and we've got three weeks before the money starts to get real."

"I'm going to think about it, Ted, and let's talk again this afternoon. Right now I'm going to tea with Entrekin. He asked me up for a D and M."

"D and M?"

"Deep and Meaningful," I said. "Entrekin is dying to stitch me up at the personal level. He wants us to slit our forearms and let our blood mingle together." I tapped McKee on the shoulder and left, saying goodbye to Fai and Peter on the way out.

I took the lift to the 27th floor. Entrekin's secretary was wearing a silk dress in a delicate shade of light green. It looked as if it had been glazed onto her splendid body.

"Hello, Simon," I said, as she ushered me into Entrekin's office.

"Making progress?" he said, while an elaborate tea service appeared and tea was poured.

I observed him carefully. He was nervous.

"Well, I had a good session with the team, Simon. It's one step forward, two steps back, of course, the way these markets are going. Every time the guys think we have a handle on things, the currencies drop, and the stock markets fall further into the shitter, and everything changes again."

"Yes . . ." he said. "Still, that's mostly our problem, since we invested in this business at much higher levels. The losses are for our account. For you it would seem to be an opportunity to buy cheaply."

"You have a point," I said. "But judging from the meeting this morning with your people, that's a controversial point of view."

Our first course arrived on a superb silver and porcelain service. Cucumber sandwiches.

"Don't like Chinese food?" I asked, smiling politely.

"Oh, would you prefer it?" Entrekin asked.

I picked up a wedge of white bread between one finger and a thumb and inserted it into my cheek. "I feel like I should be wearing white kid gloves, that's all," I said. "So, tell me about this morning. I guess I'm confused. I thought I heard some disagreement among the troops."

Entrekin dabbed at his mouth with a stiff serviette. "Well, Alexander, I suppose the thing to do is to put it in context. TransPac is the product of the hard work, and yes, the dreams, of many of us. I suppose I could be considered in some respects the guiding light,"—he dropped his eyes modestly—"but even I, despite my role as founding shareholder, consider the half dozen members of my inner circle to have been part of the very bone and blood of TransPac. And yet, having acknowledged that, nobody is indispensable."

Entrekin looked me in the eye. His eyes shimmered. "No, not even I."

British meat pies were served, and Entrekin speared one with his silver fork and sliced it with his silver knife. "And I mean that," he said earnestly. He cocked an eyebrow so that his forehead wrinkled right up to where his original hair line had been. The scalp remained serenely smooth. "I really do mean it. And I suppose what you witnessed this morning was a bit of a clash between the founding *ethos*, as I like to think of it, the sense of teamwork and a common vision, with what I might describe as a cult of personality, what in this part of the world we remember as a Gang-of-Four-type approach. Except that here at TransPac it's really a Gang of One."

"Sebastian Nin."

"Ah, you noticed," Entrekin smiled ironically at me.

"He's quite a talented, dynamic young man."

"Yes, he is young, isn't he? Impetuous. Hot-headed," said Entrekin. "You realize, I trust, that we don't necessarily have to deal with him as part of this transaction. There is tremendous value in the bond operation that is independent of Sebastian Nin."

"Well, as a matter of fact, I'm worried about some of the exposures in Nin's bond portfolio."

"That's the heart of the matter, in a way," Entrekin purred. "In certain respects, of course, Sebastian has done magnificently—he has created the first real Asian bond market, small as it is. He has begun to develop a list of regular issuers and purchasers of Asian bonds in a variety of currencies. All marvelous. Better, if I may say, than what Coldstream itself has accomplished in that respect."

"Why else would we be talking," I said.

"My point precisely," Entrekin said. "I admire your forthrightness, Alexander." He inserted a silver spoon just below the surface of the pudding that had been placed in front of him and lifted it to his lips. "But then there are the exposures, as you say, in the bond portfolio. It's the sort of thing that happens when somebody becomes a law unto themselves."

I looked at him coldly. "Managing him is your job, Simon. If he's gotten out of hand, whose fault is that?"

Entrekin held up the palm of his hand. "Quite right, quite right, Alexander. I am not ducking responsibility. I acknowledge that my neglect to exercise suitable restraint on Nin and his bond traders may prove to be expensive for myself and for my fellow shareholders. But I do want to communicate to you very clearly and frankly that we're aware of the Nin issue and that we've been developing solutions."

I was curious. "Have you thought of anything to plug the hole in his portfolio?"

Entrekin kept his eyes on his bowl of pudding. "How much of a hole do you think there is?"

For the first time that day I could see the other side of the harbor. The blue gray shadows of the winter afternoon partly concealed Hong Kong, but the rain had ceased, and the underbellies of low clouds moved slowly across the sky, trailing wisps like dragon's strands through the buildings. "Our current worst-case scenario is that the entire firm, not the bond portfolio but all of TransPac, is worth one hundred fifty US."

A struggling sound was audible in Entrekin's throat. He put down his spoon and looked at me. He was pale. "This morning we discussed a figure of five hundred million for equity that you acknowledged valuing originally at one billion dollars. Is your figure of one hundred and fifty million US dollars relevant to the same equity we were discussing this morning?"

"Yeah, it's the same thing. Adjusted for how far the market may decline."

Entrekin smiled weakly. "You realize that there can be no deal on that basis."

"Well, that's our worst case, Simon. I hope that none of us lives to see a worst-case scenario because it's likely to cause all kinds of other problems for people a lot nicer than us. People someone could actually feel sorry for."

"I know about the situation to which you refer," Entrekin said. The whites of his eyes were visible all around his irises. "I grew up during the Great Depression, and I remain convinced that the Japanese attacked Manchuria, and threw all of Asia into a bloodbath, partly because of the terrible economic conditions of those times."

"That's not going to happen," I said. "Depression, unemployment, famine—that might happen. World War III—I don't think that's going to happen."

"Nevertheless, I believe the markets are on a knife edge," Entrekin said nervously, his eyes darting.

"Oh, yes. The markets are in bad shape."

"We're going to have to prevent it."

I looked at him. His finger was nervously picking at the starched table cloth beside his plate.

"Well, that's why I'm here," I said, at last. "I have to get back to work now, but I want to leave you with one thought. Don't throw Nin off the back of the sled without giving me plenty of advance notice. Walmsley would be very cranky if I came to Hong Kong to close this deal and accidentally misplaced Nin."

"You can depend on it," Entrekin said. He seemed to have recovered. "And I would like to leave you with a thought as well—it would certainly be easier to agree to a deal if we didn't have to pay Nin for his equity, and could spread that extra money around to the rest of the team."

I dabbed at my mouth with my serviette, looking down. "Sure, but how are you going to do that?"

"You have a financial valuation model that calculates such large losses in Nin's bond portfolio that it leaves the rest of the firm worth only one hundred fifty million," said Entrekin quietly. "That means the collapse in the value of TransPac is basically his fault. Where there's fault, there's liability. And where there's liability, there are consequences. In his case, those consequences may be very grave. It shouldn't be hard to come up with a way to zero him out."

"He'll sue," I said.

"Yes," Entrekin said, looking reflectively out the window. "Yes, he may," he said quietly. "But you know, Sebastian has only been earning substantial bonuses for the past three years, not a long time to build wealth. Much of that wealth is in shares of TransPac, shares whose value he has done so much to destroy. And Sebastian has a very expensive lifestyle. He is a young man who lives large. I wonder how much there is in his personal war chest that would be available for such a project if he were shown the door and decided to litigate. I should think it would be quite expensive to litigate against Coldstream New York. Personally,

I would think over such a move very carefully before deciding to go ahead if I were Sebastian Nin. Even if I were the Prime Minister of a medium-sized country, I would think twice before dragging Coldstream New York into court; your operating budget is probably bigger than the Government of Belgium's."

He had a point.

"Okay, so maybe he won't sue. But I want to know well in advance before you do something creative," I said.

I stood up and left.

I caught a lift and rode it to the ground. I walked out and caught a cab, giving the driver an address on Hollywood Road.

CHAPTER SEVEN

IT HAD STARTED RAINING AGAIN. The taxi moved quickly through the broad streets near the harbor and started winding its way up the hill. We crested at the Midlands and soon afterwards turned in to Hollywood Road, winding along until we got to the address I had given the driver.

I paid, got out, and stepped through the misty rain into the Golden Dawn Oriental Carpet Emporium, a narrow shopfront located on the downhill side of the street. Big rectangular piles of carpets rose waist-high on either side, their subtle colors glowing in the warm light of the shop. It was like walking from winter into early summer. A tall Chinese man in an impeccable suit stood at the end of the shop, looking at documents on a desk that was pushed up against the back wall beside a staircase.

"Hullo, Craig," I said, walking slowly as I admired the carpets all around me and suspended from the walls.

The man straightened up. He looked at me and smiled. "Why, Dusty, it's you!" He walked toward me, and when we were still well over a meter apart, he stopped like a soldier on parade, raised his hand, and then lifted a forefinger in greeting. "What a pleasure."

Craig hated to be touched.

"Yeah, it's been a while," I said. "How's business?"

Craig wrinkled his brow. "Rather quiet this week," he said. "Do you reckon these markets are going to blow over or get worse?"

"Get worse, probably."

"I certainly hope you're wrong about that," Craig said sadly. "Here, let me give you my new card—I'm wired now."

"You even have a website and email address," I smiled. "Now we can stay in better touch."

"You can order a carpet over the internet now," said Craig. "I can have it shipped to Belgium, relabeled, and then sent to you in the States. US Customs will never know you've obtained Iranian contraband."

"I don't know how you live with yourself," I smiled.

"Someday the US will lift the ban on Iran and all you Americans are going to make the price of Persian carpets skyrocket again," said Craig. "Buy now while prices are good. Do you have time for a cup of tea?"

"Sure I do," I said.

Craig walked back to the desk and pushed a button. A slim young Anglo man came down the staircase. He was exquisitely groomed, and wore an open neck shirt and a pair of silk trousers. There was something almost Chinese about his refinement.

"Look after the shop, will you, Winston? I'm going upstairs for a cup of tea."

Craig introduced us as we passed and we started up the stairs.

"How's the clan?" I asked.

Craig Chin was the second youngest of seven children: five brothers and two sisters. Two of his three older brothers were in the US, one a nuclear physicist and one a mathematician specializing in fiber optics. His other brothers were in Hong Kong running a law firm together. One sister had an MBA and the other had an MD. Craig may have been the brightest of them all, but he wanted to be a painter and calligrapher when we were in high school together, and he had eventually dropped out of medical school and started the Persian carpet importing company. Craig gave me a brief update on everybody, and on his nephews and nieces as we ascended the stairs.

When we got upstairs, we entered a long low-ceilinged room, brightly lit, with spectacular antique carpets hanging from the walls. Beautiful carpets covered the floor. We walked across to a couple of leather chairs and Craig motioned me to sit down while he made tea.

"This is my private show room, where I keep the best part of my collection," he said, sitting down and pouring tea. "So, what brings you to Hong Kong?"

"Oh, this and that," I said. I sipped the strong black tea.

"Good thing you didn't go into public relations," Craig said. "You would have been an embarrassing flop."

"Do I need a special reason to come to Hong Kong?" I asked with a smile.

"It's been a while. It must be almost five years."

"Is that right?" I asked, surprised. I thought about it. "I guess you're right. The kids are older and taller. I'm older, fatter, and grayer."

"You look quite fit," said Craig, appraising me.

"The shape stays the same, but the muscle turns into fat," I said.

Craig pursed his lips and studied my face. "No, I think you're still in excellent condition."

"I wish," I said. "Look, what do you know about Stevie Nin becoming Wonder Boy over at TransPac?"

Craig arched his eyebrow and smiled. "Why do you want to know?"

"Out of a deep interest in human nature," I said. "Not to mention a profound concern for his welfare."

"Ha—well he would be a case study, indeed." Craig laughed. "I haven't actually run into him in years—he was in New York until a few years ago, you know, but some of his boys buy things from me, and, of course, his career is the buzz of the old crew from the King George V School."

"I can imagine," I said.

"His people seem to have a lot of money to spend," Craig said. "After bonus time, one of his mid-level traders came in here and bought a rug from up here." He indicated a place on the wall to the right where a magnificent antique rug now hung. "Sixty-five thousand US."

"Not bad for a twenty-six-year-old."

"If that."

"Surprisingly good taste, for that matter." I smiled.

"I've never seen Stevie in here," Craig said sourly.

"So, what's the deal? Is Sebastian Nin God's gift to investment banking?"

Craig sipped his tea, making a deprecating mouth. "Well, I don't know, Dusty. He isn't well liked, of course. But nobody that successful is. The thing is, people don't say he's brilliant. They say he's brash. Creative. A visionary."

"Hmm."

"Of course, he's bright."

"He was bright, alright," I said. "But he was never as smart as Jacqueline, for example."

"Have you seen her?" Craig asked. His eyes were fixed on me.

"No," I said. "Haven't heard from her in almost twenty years."

"Ah, so you never got back into contact?"

"Nope," I said.

"I somehow thought for years that you two would get back together and get married. Return to Hong Kong as one of its most brilliant couples. Raise a whole brood—a new dynasty," said Craig. "But what do I know?"

"You didn't get that one right."

"I hear she's married and living in Seattle."

"I think Bill Gates's wife's name is Melinda," I said. "I'm surprised Jacqueline settled for less. Of course, maybe she's one of Bill's top people."

"I think not," said Craig. "I seem to recall that she married a doctor. I think she might be one too."

"Just like her daddy," I said. "Well, anyway, so the word on Stevie is he's a visionary, huh? But nobody's saying he's a genius."

"Not this week," said Craig with a small smile.

"Well, thanks, Craig," I said. "Great to see you. If I'm here for more than a couple days, let's have dinner."

"I'd be delighted," said Craig.

He accompanied me down the staircase and we walked through his gallery where I made admiring comments about his goods.

"Just one thing," Craig said, as we halted at the door. Tiny droplets dotted the glass of the door, shimmering golden from the light of Craig's shop, with the gray winter afternoon behind. "Stevie's business seems to be founded on getting new borrowers into the bond market. People who haven't ever been able to borrow money before. Not all of those new borrowers are very nice people."

I nodded. "See you," I said.

CHAPTER EIGHT

I CAUGHT A TAXI BACK TO TRANSPAC. I had wanted to see Craig because he was an old friend whom I could trust, and he was always exceptionally well-informed about what was happening in both expatriate and Chinese circles in Hong Kong. I had been joking about Iranian contraband, but the fact is rugs use certain established shipping routes between Central Asia and the rest of the world. There isn't much else besides oil and gas, and light manufactured goods, like cotton textiles, that the rest of the world buys from Central Asia. Legally, that is.

Much of the world's heroin comes from poppies grown in Afghanistan, refined from resin into opium and heroin in Pakistan, and then shipped across the ancient trade routes overland through Samarkand and Bukhara or by freighter across the seas.

Drugs, weapons, human beings are all moved along these routes. Hong Kong has been traditionally one of the great heroin-refinement centers of the world, and Thai poppies are a major factor of production. Thai opium is controlled by the same people who control the international trade in tropical hardwood, and these warlords, who are often ethnic Chinese, find it easier to move back and forth along the borders of Thailand, Myanmar, and Cambodia with the tacit understanding of the Red Army.

The cash produced by these activities is sterile, useless, unless it is reinvested into ordinary commercial enterprises. These new companies become investors in bonds, and they find it convenient to issue bonds as well. I knew Craig Chin knew a great deal about all this, while maintaining a sensible distance from it.

I arrived at the War Room, where I had a planning session with McKee and his team. We agreed that a price was needed by tomorrow morning.

50

Mergers and acquisitions is a high-grade form of buying and selling apples out of a pushcart. The whole point is to decide what price to pay, or to accept if you're the one selling the company. Mergers and acquisitions are described by white knights and poison pills and battles and defenses, but it's really just a question of how much money to offer for something you want to buy. Our clients are shoppers, or to invoke the dignity of the 19th century, merchants. That's why the profession is called merchant banking, because the industry grew out of financing ships full of cargo from the Far East and other places.

Once you learn how to manage risk, you acquire a taste for it.

A modern investment banker's job is to collect all the information possible on a company, and quantify it. The hopes and dreams of the company's work force, the glamour of its brands, the fascination and desirability of its products, the strategies of its board of directors for expanding into new markets to sell products to millions of new people, these all get turned into numbers by an investment banking team working on an acquisition.

We look for the bad news too, the risks, and we turn those into numbers as well. Has a huge pollution problem triggered environmental litigation? Are there occupational diseases in the workforce or excessive deaths on the job? A demoralized distribution channel and an incompetent board of directors? An aging product line that nobody wants to buy?

Everything is turned into a number. Every number is weighted with the risk we assign to it, and then compared to the cash flow we think the company can generate for our clients. It's simple really. If the cash flow exceeds the expenses and risks, we do the deal at the price that we have calculated. If it doesn't, we don't.

An acquisition team loads all the numbers they have collected into a computer program called a financial valuation model. The model starts as an off-the-shelf mathematical program we've built for previous acquisitions and is customized for each deal. It's a crystal ball, except that it's loaded with banks of elaborately detailed data, powered by an analytical engine of complex formulas that crunch through countless iterations—and, in the end, it isn't as accurate as a crystal ball.

A financial valuation model projects years into the future, often ten or twenty years. The model's focus on the future makes an acquisition unlike almost any other category of human activity.

A surgeon uses an MRI— an analytical tool with some similarities to a financial model—to look at a patient's organs in order to diagnose the illness and decide to operate. But the operation is performed on real flesh and blood.

A general planning a military campaign studies a map and satellite photos when he decides how to attack—just as we peer into our financial model. But when the war starts, real men move forward to kill other human beings.

An acquisition is different because it often takes years before it will be known whether or not the deal was a success. So when we do a deal, the financial valuation model isn't just an image of reality; for all practical purposes, it *is* reality. We can't know what is really going to happen to the actual company, or the markets and communities it operates in, or the actual people who work there or who buy its products. So we do our work, and generate our best analysis, and try to close a deal at the price we've calculated the company is worth. But it takes a year or two, and sometimes more, before it is clear whether the acquisition is a success or a failure.

The reality of how an acquisition gets done means that there is tremendous pressure to influence the financial valuation model. It only takes a few keystrokes to change a number that might make a bad deal look like a good deal. The assumption that gets changed might relate to an event five or ten years away, which means that nobody will be able to prove for a long time, even if the deal goes bad, that the guy who changed the assumption did something wrong. Fortunes are at stake, and it is so easy to turn light into darkness, or darkness into light. It's like discovering the secret to perpetual motion, or a technique for committing a perfect murder. It's so easy, and hundreds of millions or billions of dollars hang in the balance. The temptation is palpable, a presence in every War Room.

Ted and his team were gearing up for another six hours of work that night. I worked alongside them for a couple of hours until the team decided to order in dinner. I was starting to feel dead on my feet, and I decided to go back to the hotel and get some sleep. There was no point staying up while the basic computer modeling was being run. I could have gone over to our lawyers to run through the documentation, but I'd read everything I felt I needed to know on the plane. So I gave Entrekin a ring to tell him I was going back to the hotel.

"Are you free for dinner?" he asked.

"No, sorry," I said. "I'm still dragging a bit from jet lag. The guys are ordering in food here, but my stomach is still in a different time zone."

"You looked tired at lunch," he said.

"Yeah, I need a good sauna tonight," I said. "My whole body is aching."

"I would be delighted to make my club available," Entrekin said. "Let me just put you on hold for a moment while my secretary makes the arrangements."

"Thanks, Simon," I said, "but the Peninsula has a great health club where I'll work out for a while and a sauna straight from Finland. Afterwards I'll just go up to my room and get some rest. Thanks, maybe some other time."

CHAPTER NINE

I RETURNED TO THE PENINSULA, went to my room, and changed into gym clothes, removing my watch and wedding ring. I've seen guys who take off their wedding rings and slip them into the pocket of their suit coats before they go into a bar or a club, especially when they're traveling on a business trip. Someone who loses their wedding ring on a business trip is likely to catch hell from their wife—and deserve it—but there are plenty of innocent reasons to lose your ring as well, like in a swimming pool, or in a whirlpool at a hotel health spa. I always play it safe.

It was just after seven o'clock when I got to the health club, and at first I thought the only other people in the gym were two guys sitting on the exercise cycles, their legs pumping. One was a guy in his mid-thirties by the look of it, trying hard to avoid ending up looking like the other guy, who was disconsolately pushing the pedals of his exercise cycle, red faced and covered in sweat, as if his over-indulged wreck of a body could be resurrected.

I found a rowing machine and started my work out slowly. In the wilderness of mirrors I saw a woman in the far corner of the gym, her back to me, apparently doing yoga.

After twenty minutes I finished with the rowing machine. About that time the heavy, older guy clambered down from his exercise cycle and left. I went over to the incline board and started the first of six sets of thirty sit-ups. When I was finished, I noticed that the other guy had gone.

The health club was beautifully appointed, and among other pieces of equipment, it had a full competition-class set of free weights. I walked over and got a pair of forty-five-pound dumbbells and sat on a bench doing some arm and shoulder work.

The woman came over, confident and relaxed, and put thirty-pound plates on the bar of the other bench. One hundred and five pounds is a lot of weight for most guys, and it is quite a lot for a woman to attempt. She was tall and in great shape, but she didn't look like a powerlifter either. She held my eye a heartbeat longer than necessary.

I realized I felt the faintest flash of pleasure while looking for that extra moment into her eyes. It was a tiny luxury, a civilized sensation far removed from time zones, valuation models, and collapsing currencies.

"Would you like a spot?" I asked. I was offering to stand over her and ensure I would pull the weight off her if anything went wrong.

"Sure, thanks," she said.

She was much better looking than the average user of a hotel health club.

I finished my set, put the dumbbells on the mat, got up and walked around to the head of the bench, looking down on her. She lay on her back, her hands resting at her sides, waiting for me. She looked up at me, and then focused on the bar between us, and grasping it with both hands, she lifted it from the bench.

She did pretty well with the first three or four repetitions. Then her left elbow shook as she lifted the weight off her chest, and my hand hesitated, floating out a few inches so that the tips of my fingers hovered just under the bar, but she got the weight up and locked her elbows.

"That's enough," she gasped.

My hand floated under the bar as she directed it back over the supports of the bench and clanged it into place.

"Nice set," I said.

She took a couple of deep breaths and then sat up, swiveling around with her elbows on her thighs and her hands hanging between her knees. "Want to rotate in?"

I looked doubtfully at the bench. It was only 105 lbs, and loading up the bar would be a hassle, still, even a set of reps with a light bar would keep the blood flowing. Probably perfect for seeing off jet lag. "What the hell," I said.

We exchanged places. She stood at my head, and I was now looking up at her thighs as they disappeared with a well-turned curve into her brief shorts. I shifted my focus and gazed past the iron bar, and beyond the swell of her breasts, to her intelligent blue eyes. I savored her glance.

"What kind of accent is that, by the way?" I asked.

"Australian."

"Where are you from?"

"Sydney."

"My wife is from Perth," I said, lifting the bar off the bench and beginning my set.

I did twenty-two or twenty-three reps before setting the bar back onto the bench. I never needed her assistance.

"Thanks," I said, sitting up. The blood was pumping through my chest and upper arms, tightening the muscles and giving me a slightly heady feeling. I looked up at her and smiled.

"You're an American, aren't you?" she said.

"No, I actually carry a Dutch passport," I said. "But I live in New York now."

"I'm so glad you didn't say that you were a Canadian," she said. "Canadians always get so upset when you ask if they're Americans. I would have felt so self-conscious. My name's Alex by the way."

She smiled, and it was not possible to ignore her beauty.

"What a coincidence," I said. "So is mine."

We did a couple more sets, and by the end of the session, I was becoming uncomfortably aware of how close her warm, sweating body was to mine. It was a pleasant feeling, but it wasn't a comfortable feeling.

"Well, I'm off," said Alex. "Thanks so much."

I looked at her, but her eyes slipped away, bearing away her glance like an ineffable scent on a shifting breeze.

"My pleasure," I said, as she strode out of the equipment room. I did a few more exercises with the medicine ball and then went to the showers.

I went to the shower feeling a mixture of disappointment and relief.

The shower was excellent. Hot water thudded against my skull and rang in gobbets down the back of my neck and shoulders as I thought about what had just happened.

I had had no intention with sleeping with Alex. It was pathetic of me really to have indulged in even a mild flirtation in the health club. I looked down at the water flowing over the muscles of my shoulders and chest. I didn't need a stranger to reassure me; I was cross with myself at my human weakness, the childish desire I had permitted myself to indulge, enjoying the attention of a beautiful woman.

I thought to myself that I was already being unfair to my wife, Samantha, in a sense, because it was she who had transformed my personality and made me attractive to women who are drawn to healthy men, not to the dark person I had been, obsessed with the past and drawn to death, when Samantha and I first met.

When we first met in Rome, she said I wore a permanent scowl. She told me I was harsh and sarcastic. How she saw the potential in me or decided the task was worth all the aggravation it was going to take, I'll never know. But I understood enough about the change she had made in me to feel that Alex, or any other woman I chanced to meet, was unconsciously enjoying the benefits of a tremendous amount of work and faith and love that had been invested in me by my wife.

I left the shower feeling clean and relaxed and, tying a towel around my waist, I made my way toward the goal I had been anticipating for hours, the Peninsula health club's magnificent sauna. When I had arrived earlier that evening, before entering the exercise room, I had checked with the attendant to make sure that the sauna was cranked up and would be perfectly hot.

I opened the door and stepped in.

Alex was sitting in the sauna, stripped to her waist, a streak of blond hair across her forehead, her magnificent breasts beaded with sweat that shone like pearls. A Peninsula towel clung to her hips.

"You don't mind me like this, do you?" she said languidly. "This is how I sunbathe on Bondi Beach."

"No, you look great," I said.

I sat down and smiled at Alex, and I could see she had brought back the luxury she had taken away. Her blue eyes looked into mine, and I could feel my body involuntarily react to the unknown promise of her eyes.

The tip of a pink tongue licked the corner of her mouth where a strand of blonde hair had fallen across her nose and nestled into the place in her cheek where her lips narrowed like the point of a star.

I closed my eyes. The image of her breasts and her taut belly floated before my closed eyelids.

I opened my eyes again.

"I don't suppose you surf when you're at Bondi, do you?" I asked, glancing at her, and then allowing my gaze to move to the wall of wooden beams behind her.

"Not really," she said. "But I do like to body surf."

It was a perfectly reasonable thing to say, and perfectly plausible. But something about the way she slowed the rhythm of her words as she pronounced the sentence brought the words "body" and "surf" across her lips in a way that gave them a totally new meaning.

It's often thought men are tempted to sleep with women who are not their wives because of the boredom and routine into which a sexual relationship between two married people inevitably settles.

That idea confuses two separate aspects of adultery. The first is the thrill of seducing, or being seduced by, an attractive stranger. It's an age-old temptation.

The other element that makes adultery so appealing, however, is the chance it offers to apply the lovemaking skills one has acquired in one's marriage. Different lovers can teach different skills, but brief sexual adventures involve so many distractions and inconsistencies, and such a low level of real intimacy, that aside from a few techniques, it is difficult to get beyond a certain level of lovemaking in the early years.

By contrast, the emotional security of a marriage, the lack of any need to pretend, the level of understanding that develops over time between a man and a woman, provides an excellent regimen for turning even an ordinarily sensitive man into an attentive and satisfying lover.

The sexual dimension of a marriage either starts to bleach and wither as the years unfold in an unimaginative and dutiful routine, or it develops into a long-lasting life force, an adaptability and capacity for renewal that both nurtures and is nurtured by the marriage.

Of course, neither the husband nor the wife in such a marriage is always sexually fulfilled, or even especially content in their marriage. Pregnancies, long absences, and excessive work schedules all produce situations in which at least one partner may feel resentment, a certain loosening of commitment, to their spouse. And the fact that dissatisfied partners may recognize they are better lovers than they were when they were single and able to enjoy others, and that they are therefore more likely to give pleasure to an exciting stranger, represents a compelling temptation.

"I'll bet the waves enjoy it just as much as you do," I said, watching her figure that one out.

"Hmmm," she murmured, licking a drop of sweat off of her lip.

"Do you have a boyfriend?" I asked, leaning back against the wooden step and closing my eyes again. I was going to have to stop looking at her, or my body was going to assert itself.

"Not at the moment," she said. "We just broke up."

"How sad," I said. "Were you going out for a long time?"

Alex seemed surprised by my interest, but happily answered a long series of questions I asked about her relationship with a guy in Sydney who owned a couple of nightclubs, but wasn't really ready for a serious relationship.

I was only half listening because the heat and the proximity of our nearly naked bodies in the dim sauna was creating enormous stress for me. So, as I led Alex through a long catechism about her failed relationship with Darren—and I couldn't tell for sure whether what she was telling me was real or fanciful—I was also concentrating with increasing desperation on memories of my wife because as I began to smell Alex's hair and skin, my desire for her grew.

I thought back to when we first met, when Sam and I rode motorcycles around Rome. she would gleefully cross into the oncoming lane when our side of the Lungo Tibere was congested, laughing in the Roman sun over the roar of our motorcycles, her loose linen top flapping against her brown breasts in the rush of the wind.

It was summertime, and we often rode up to the Lago di Albano, next to Castel Gandolfo, to go swimming. The Italian women were mostly topless, and Samantha stripped off her linen shirt and swam the same way. Afterwards I would rest my head in her lap while she massaged my forehead, whispering soothingly to me about rubbing away the worry wrinkles.

"They're from concentration," I would say.

"They're from worry," she'd reply, "or anger."

"What do I have to be angry about?" I said.

"Someday you'll tell me," Sam had replied.

I wanted some steam, so I opened my eyes, leaned forward and grasped the dipper, and turning to Alex asked, "Do you mind?"

"Not at all," she said languidly. The steam hissed from the hot rocks and swirled around my head. The sauna was beginning to feel too hot.

Alex was leaning back now, her body covered in droplets, a streak of damp hair across her eyes. I suddenly thought Alex was about to fail. I was not going to be seduced, and my struggle to overcome my desire for her burnished, shimmering body would seem to her like a total rejection of everything she was.

As I thought about Alex and tried to put myself in her place, it occurred to me that the whole situation was highly suspect. I've spent almost twenty years staying in expensive hotels around the world, and my experience is that beautiful women are found in the foyer, in the restaurants and bars, occasionally in the lifts, but very rarely, unaccompanied, in the exercise rooms. It does happen, but Alex would have to be one of the half dozen most beautiful women I had ever run into in a hotel health club, and the first one who had sat next to me, half-naked, in a sauna.

I had told Entrekin exactly where I would be.

It was time for a cold shower and some dinner from room service. "Nice to meet you," I said, as I left Alex in the sauna.

"Bye," she said faintly.

Chapter Ten

I WENT BACK TO MY SUITE, changed into a bathrobe, and ordered room service. I was feeling cross and humiliated that Entrekin had thought I could be so easily corrupted.

It was just after eight thirty in the evening. It was seven thirty in the morning in New York.

I called Samantha.

"Hello, darling," I said. "You've caught up to me again. At least we're living in the same day."

"Oh hi, sweetheart!" she said, but I could hear the fatigue in her voice. "Are you alright? I was so worried the other day when the phone went dead."

"Yeah, I'm sorry—"

"No, no—no need to be sorry. I was just worried. But I remembered that you'd only just arrived in Hong Kong that day and I thought you must have fallen asleep while waiting for the kids."

"That's right," I said. "I'm sorry."

"No problems," she said, using one of her Australian expressions. "The kids got over it."

"That's what worries me," I said.

"Well—" she paused. "Look, it's something we can talk about when you get home. CNN is full of what's happening in Asia. No wonder they wanted you in Hong Kong. Is everything okay?"

"I'll probably be back in New York by the end of the week," I said.

"That bad, huh?"

I loved her quick insight.

"Yeah, there's something wrong with this deal," I said. "It reminds me of those early privatizations in Eastern Europe just after the Wall fell, when the KGB just used a front company to put in a bid, and killed the accountants, lawyers and investment bankers, one by one, if their bid wasn't accepted."

"Oh, darling—you're not in any danger, are you?"

"No, I'm not," I said. "But I just walked out of a honey trap a couple of minutes ago, and I'm starting to wonder if somebody involved in this deal is going to end up dead."

"Darling, I want you to get out of there now! I mean this is the last straw. I'm sick of having my husband ruining his health, working until all hours in God knows what part of the planet, without having to worry about you getting hurt as well."

A note of pleading came into her voice.

"Sweetheart, what are you thinking?"

"I'm sorry I said what I did," I said. "I'm just shaken up by having this blonde walk into my sauna in the hotel this evening. It just feels like some creepy mob or KGB deal, or something. I'm so tired I must be starting to hallucinate. I'm sure everything will be fine in the morning."

"So what did this blonde do? Strip off her tiger-skin skirt and try to tackle you?"

I explained briefly, asked to speak to the kids, and rang off. They were in the middle of packing the car to go to Vermont. I could imagine the morning news on the television, the smell of coffee in the air, dazzling winter sunlight coming through the kitchen window as Steffie and Timmy talked.

I made a drink and was just sitting in an armchair when room service arrived. The phone rang. I looked longingly at the dinner tray for a moment and answered the phone.

It was Nin on his mobile.

"I thought we might have a drink," he said. There was a commotion in the background.

"I'm having a drink," I said.

"Yeah, but I thought we should talk," he said.

"It's up to you," I said. "I'm at the Peninsula. I'd come meet you but I'm too tired, so if you want to talk, we'll have to have one here."

I listened to the music and the tangle of voices coming through the telephone.

"Alright," he said. "I'll see you at the Peninsula in half an hour."

"Meet you at Felix," I said. "I'm hungry."

I was sitting at a crisply covered table, nursing a martini, when Sebastian Nin was ushered to my table.

I nodded without getting up. "Make yourself at home."

He sat down. "I am home. This is my town." I watched him light a cigarette.

"How's morale among the troops?" I asked.

"Fine," he said. "They're hanging in there."

"They looked pretty discouraged to me when we went to the trading floor," I said.

Nin shrugged.

The waiter came and we ordered courses prepared from the animals, seafood, plants and herbs of the Pacific Rim. I chose a bottle of old burgundy to accompany the meal. "The Sebastian Nin combination," I said, smiling at him.

He looked at me quizzically.

"Chinese food and French wine," I said. "Like your dad and your mom."

"Oh, right," he said listlessly. He lit another cigarette.

"Smoking between courses," I said. "Not a good sign."

"Oh, signs are all around," Nin said. "Signs of the times. Bad signs."

"It is what it is," I said. "I'm sure I'm not telling you anything you don't know if I say that Coldstream is more likely than not to walk away from TransPac," I said. "That's why I'm here. I only get called in when a deal is in deep trouble."

"Terrific," he sneered. "I hadn't seen the Grim Reaper yet, but I guessed he was due any moment. I just didn't expect him to be you."

"The Reaper's got a different gig," I said. "I'm here to keep the deal alive."

"Thanks—worlds." He looked out the window at the lights of Hong Kong.

"How did you end up in the middle of this?" I asked.

"What do you mean?" he asked.

"We haven't seen each other in twenty years," I said. "How'd you get from there to here? Mixed up with a crew like Entrekin and his boys?"

"They're not such a bad bunch," Nin said, not looking at me.

I laughed shortly. "There was a blonde at my hotel this evening," I said. "In the sauna, where I told Entrekin I was going to be. It's an old trick, played without much subtlety."

Nin smiled grimly. "You're saying Entrekin arranged it?"

"I'm not saying it," I said. "But the thought did cross my mind."

"Could be," he said with a shrug.

"Nice bunch to be in a tight spot with," I said.

"Well, you know, you take what you get in life," said Nin a little angrily. "In my case, I don't think it's such a bad place to be. When I was at school, I didn't work as hard as Jacqueline. I didn't give a shit basically. As a matter of fact, I wanted to go to university in Canada so I could go skiing."

"When did you learn to ski?" I said. Skiing is not a typical accomplishment of natives of Hong Kong.

"I was going to learn in Canada," Nin said with a grin. "But there was entirely too much fucking snow for me. I mean, that's a country that could stand to seriously benefit from global warming.

"So after the first semester—the weather started to get cold at the end of September and I immediately started sending out applications for a transfer—I went to UC Santa Barbara. I figured the beach was the next best thing. My dad wanted me to go pre-med, which I did. But I hated all the chemistry and biology courses, and life was good in Santa Barbara. After college the only place I got accepted was the American Medical School in the Caribbean. It's not accredited in the US, but you'd be surprised at the number of good doctors it turns out. A lot of the students were fuckups, of course, like me. Mostly the sons of doctors whose fathers were determined to turn their kids into doctors, by hook or by crook—and were willing to pay all the way."

"What was it about being a doctor that appealed to you—the chance to serve mankind?"

"That's not as funny as you fucking think," Nin flared. "As a matter of fact, I didn't want to be a doctor. Couldn't stand the idea, actually. And not just because I was coming in second string behind my sister, who, of course, not only went to Stanford undergraduate, but medical school there as well.

"So there I was, sitting on this little island in the Caribbean with a bunch of third-stringers while Jacqueline was in her third year of medical school and trying to decide whether to go on for a PhD in Genetics or accept a position as a research fellow at the Einstein College of Medicine in New York."

"I knew she was smart, but that's really impressive," I said.

"Sure," Nin said. "I was just busting with pride about my fucking sister as I dissected the corpse of a poor dead sharecropper in a half-air-conditioned anatomy classroom at the American Medical School. That was ripe, let me tell you. The one time I'd be willing to spend a year in Canada would be if I had to take another anatomy class. Lots of formaldehyde and very low temperatures is what you want, trust me, when you work on a body for twelve months."

"So, is that what turned you off medicine?"

"It wasn't the highlight," he said. "No, what happened was that when I was at the American College of Medicine, that was exactly the time that a lot of cocaine was starting to filter up through the Caribbean. The price of sugar in the world markets was collapsing. So the planter class on the island was in a tight spot and some of them started to diversify into cocaine transportation. Traditionally, the medical students mixed socially with the young sons and daughters of the planter families, and the guys I met were starting to get involved in the drug trade behind their dad's backs. So, it was kind of a wild scene."

"So that's the link to bond trading," I said, smiling.

Nin scowled and shook his head.

"Actually, what happened was that there were about twenty families who owned like seventy percent of the island, and everybody else worked for them in their cane fields, which is hot, back-breaking, often dangerous work. Not only do you have to chop away for hours with these heavy cane knives at sugar cane that is as thick as a man's arm, but the cane fields are full of spiders, rats, poisonous toads, and snakes."

"The guys I knew, of course, rarely got out of their air-conditioned Land Cruisers when—and if—they took a quick trip down to the cane fields. They weren't like their fathers, who were tough sons of bitches, but knew their business. The young guys just ran around spending their families' money, and either screwing the poor black girls from the villages or the white tourist girls in town. And then a few of the guys I knew started getting involved in the drug trade: setting up piers at small inlets, and agreeing to store cargo in camouflaged warehouses, that kind of shit.

"And I got to thinking about my dad back here in Hong Kong, sending his hard-earned money to me so I could go to medical school in the middle of this shit, with these plantation owners' sons running around practically acting like everybody else on the island were slaves, except themselves and the white students going to this fourth-rate medical school. I couldn't explain it to my family. All they wanted me to do was get my MD, even though my degree would be practically worthless in the US anyway.

"I was in agony thinking about how disappointed my parents and uncles and aunts and everybody would be. I didn't want my dad to lose face. That's why I hung in there as long as I could. But I figured the ancestors would understand, even if nobody else did, and so I decided to leave the island."

Nin looked at me, his eyes burning. "So I just left and went to New York. I couldn't tell my family I had dropped out, and I had almost no money. But I got a job writing sales tickets on the trading floor of a big bond house after I ran into a guy from King George V on a bus going up Lexington Avenue. Remember Clinton Gage?"

"No," I said.

"Great guy," Nin said. "Nicest guy I ever met. He'd gotten his MBA and was working as bond trader. He got me my first job."

"So that's how I ended up working at TransPac, feeding the hungry, healing the sick, and defending the oppressed," Nin said with a grin, shaking another cigarette out of its packet. "As a matter of fact, I won't bore you with the details, but over the years I decided it was time we Asians broke free from dependence on the British and Americans for the investment capital needed to develop the economies of Asia. I didn't learn much about medicine at the American College of Medicine, but living on the island of St. Philippe was like experiencing a microcosm of what it must have been like in China a century ago. You guys are the direct descendants of the opium traders and gun runners who made war on China a hundred years ago," he said.

In my case, he wasn't far wrong, at least on my dad's side. I didn't know if he knew it. "Plenty of Chinese would rather live under *gweilos* in Hong Kong than under their Chinese brethren on the mainland, not that they have the choice anymore."

"I don't think it's realistic to expect the first Chinese governments to come to power after centuries of European and Japanese imperialism to be the most rational regimes in the long history of China," Nin said calmly. "It will be interesting to see how China develops over the long term—not that we'll be around to see it.

"But in the meantime, I've built here what is the first investment banking operation that raises Asian capital for Asian borrowers," he said. "In a way, going to that shitty little island in the Caribbean woke me up. It gave me a mission."

"Well, that's why Coldstream's interested," I said simply. "You've done a great job."

"Yeah, I know a lot of guys at Coldstream think so," he said, looking at me narrowly. "What about you? I want to ask you something man to man: do you want to get this deal done? Are you here to make it work, or to kill it?"

I smiled. "The last thing this deal needs is someone else trying to kill it," I said. "Every trader in every market on the planet is seeing to that. Not that they even know or care about TransPac, but the way traders are dumping everything they've got that has the remotest link to Asia, it's hard to say whether Coldstream will be able to close this deal."

"Look, Street," Nin said, glancing around the restaurant. "Entrekin acts like he's got the shareholders all stitched up, but that's bullshit. The two key silent investors are Sheikh ibn Massoud from the Gulf, and an ethnic Chinese Malaysian with a name you don't want to have to pronounce."

"You mean Perkhidmatan Pendidikan?" I asked. The share register was in the due diligence material I had read on the flight from Buenos Aires, and I've done a couple of acquisitions in Malaysia, spending enough time in Kuala Lumpur to learn how to pronounce Malaysian names.

"That's him," said Nin. "Massoud and Pendidikan between them have forty-two percent of the shares of TransPac. I've got seven percent. All you need is just one of those stumblebums on Entrekin's team to have the majority votes. Surely you can figure that out. If you cut one of them a deal on their shares or give them options on Coldstream shares or some kind of upside, you can cram any deal you want to down the throats of Entrekin and the rest of them."

"They won't be happy," I said.

"That only matters if you want them to stay after you've done the deal," Nin said.

"Good point," I said.

"And you can screw them to the wall, basically, for their shares, which would leave you more cash to sweeten things for Massoud and Pendidikan."

"And you," I said.

Nin shook his head impatiently. "I'm not that worried about what I make on this deal," he said. "It pales in comparison to how rich I'm going to get in the next five years as I continue to build TransPac."

"Well, I don't like it," I said. "It's unethical. It's pushing the security laws to the very limit, at best, and it'll drag Coldstream into nasty litigation that we'd just as soon avoid. It's not the right way to do business."

"Don't tell me the right way to do business," Nin said. "Especially not in this part of the world."

"As long as it's my money, I'll do things my way," I said.

"What are you worried about?" Nin said. "Entrekin won't sue. Those guys couldn't even get a deal done with Coldstream in almost twelve months. They thought that they could get a better price by playing hard to get. What fuckups! I only got involved in the last two months when Entrekin started to panic. He kept me frozen out of the negotiations until then. They won't be able to put together a half-decent lawsuit. They're pushovers."

"I'm not going to run my deal that way," I said.

"Okay," Nin said, lighting a cigarette. "Coldstream wants my bond-trading operation, and I was just trying to show you how to get it. But go ahead and do it your way—good luck."

Neither Nin nor I were in the mood for dessert, but I ordered a bottle of Château D'Yquem.

"There's nothing like a good sticky to resolve the differences that emerge over dinner," I said, as the sommelier opened the bottle and poured the golden wine.

Nin sipped the wine, not looking at me, and said, "I've been wondering all day. When are you going to ask me about Jacqueline?"

"I don't know," I said. "You told me what an outstanding medical student she was. You said she's married to some guy who runs an oncology department at a hospital in San Francisco. Is there anything else I should know?" It was interesting that Craig Chin's information hadn't been quite accurate; perhaps Jacqueline and her husband had moved from Seattle to San Francisco only recently.

Nin was looking at me carefully.

"Okay," I said. "How's Jacqueline?"

"Come on, Dusty," Nin said. "I mean, you and Jacqueline went out for a year when you lived in Hong Kong, and then you wrote letters for another five years or something. Did you ever see each other again?"

"No, we didn't," I said. "We almost did, halfway through college, but it didn't happen. But as you say, we wrote to one another for a long time, and we used to talk on the phone when Jacqueline was at Stanford and I was at Princeton."

"I don't give a shit about what did or didn't happen between the two of you," Nin said. "But surely you have some lingering interest, even after all these years, in what became of my sister. Don't you at least want to know that she's happy?"

"Of course, I want to know she's happy. Cut to the chase, Sebastian," I said. "I've already asked you how's she doing."

"Yeah, but you didn't sound as if you gave a shit," said Nin.

"I don't live in the past," I said. "I don't like to be reminded of the past as a matter of fact."

"Sometimes the past gets between the present and the future," Nin said. "You can't get to where you're going unless you go back through your past."

"It doesn't work that way," I said. "I certainly wouldn't price a bond, or a company, that way."

Nin looked at me coolly.

"There's more to life than what you see in a financial model," he said. "In any case, Jacqueline is doing great. She took the position at Einstein for a while. She never really liked having patients or too much dealing with real people, as opposed to theories and data and the latest equipment. She met her husband there and they got married and moved to San Francisco and have their daughter—who's also a real beauty, and scary smart."

"I'm glad that there's a doctor in the Nin family after all," I said, surprised Craig Chin had so completely misinformed me.

Nin looked at me.

"Do you want to know anything else?" he asked at last.

I thought about it. "No."

"Really?" he asked.

"Yeah," I said. "What else is there to know?"

"You're not angry about something, are you?" Nin said. I could see his brown eyes glowing through the wreaths of cigarette smoke.

"What a strange thing to ask," I said.

"Maybe, maybe not. It's kind of strange that you don't seem to have any interest in her. People tend to be a bit more sentimental about their first girlfriends. My trader's instincts tell me there's something more to your position than you're letting the rest of the market know about."

I smiled. "Let's put it this way, Sebastian. If I were in the mood to get sentimental, I would restrain myself."

It seemed to me a little sad Sebastian still thought the brief past that we shared in common could have any lingering relevance. His sister had been a beautiful girl, but she was also cold and reserved, the perfect first love for a boy who wasn't eager to turn into a man. I had always thought of Jacqueline as possessed of the beauty of a graceful tree or an ocean wave, rather than something bred of flesh and blood. She had seemed to me like some highly refined mineral, or the most elegant plant in a garden. In addition to her great beauty, Jacqueline had a fine mind and she was a kind person, but Sebastian was delusionary if he thought that his icy, distant sister had somehow established an enduring hold on my imagination or my affections.

I waved for the check.

"Now, listen to me, Sebastian," I said. "All joking aside, I want to help you. I've been in Hong Kong for less than two days, but you have a couple of problems at TransPac you need to know about. First, the way these markets are heading I think the banks are going to start calling TransPac any day now and pulling their funding lines. You've got to build up some cash fast."

Nin looked at me coldly. "I know that," he said.

"Well, what are you doing about it?"

He looked at me. "Why should I tell you? How do I know you won't run off to Entrekin and report back every word I've said tonight?"

"Does it matter?"

"You tell me," Nin said.

"That's your second problem," I said. "Entrekin and the boys are trying to figure out how to cut you out of the deal."

Nin laughed bitterly. "They're such limp dicks. They wouldn't know how to cut me out."

"I suppose that's right," I said. "Although, as a matter of fact, I don't think it would be difficult."

Nin's face was expressionless.

"Of course," I said, "I've got a couple of good reasons not to do it."

I looked at Nin.

"You're actually the guy we want," I said. "That's obvious from all the analysis I went through before I even got off the plane. Everything I've seen and heard in Hong Kong only confirmed it."

Nin was smoking another cigarette.

"I hope you're not expecting me to throw myself at your feet in gratitude. You'll only be disappointed," he said, looking out at the extraordinary view of Hong Kong.

"It's been a long time since we knew one another," I said. "All that crap you were saying about the past does remind me of one bit of unfinished business between us. Even though it was a bit of schoolboy silliness, I guess I owe you an apology. I want you to know my word is my bond, even though I lied about calling you a bastard years ago."

Nin's eyes narrowed. "I'm not sure I know what you mean."

"You mentioned it yesterday," I said. "I'm sorry I denied to Jacqueline that I called you a bastard on the playground all those years ago. We both know I did say it, but maybe I'm the only one who will ever understand I meant it in a friendly way."

Nin looked at the view.

"Oh no," he said. "I've always understood that."

"You did?" I asked, surprised.

"Sure," he said, sipping his glass of Domaine de la Romanée Conti.

I thought about it.

"Jacqueline didn't," I said.

"No," he said. "She didn't."

I looked at him. He smiled.

"Well, you didn't expect me to explain it to her, did you, after you called me a liar?"

"No, of course I didn't," I said. "But I never realized you understood what I said in the first place. If you knew I was being friendly, why'd you get your friends together and jump me?"

Nin laughed shortly. "Oh, I didn't know it until after you managed to throw us off you in the fight after school. After you pulled us apart, I looked back at you because I thought you might come after us. But you just stood there. As I looked at you, there was something about the way you looked at me, blinking the blood out of your eye. There was some kind of look of surprise in your eyes, but even more, something offended and shocked about the way you were staring at me. It made me realize it was all a misunderstanding."

It was my turn to look out the window. I looked up toward the Peak in the direction the Nins used to live. I thought I could see among the scattered lights on the dark mountain a tiny cluster of lights that might have been their house.

"You're a good poker player," I said.

"You told my family I was a liar," Nin said. "I had no reason to be nice to you."

"Well, it's all pretty silly and meaningless, now, isn't it?" I said, as I signed the check and stood up. "Thanks for coming by. I'm going to get some sleep."

We entered the lift together and stood there as it descended to my floor. The door opened, and Nin said, "Let me know if you change your mind about my idea."

"If I were you, I'd be raising as much cash as possible to prepare for the run on TransPac that is about to happen," I said. "Leave the harebrained conspiracies to Entrekin."

CHAPTER ELEVEN

THE NEXT MORNING, MCKEE HAD ORGANIZED a meeting to discuss our conclusions about the risks in TransPac's bond portfolio. The guys had prepared an excellent presentation that sliced and diced TransPac about four different ways, looking at the risks of the currency, interest rate, liquidity, and credit standing of the borrower. It was grimly fascinating.

Liquidity: oceans of other people's cash sloshing around inside your investment bank. What a lovely, privileged position—until all that cash floods back to its owners. That's why banks consider cash a liability. Potentially my new friend Simon and my old friend Sebastian had a billion-dollar liability—their obligation to repay the cash inside Transpac on demand.

I looked around the boardroom as the computer-generated slides flashed one after another across the recessed screen, and Ted gave his presentation, speaking to each slide with a comment or two. If banks and other funders panicked, Transpac's liquidity could go bone-dry in days, leaving nothing to fund Nin's bond positions. Within hours Transpac would change from being an apex predator dominating the Asian bond market to a skeleton too bare for even a taxidermist—much less for Coldstream Holdings.

Entrekin was composed, but very pale. He seemed to lose interest halfway through and began running a finger under the bracelet of his gold watch, back and forth between the metal and the skin of his wrist. The Old Asia Hands on either side of him looked bewildered and ill. Only Sebastian was generating the kind of intensity the images on the screen justified. He kept up a steady stream of sharp questions, qualifications, and comments. He didn't catch Ted out once, but it was good to see somebody at TransPac still had some fight.

When the presentation was over, everybody looked at me.

"Simon, any comments?" I asked.

Entrekin shook his head.

"Thanks, Ted, for the analysis," I said, nodding to McKee. "Gentlemen, I think it's obvious from what we've just seen that we have entered a new phase in the deal. A crisis phase. It no longer matters whether TransPac is worth five hundred million or one hundred million—"

"Bloody oath! It does to us!" snarled Pelham.

"The real problem," I said, "is that the market has little pieces of the same big puzzle we've just seen this morning. Some players will have a couple of pieces, some players will have many more."

I glanced around the room. "And they're going to come up with a picture that looks like the one we've just seen, or worse. And when that happens, they're going to pull their funding and cancel their credit lines to TransPac so fast it'll make your eyes water. And then it won't matter what the firm is worth anymore, because it'll die from a lack of liquidity."

Entrekin cleared his throat. "What is the solution, Alexander?"

I looked at McKee. McKee was expressionless.

"We've got to raise cash fast, Simon, or counteract the signals out there in the market, or both."

"Is there any possibility of a guarantee from Coldstream New York?" Entrekin asked softly.

I smiled coldly. "Nice try. We are not going to assume all the risks of ownership without an agreed deal on what we're paying for TransPac. And that leaves you gentlemen to pick up where you left off last time, and decide at what price you're willing to sell to us."

Another uproar erupted around the table. Finally, I brought it to a halt. "Let's see if we can raise some cash," I said. "Does anyone have any ideas?"

I looked around the table at silent faces.

Then I turned to Nin. "Sebastian, I was thinking that Lobo Global Power is in a position that might be interesting for us. They've got a billion dollars US in debt they've issued to build a half-finished power plant in Indonesia. Maybe they'd agree to swap some debt with us, push up the price a little. Do you know Bill Dorfman?"

"Sure," said Nin. "I know him well."

"I didn't notice any of their bonds on your books," I said. I looked at McKee, who shook his head slightly.

"No, but I've spent a lot of time with Bill and his CFO, Wayne."

"Warren," I said. "The CFO's name is Warren. Okay, Lobo's based here in Hong Kong. Why don't we go over this morning and have a chat?"

"They won't see you without an appointment," said Nin. "I doubt we'll get in to see Dorfman for a week."

I looked around the room. "Why don't we divide up the work, gentlemen? Sebastian and I will try and stop the market from trashing TransPac's credit rating, and you all can get together and decide how much you're willing to sell us your shares for."

I rose, nodded to the set faces staring at me from around the table, and motioned for McKee and Nin to follow me out.

Dorfman's secretary put me on hold for fifteen seconds before coming back on the line and asking me to come by at eleven o'clock that morning if that was convenient for me. I said that would be fine.

McKee and I went back to the War Room. We closed the door and I sat down between Fai and Peter. "Okay, guys, if we're going to save this thing, I need some flexibility in the financial valuation model to run some extra scenarios. I want to do some serious stress-testing as well."

The guys nodded. Fai rang his long, elegant fingers up and down a pencil he held in his left hand.

"I'd like you to put some switches in the model so that we can figure out what happens if some of the issuers of the bonds on TransPac's books prepay their bonds at a discount."

"You mean buy their bonds back?"

"Yes," I said. "We need the cash flows up front, at a discount to face value, and then no further cash inflows from the coupon on the bonds that have been redeemed."

I was proposing we bring forward the cash projected to be received over many years from the bonds into this current period, but reduce the total amount of cash received by applying a discount. I was gambling that the time value of money, and removing the risk weighting the model assigned to outstanding bonds—which was getting more and more extreme as markets declined and destroying the value of Transpac projected by the algorithms in the model—would offset the reduced amount of total cash.

Peter's shoulders slumped. An expression of anxiety briefly crossed Fai's face. "That will take a lot of work."

"Yeah, it's not difficult conceptually, but you're going to have to write the new logic into every line of every bond in the portfolio," I agreed. "I know it'll take a while, but you're going to do it. It's the only strategy that might save TransPac, and I have to understand the financial impacts of the strategy."

Fai blew out through his cheeks. "Okay," he said, rubbing his hair.

McKee was watching. "How long do you think it'll take, Fai?"

Fai looked at Peter. Then he looked at me and finally he looked at McKee. "Maybe fifteen or twenty hours. We may be able to divide some of it and work on different parts of the portfolio at the same time. We may be able to do it sooner that way."

"That would be good," I said. "Time is running out."

Ted looked at me wearily. "The thing is, Dusty, we thought we had this deal cracked a month ago when we were working like dogs to achieve financial close before year end. We were pretty strung out then. But then the rupiah crashed and took every other Asian currency with it, and we've been going like maniacs since then. The guys and I have been averaging about three hours a night of sleep for the last week."

I looked at them. Their skin was pale and blotchy. Their eyes were red-rimmed. The expressions on their faces were slack and lifeless. There was a faint smell of stale sweat coming off their suits. Worsted wool trousers weren't meant to be worn twenty-one hours a day, day after day, and sweated into the way athletes sweat into their uniforms. But that's what happens on a deal. Their suits absorbed the odors of tired, anxious men, an aroma of the locker room mixed with the toilet, and exhaled it again into the neutral air-conditioned atmosphere of the War Room. This was a team at their limits.

"You guys have done a great job," I said. "But I've got to have this analysis. Asia is on the brink. Otherwise we're dead, and all the work that you've done on this deal will have been useless."

McKee nodded. "Right," he said. "Okay, guys, let's get to it."

Fai and Peter swiveled slowly in their chairs and began working on the model, their fingers tapping slowly and tentatively at their keyboards as screenfuls of the model skidded by on their monitors.

I read legal documents until sandwiches were brought in. It was time to find Nin and go pay a call on Lobo Global.

Nin and I walked the few blocks to the office tower where the Asia-Pacific headquarters of Lobo Global Power was located. Lobo had the penthouse floor, and as we stepped off the elevator, I felt as if we were treading on a cloud that was floating past the Peak. The views were breathtaking.

We were led into a corner conference room with views north and west and offered tea and water. Then the door burst open and Bill Dorfman strode in with Warren Brightling padding silently behind him.

"Dusty! It's good to see you. Damn, you're looking good. How's bidness?" Dorfman's drawl filled the conference room as he grabbed my hand and pumped it. His hand was hard muscled, and a heavy gold bracelet rattled around his wrist between the starched French cuff of his shirt and his tanned hand.

"I'm fine, Bill," I said smiling. "How's Trixie?"

"Aw, she's great," Dorfman said. He had a set of long, straight, yellow teeth, stained from the incessant flow of pipe smoke across his tongue and palate. "Trixie's always great. Maybe that's why I'm always fucked up!"

"Ha ha," I said. I turned to Brightling. "Hi, Warren, how're things?"

Brightling held out his dry, loose hand and gave mine a brief shake. He moved with a silent, smooth looseness that lingered from his days as an All-American forward at the University of Kansas. "How ya doin', Dusty," he said quietly.

Dorfman spun on his heel, his honed chest muscles bending the candy stripes on his shirt into long curves, and looked inquiringly at Nin. "Hi, Bill Dorfman," he said, putting out his hand.

"Sebastian Nin," said Nin, taking his hand.

Nin was the shortest one in the room. Dorfman cocked his head and looked at me. Then he snapped it around and looked at Brightling. "Ha!" Dorfman exclaimed.

One of Brightling's sinister grins split the side of his face, starting from the corner of his mouth. "Heh, heh, heh."

"So . . ." Dorfman's head spun around, and he leaned his head forward and peered at Nin. "You're Sebastian Nin, from TransPac?"

"Yeah, that's me," said Nin.

Dorfman looked at me and laughed. "Hell, Dusty. Have a seat, you and your friend. Pull up a chair and tell us what you've come to see us about."

"I take it you've met," I said, as we all settled in around the conference table.

Dorfman pulled his pipe out of his pocket and was filling it with the cheap and cloying tobacco he favored, a relic of the years before he made his millions developing power projects around the world. He jerked his head in Brightling's direction without looking up.

"Nooo," said Brightling. "We talked though . . . once."

Dorfman looked up as he jammed the pipe between his teeth. His gaze was level, his expression serious. "But Mr. Nin here has been burning up the wires for months trying to get through ever since. Thirty, forty calls."

He lit his pipe, sending big puffs of smoke into the common air above the table. "Hey, he's a persistent guy. That's okay. What's up, Dusty?"

I hadn't looked at Nin since we sat down and didn't now. "Well, Bill and Warren, first of all, everything I say today is confidential. There's no time to sign a confi agreement, but can we agree on that? Everything is commercial-in-confidence?"

Dorfman and Brightling nodded solemnly.

"Good. Now as you know, TransPac has some bonds out in the

market. They're getting pounded. Today they're down to half the value that they were issued at. Meanwhile, Lobo Global has got a billion dollars in bank debt out there which the banks are going to be feeling pretty nervous about right now."

"I don't know about that—depends on whether they take the short view or the long view," said Dorfman, his voice booming. His head snapped back on his shoulders combatively and he grinned. Dorfman's face was an unsettling mixture of vigor and wear. The rich brown color he dyed his hair, and the way his eyes sparkled at moments like this, almost counteracted the network of lines that had scoured his features and the loose skin of his neck.

"Come on, Bill," I smiled. "Don't kid me."

"Now, what you don't know," I continued, "is that Coldstream Holdings represents a party who is considering an investment in TransPac. What I don't want to happen is for somebody to start getting their hands on those bonds and use them to try and grab an ownership interest from my client. So I thought, if you ask your banks for the right to make a market in Lobo Global's debt, Sebastian here can run an orderly trading operation for you, and maybe we can swap some of your debt for our bonds and get our bonds out of unfriendly hands."

"Hmmm," said Dorfman. His glistening eyes tracked from my face to Nin's, up the wall and across the ceiling, along the horizon, and then back to Brightling. "What do you think, Warren?"

"Yeah," Brightling nodded, his head bobbing loosely on his neck from shoulder to shoulder. "Yeah, maybe there's somethin' there."

"Okay," Dorfman said. "Let's talk about it. When can you shoot us something?"

I looked at Nin. "Got some time?"

Nin nodded, his face dark. "Yeah, I'll get somebody on it."

"Now, remember, gentlemen," I said. "From first to last, this is confidential. Coldstream's discussions with TransPac. The idea of buying up TransPac's bonds. The swap for your paper."

"Sure, Dusty, no problem," said Brightling.

"You can trust us, Dusty," said Dorfman.

We shook hands all around. Dorfman winked at Nin. "Nice to meet'cha. Warren, take the kid's phone call next time."

Warren smiled at Dorfman. "Heh, heh."

We threaded our way through the crowd on the sidewalk toward TransPac. I shook my head and looked at Nin. "So, you know them well, huh?"

He grinned at me. "If I hadn't said I knew them, would you have taken me to the meeting?"

"I might have," I said.

"But probably not," said Nin. "By saying I did know them, I got you to take me. And so what if they've been treating me like something they'd scraped off their shoes? Now, I know them and they know me. And we're going to do a deal."

"I'm not sure you're the kind of guy who should be running a major bond-trading operation," I said.

"Too late," he grinned.

"Be careful with those guys," I said. "They're the two hardest operators in Hong Kong—Triads and Red Army front men included. It's worth your life to mess with them."

Nin looked at me in surprise. "Why'd you tell them all that confidential information?"

I smiled.

I got off at the floor where the War Room was located, walked in and asked how it was going. Fai and Peter were hunched together looking at Fai's screen. They turned and looked at me. "Making progress," Peter said faintly. Fai looked dazed.

My mobile phone rang. It was Craig.

"Can you take a break for a quick lunch?" he asked.

"Sure," I said.

He gave me an address on Glenealy Road.

"Okay," I said to Peter and Fai, "tell Ted I'll be back in a couple of hours."

I left the room went down the lift, and caught a cab for Glenealy Road.

CHAPTER TWELVE

THE TAXI DRIVER MISTAKENLY LET ME OFF a few doors down from the restaurant and I walked up Glenealy Road, searching the signs for the name of the restaurant. The sidewalks teemed with people, and I passed several restaurants that obviously catered to expatriates. Through the windows I saw their healthy faces, their well-groomed heads and shoulders, and I saw in their smiles and in their gestures as I hurried up the hill the sleek, self-satisfied air of predators.

The restaurant Craig had suggested was a narrow place nestled into an odd nook where Glenealy Road suddenly hooked to the right. I entered, and the interior was old and dark, full of Chinese businessmen. I was greeted and ushered to the back where Craig sat in a dim alcove ten feet opposite the kitchen door, ten feet from any other table.

He raised his finger in greeting, his faint, friendly smile just visible in one corner of his mouth.

"We'll get a little noise from the kitchen here," he said. "But no one else will be able to hear us. And the service is superb—the staff has to pass us every time they leave the kitchen."

"Good choice," I said, looking forward with satisfaction to the prospect of a delicious meal. Craig had always insisted on the best of anything he chose, and even as a kid, had stinted no effort to locate and obtain it.

The dim sum began to be brought to our alcove, and shortly the bamboo canisters began to pile up on our table as we talked.

Once my eyes had adjusted to the darkness, it was distracting to have the sudden glare as the kitchen doors opened and shut.

"I've had an interesting time making inquiries since you directed my attention to young Sebastian's career," Craig said. "I hadn't paid much attention until you visited yesterday."

"He was never really your type," I said.

Craig smiled thoughtfully. "I've got a story to tell you about that later," he said.

The dim sum was extraordinary. It had been too long since I had been to Hong Kong.

"I had drinks with a young fellow who has been trying to get himself invited to one of my classical Chinese music evenings for some time," Craig said. "Rather attractive boy, a bit pushy. I was going to let him wait a while longer, figuring he would either acquire some manners or go away. But after you and I spoke yesterday afternoon, I thought of Anthony."

"What's the connection?" I asked, puzzled.

"Oh, sorry," Craig laughed. "I suppose I should start from the beginning. Anthony works for Sebastian Nin. He's a foreign exchange trader, but his real job is to act as one of Sebastian's assistants. Sebastian has about three, I think."

"So, did he have much on his conscience?"

"What conscience?" said Craig. "He works for Sebastian."

"Is he that bad?" I asked, carefully selecting another dim sum.

"Oh, my hair stood on end," said Craig. "Truly. I was amazed what a few pink gins can accomplish to loosen youthful tongues. Sebastian is running a brothel over there. Anthony was talking about tapping phones, setting honey traps . . ."

"Women, you mean."

"Women—when appropriate," said Craig. "Anthony said that it's amazing how senior executives come to Hong Kong and think because they're ten thousand miles from New York or London they can get away with anything. As if no one lives here."

"As if no one is watching," I said.

"More to the point," Craig agreed. "But yes, it's absolutely standard. They have whole strings of them, like ponies, English, Europeans, Chinese, Southeast Asians, Americans—"

"—and Australians," I said suddenly.

"Whatever they think will appeal to the visiting mark." Craig shrugged.

"Son of a bitch!" I said. "And I thought it was Entrekin who set that up."

Craig arched an eyebrow, and I explained my encounter with 'Alexandra' the night before.

"You've entered the charmed circle," Craig said. "Sebastian obviously wants you to do something for him."

"Oh, he wants me to do something, alright. He wants me to pay him too much money for his fucking company," I said, mindful of the mistakes Craig had made about Jacqueline and her husband.

"If Sebastian pushed that girl my way last night, it meant he's seen a dossier on me and knew I had an Australian wife," I said, playing along with the possibility Craig was right. I wanted to ask Craig about how he got Jacqueline's career details so wrong, but I decided to wait until later in the conversation. First, I wanted to hear more about what Craig did know—or thought he knew. "Guys often stray with women who remind them of their wives. The funny thing is, when we met for the first time two days ago, he pretended he didn't know for sure that it was me. But he must have known, and he probably already had last night's honey trap set up."

I had to think this through. After everything I had read in the analysis of the TransPac acquisition, and after my three days in Hong Kong, I was convinced the deal made sense. Acquiring Nin's bond-trading operation would be a significant boost to Coldstream Holdings position in Asia. I knew that Houghton, the managing director of Coldstream Holdings Hong Kong, badly wanted TransPac, and I was inclined to agree with him. The major obstacle to getting this deal done was determining the fair value of TransPac as the cataclysm in the markets lowered its value hourly. But that was what I was in Hong Kong to figure out. Perhaps Sebastian just couldn't help himself—he wanted to improve his odds in any way he could. On the other hand, maybe Craig was wrong. Or maybe Craig was right and Sebastian really wanted to do his version of the deal with Massoud and Pendidikan, but when he told me about it last night, it had struck me as a mere gambit, too far-fetched to be what he really wanted. Catching me compromising myself could be one way to get whatever it was he wanted, an ace even if he didn't need one.

I remembered Mark Twain's description of "the calm confidence of a good Christian with four aces". That was how Sebastian would get religion too. Perhaps he figured there was too much at stake not to try and acquire some leverage over me. The other alternative was that, given the poisoned situation with Entrekin and his team, perhaps Sebastian was just trying to buy himself some insurance that I would support him, instead of Entrekin, when push came to shove. Perhaps he had mentioned the silent partners as a way of testing me to see what I knew about them, in case Entrekin was trying to cut him out, which, of course, Entrekin was trying to do. As I reflected on it, though, something bothered me.

Maybe it was Sebastian's method to try too hard. Perhaps it was just the way he did business. He'd called Dorfman and Brightling thirty or forty times when they wouldn't take his calls.

But maybe he wasn't trying too hard: maybe there was something rotten in the deal I didn't know about yet. Maybe Sebastian was trying to get leverage over me so that, in case I did find out what it was and decided to pull Coldstream out of the deal, Sebastian would have a chance to get me to think again. The idea there was something very wrong with the deal, and Sebastian knew it and was trying to get me to do the deal anyway—that worried me. Seriously worried me.

I wanted Craig's advice, but I couldn't tell him any of this. Nothing is more confidential than an acquisition of this magnitude in a collapsing market like the one we were in. One leak anywhere would be magnified by the general hysteria already out there a million—or a billion—times over. Everyone in the market was frantically scanning the horizon for a sign, any sign, that would tell them what is going to happen next. A whisper in such conditions could rapidly and monstrously boil up into a typhoon, blowing away the deal and devastating everything else in its path. No, I couldn't confide anything about the acquisition to Craig, so I permitted myself anger.

"That little son of a bitch Sebastian just won't let me alone," I said. "He hounded me and harassed me as a kid, and now he's doing it again. Poisonous bastard. What the hell does he have against me?"

Craig sat back in his chair and crossed his arms. "Don't be too hard on poor Sebastian," he said softly.

I was stunned. "What do you mean?"

"Well, look," said Craig, "he may not mean it entirely in a bad way."

"I don't know what you're talking about," I said. "The guy has been a pain in the ass since we were kids. I can't believe he's still carrying on like this when there's so much at stake."

"Well, I don't know what the two of you are up to this time—"

"Sebastian and I are trying to get something done despite what's going on in the markets," I said. "It would be a lot easier if he and I cooperated, that's all."

"I don't think it's a big secret Coldstream has been talking with TransPac for some time about investing in them," said Craig, looking at me thoughtfully. "Hmm. But you tell me what you want to tell me. Well, let me put it this way. I think that Sebastian had a bit of a schoolboy crush on you. Did you ever notice?"

"You're kidding me."

"No, I'm not, actually," Craig said calmly.

"I don't get it. Sebastian did everything he could to torment me back then."

"And how can you tell when a kid likes another kid?" Craig asked. "They tease, they pinch, they shove and hit each other on the playground. Don't ask me why, but that's the way it is."

I shook my head. "I think you're mistaken, Craig. I think it was all mixed up with Jacqueline. Maybe he didn't approve of me. Maybe I was jealous. But I can't believe he had a crush on me. That's crazy. Is he gay now?"

"Everybody's gay," Craig said, smiling. "Some of you just don't know it yet."

"Well, if Sebastian's gay the way I'm gay, you don't have much of a case," I said.

Craig laughed. "One can always hope," he said. "To be honest, I don't have any hard evidence about Sebastian. The out-of-the-closet gay community in Hong Kong is fairly small, and Sebastian doesn't hang out in the clubs. I don't know anyone who's slept with him. But I did have a funny experience with him years ago, probably the last time I saw him, when I came back from the States after dropping out of Cornell. I was walking down Ladder Street, and at the last minute I saw Sebastian Nin walking up Ladder Street. I recognized him and stopped. He caught my eye and stopped too."

Craig stopped and smiled with mock modesty. "If I do say so, I was looking pretty good. I had lost weight and was cutting my hair differently than I had when I was King George V. In any case, Sebastian gave me the eye, and asked innocently if Hollywood Road was up the hill."

"Why did he ask that?" I said. "What could be more obvious? He knew Hollywood Road was right at the top of Ladder Street."

Craig chuckled. "He obviously hadn't recognized me, and when I stopped, he thought I had something else on my mind. The boy tried to pick me up! He would have been twenty-two or twenty-three by then. I was so flabbergasted, I just nodded and kept going down Ladder Street. To this day, I don't know if he later figured out it was me. In any case, he has certainly never come by my shop."

I thought about it. "Okay," I said. "Maybe there's something to your theory. But I still don't get it."

"I don't know if it has anything to do with anything," Craig said. "You and Sebastian play with millions and billions, and presumably what you guys do relates more to that than to anything else. At least I hope so—it's other people's money you're playing with. A little of it's even mine! Very little. But it was as clear as day to me back then that Sebastian had a crush on you. Think back—you were a tall, blond-haired, blue-eyed *gweilo*. There was something sort of adventurous and corrupt about you . . ."

"In your dreams," I grinned. "Jacqueline wouldn't have agreed with that. And I didn't get laid for another five years after that."

"You were a diamond in the rough," Craig said. "I stand by my analysis. The thing is, for a Chinese kid like me, or for a Eurasian kid like Sebastian, you looked like everything the advertisements and the movies and the photos in the magazines were telling us was the ideal."

"Sorry, but that's bullshit." I said. "I mean, I would like to believe you in a way. It's flattering. But do you remember 'Enter the Dragon'? Remember Bruce Lee? At the King George V that I remember, every school boy, *gweilo* foreign devils and Chinese, wanted to be Bruce Lee."

Craig shrugged. "Well, speaking personally," he said. "I wanted to be Bruce Lee so I could sleep with someone like you. Of course, that was all in kind of a vague, half-conscious way."

"So you're saying I was in love with the wrong Nin kid." I smiled.

"Were we talking about love?" said Craig, arching his eyebrows.

"No, I suppose not," I said, knowing as I said it I was lying to Craig. "I don't really know how I felt. Jacqueline and I were too young."

I did love Jacqueline back then, deeply. And I was still a liar.

Craig looked at me skeptically. "Didn't you and Jacqueline write for years after you left Hong Kong?"

I nodded.

"Well?" he said.

I shrugged. "The point is, I don't think Sebastian tried to set me up last night with that Australian bait, if he did, because he had a crush on me as a schoolboy or because he had some weird feeling of inferiority. I mean, from what I remember, King George V was basically a race-free environment. That was one of the things I remember best about the place. I've always respected those Brit administrators and teachers for enforcing that kind of environment."

Craig sighed. "Look, it's a complicated subject. I agree with you in a sense. King George V wasn't about the English upper class—the teachers and the kids were from the most intrepid element of the English commercial middle class—traders and brokers and businessmen from Leeds and Manchester and Bristol—they certainly weren't aristocrats. The school wasn't too bad in that sense. Almost class-free in an imperial sort of way. But you have a different perspective having been there as a *gweilo* than I do as a Chinese. I'm not sure it's worth going into."

"But what about the fact the Nins were a mixed couple themselves?" I asked. "And it was Sebastian's mother who was the *gweilo*. By your logic, Sebastian should have been totally fine, no chip on his shoulder. First, he was Eurasian, and second, if he had any problems with *gweilos*, it was his Chinese dad who had taken a *gweilo* wife. That should have reassured him if he had issues about the respective power of Westerners and Chinese."

Craig threw up his hands. "For all I know, it may have made it worse," he said. "My parents had eight children, but they were hardly an advertisement for marriage. The last thing in the world I would want was my dad's or my mom's life. Who knows what went on in the Nin's house?"

I broke out laughing. "I don't know what it is about you Hong Kong natives, but all this old gossip from our childhoods just doesn't make a rat's ass worth of difference any more. Our destinies were not determined by the moment of our births, or by the stars, or even by the years we studied at King George V. I know the English like to say that the battle of Waterloo was won on the playing fields of Eton, but the older I get, the more I think of that idea as just another unchallenged piece of imperialist propaganda. You should have heard the way Sebastian Nin was carrying on yesterday about his sister! I couldn't believe it."

Craig looked a little hurt.

"In any case," he said, "the real reason I wanted to have lunch with you is to tell you that—"

I wondered why the restaurant allowed meter readers from Hong Kong Electric to read the electricity meter during one of the busiest times of the day. But the torches pointing at the alcove wall weren't ordinary torches. As two beams of light traced across the wall between us and came to rest on Craig's chest, I saw they were shining from two tactical lights affixed beneath the barrels of silenced Heckler & Koch universal self-loading pistols.

Craig's shirt began to ripple violently away from dark holes that appeared obscenely to the abrupt hisses of the silenced pistols. Craig didn't weigh much, and the sound of his head and shoulders smacking against the wood was as loud as the bullets knocking against the wall behind his body.

As they killed Craig, the two men stood with their backs to the other diners. A cry was caught in my throat, but I flung my hand out, trying to chop at the forearm of the man standing closest to me. He half turned and suddenly I was looking, partially blinded by the torchlight in my eyes, into the deep ugly hole at the end of his silencer. I froze. His partner squeezed two more hissing shots into Craig, now slumped in the booth, and the ugly knocking of the bullets ceased.

The two men burst through the kitchen doors and were gone.

CHAPTER THIRTEEN

I SAT IN MY CHAIR. I was staring at Craig's shoulder, which was dark with blood, all that was visible of his body.

"Craig," I said, lurching up. I pulled the table back, thinking to make more room so that I could get close to Craig and prop him back up.

Craig's body rolled under the table. I frantically tried to pull him back up to the seat, but my hands sank into a morass of flesh and torn fabric and splintered bones.

They told me later I was shouting, that I kept fighting off the kitchen workers with my elbows as I tried to lift Craig up. His entire upper torso had been ripped and rendered into loosely connected pieces, and I couldn't get a proper grip.

The lights went on, and I was pulled off of Craig's body and forced into a chair at one of the tables closest to the alcove where we had been seated.

I was fumbling for my wallet with hands covered in blood when the police came. I still had the business card Craig had given me the day before. I wanted to call Winston and tell him what had happened to Craig. I didn't know any of his brothers and sisters. I kept thinking it was the least I could do.

The police had arrived after only a few minutes. I remember thinking Hong Kong seemed to offer its citizens the same deal New York did; they couldn't prevent you from being stabbed, shot, burglarized, beaten, or raped, but they could get there as quickly as possible to pick up the pieces once it happened. I told the police everything I could. It wasn't much.

As I answered their questions, I looked at the scarred, bloodstained wall against which Craig had been seated. I couldn't tell because of the silencers, but the killers must have been using forties, or maybe even the forty-five caliber H & K, originally designed for the United States Special Operations Command. The carnage they had wreaked, and the fact the killers didn't bother with head shots, looked like they had been firing hollow points.

About the time the police photographer was finishing up, the police said I could go. The medic had had the stretcher organized for almost an hour by this time, and he had been mostly standing around waiting to take Craig's body to the city morgue. He asked me if I would like a sedative. I told him no, thanks.

I stepped over the police tape and went into the kitchen to wash my hands and the sleeves of my suit coat. A policeman nodded and said, "You have blood on your face, too. Nose and forehead."

A kitchen hand wiped my face with a wet cloth. I found if I buttoned all three buttons, the jacket of my suit covered most of the bloodstains on my shirt.

Somebody told me a taxi was waiting outside, and I made my way through the restaurant. Outside on Glenealy Street was more police tape, police cars and an ambulance with flashing lights, and a big crowd.

I was escorted through the crowd and got into the taxi.

"The Peninsula, please," I said.

I must have been in a daze as I made my way through the lobby to the lifts, and then when I got to my floor, along the corridor to my suite. The maids were still in the hallway, and as I walked by, they stopped and looked at me in shock, the beginnings of friendly smiles frozen on their faces.

I think my brain started working again in the shower, as tides of hot water flowed over my head and shoulders. I was starting to feel clean until I looked down and saw Craig's dark blood still swirling in the water, and I stayed in the shower until I was completely waterlogged.

I thought of calling Sam, but it was three in the afternoon, so it was two o'clock in the morning in Vermont. I started thinking about where everything I had brought to Hong Kong was located around my suite, and I must have stood in the shower of several minutes, imagining in perfect detail the process of getting packed for the airport. Then I thought of sending an email to Walmsley; I would never be able to forgive myself if I telephoned him at this hour like a panicked kid. The simple procedure involved in turning on the computer and logging into the Coldstream network just seemed so hard. Too hard.

I got out of the shower, dried off, and mechanically started to shave, even though it was the middle of the day. The feel of my familiar things began to comfort me, and for the first time the tense, strained feeling in my chest and the numbness in my head started to lift slightly. I finished shaving, and then continued with my morning routine exactly as I always did. Years ago, I had evolved these habits as a way of providing a centering, a familiar order to the day, regardless of where on the planet I happened to be that morning. It was working.

I had only brought one other suit, but it was fresh and dry-cleaned. I had plenty of everything else. Still naked, I sat on the bed and rang Coldstream's Hong Kong offices.

I got put through to Houghton, the managing director. Houghton was the biggest supporter of the TransPac acquisition, and I had been planning to meet with him as soon as I got a break in the action. Now seemed like a good time.

"Dusty! How the hell are you?"

"Oh, I've been better, Rick. Do you have half an hour for me to come see you? We need to have a chat."

"Absolutely," he said. "I meant to ask you out for dinner last night, but ended up working until two in the morning. Sorry I've left you on your own with the TransPac mess. I've been fighting a whole host of fires trying to deal with the effect of the financial crisis on our regular businesses."

"How does it look?" I asked.

"Bad," he said. "I'm afraid this could knock Asia back ten, maybe twenty years."

"I hope not," I said.

"Me too," Houghton said. "But it's pretty ugly out there, every day a new record low for every Asian currency, prices for stocks back where they were in the late '70s, bond prices—"

"I know," I said. "Why don't I show up at your office in the next half hour?"

"Fine," Houghton said.

When I arrived at Coldstream's offices, I was given a special temporary pass that was valid for a week. The offices were predictably amazing, with sweeping views across Hong Kong. When I was shown in to his huge office, Houghton was seated at a conference table to the left of his massive desk, poring over some documents with several people. They left after brief introductions.

Houghton and I sat down at the table. Houghton shook a couple of cigarettes out of a pack and offered one to me.

"No thanks," I said.

"I quit smoking five years ago," said Houghton ruefully, squinting as he lit up. "I started bumming my secretary's cigarettes last week, and I finally sent her out to buy me some yesterday. I'll have to quit all over again when this is over."

He peered at me through the smoke.

"I hope you don't mind my asking, but are you alright? You look a little pale."

"Oh, I was having a just fabulous time until lunch," I said. "You know what fun this TransPac deal is."

Houghton grimaced.

"But an old friend I was having lunch with at this little place on Glenealy Street got shot in front of me right as we were sitting there."

Houghton froze. "You're kidding me."

"No," I said. "I'm not."

"My God," Houghton said. "What was it—some kind of bungled robbery? We've had some amazing shit happen in Hong Kong the last couple of years."

"No, no," I said. "A couple of guys just pulled out H & K's—you know, high-end military class semiautomatics—with tactical lights and silencers on them, and just blew him to pieces. I mean, it was fucking terrible."

"That's extraordinary," Houghton said. "Who was this guy?"

"Craig Chin, an old friend of mine from King George V—"

"Not the rug guy," Houghton said.

"Yeah, he owned the store on Hollywood Road," I said.

"Shit, my wife got us some rugs from him," Houghton said. "She's not going to believe it." He rubbed his forehead. "Holy shit, what a week this has been.

"Look, are you all squared away with the police and the authorities? Is there anything we can do? I can arrange to have our in-house counsel give you a briefing on Hong Kong criminal law or anything you might want to know. I suppose you're a material witness to the murder."

"Thanks, Rick," I said. "I've given my statement to the police, and they've got my address at the Peninsula. I had the concierge send over to them all the clothes I was wearing, in case they want to do any further analysis on it."

"Okay, right," Houghton said. "You might want to contact the US Consulate as well, just to keep them in the loop. Wait—you're not an American, are you?"

"No, I'm Dutch on my dad's side and Swedish on my mom's side," I said. "But I went to college in the States, and after I got out of college I enlisted in the US Army for a few years to piss off my father—it worked, Dad just about went nuts, it was almost worth it—but I still don't have a US passport, just a green card."

"Ah, so that's how you knew about the gun gizmos you saw today," Houghton said.

"I guess that's right," I said. "Look, Rick, I know that this sounds paranoid, but there is a possibility—a remote one, no doubt—that Craig's death has some connection to the TransPac acquisition."

Houghton looked at me. "You're under a great deal of stress right now, Dusty."

"Yeah, yeah," I said. "I know. I know it sounds crazy, too. But Craig did go to school with Sebastian Nin, and he knows everybody who is anybody in Hong Kong—"

"Do yourself a favor, Dusty," Houghton said kindly. "Leave the murder investigation to the Hong Kong Metropolitan Police and concentrate on getting the TransPac deal done. You've got enough on your plate."

"That's sensible," I said. "But the thing is, Craig didn't seem the least bit worried when I saw him yesterday and today. If he had some gambling debts, or who knows what else, that were serious enough to get him killed by obvious professionals, it would have been building up for some time. He would have seemed more nervous, more upset—"

"Dusty, you're in shock," Houghton said, "and he was your friend. Jesus, my heart goes out to you. But you've got to be able to separate your job from this—this terrible tragedy you've just witnessed."

He looked at me intently. "I mean, do you think you're capable of going on—or do you think you should take a break?"

It brought me up short. "A break? What break? This deal won't be around when I get back from a break. I could blink and the deal might be dead."

"Oh, no," said Houghton quietly. "No, if we didn't have your expertise available, we might just have to accept a little more risk and go ahead and do this deal. I know Walmsley sent you out to kind of audit the work we've done here on behalf of the Executive Committee. But Walmsley's days as the managing partner of Coldstream Holdings aren't going to last forever. He sure as hell doesn't have the right to get into the middle of the strategy we've put in place for building our presence here in Asia. He's way out of line if he thinks he can do that."

"I think there's some kind of misunderstanding," I said. "I got yanked out of Buenos Aires and told by Walmsley to get over here to save the TransPac deal."

"Well, it's nice to know Jim wants the deal saved," Houghton said, "but it's kind of disappointing to hear he thinks it needed saving."

"Rick, I don't know what you're talking about," I said. "These markets are shit-canning every deal on the planet. Have you checked your emails the last couple of days? I don't know if you're copied in on all the international M & A traffic, but it is fucking bleak out there. And we're at the epicenter. The TransPac deal is ground zero."

"I know this is a crisis," Houghton said, "and I appreciate your help."

"This isn't a crisis," I said. "This is a crisis deluxe."

"Don't be penny wise, pound foolish," said Houghton. "Entrekin called me last night and said he was concerned that you were really putting the screws to them on price."

"My obligation is to ensure we don't pay too much," I said. "Especially for an asset that looks like it might have been gutshot by what's happening out here."

"You don't know what the future holds," Houghton said. "Your valuation model is just a house of cards."

I stood up. "I've got to get back to the War Room."

"Don't let this deal get away, Dusty," Houghton said.

CHAPTER FOURTEEN

ON THE RIDE BACK TO TRANSPAC, I thought over what Houghton said. It was obvious he wanted to do the TransPac deal, but I knew that before I arrived in Hong Kong. His name was all over the material I had read on the flight. I remembered now that there had been a Houghton faction three years ago when Walmsley was voted in as managing partner of Coldstream Holdings. At the time, Houghton wasn't considered a serious contender, but he obviously nursed ambitions to make it to the top slot one day.

I had no desire to get caught in the middle of a political struggle between Walmsley and Houghton, and what Houghton had said about Craig's death was reasonable. I had been in Hong Kong for less than seventy-two hours, and I had no chance of unraveling a murder.

I did decide one thing—I was not going to get run out of Hong Kong.

When I got back to TransPac, I went to the War Room and checked on progress.

"It's ugly out there today," McKee said. "Markets down again across Asia."

Fai and Peter were sitting despondently at their table in front of their computers. I saw red-colored numerals running along the delta rows of the valuation executive summary. A wipeout in the Asian market. London was just opening, and then New York would fire up five hours later.

"How's the restructure of the model going?" I said.

Fai and Peter shrugged. McKee observed them silently and then looked up at me. "We're running behind, Dusty. I'd say about half way through. We'll be working on it for most of the night."

"Okay," I said.

I took McKee aside and told him about the killing.

He nodded his head solemnly. "You didn't look too good when you came in," he said.

I waited for him to ask whether I thought there was some connection to the TransPac deal.

"Is there anything else you want done with the model?" he asked. "Maybe you should get some rest."

McKee had one of the most logical minds I had ever come across, and the idea that Craig's killing was somehow linked to the TransPac deal hadn't occurred to him. Houghton was right; I must be in shock.

I called Nin.

"It's Street," I said. "How's it going?"

"Okay," he said. "Not great. It'll pick up."

"I'm going to come up to the trading floor."

"Sure, why not."

I caught the lift and punched the button for the trading floor. Nin came out to meet me at reception and escorted me through the security doors onto the trading floor. As we stepped onto the floor, before the doors closed behind us, I knew something was wrong. Hundreds of people were in that room. I walked among the positions. The traders and salespeople spoke in low murmurs among themselves and then fell silent as we approached. Assistants were reading gossip magazines. It was like a train station filled with people waiting for the train to a place they didn't want to go.

"I built this from the ground up," said Nin. "When we got here, there was nothing. We did our first six bond underwritings using nothing but some phones and accounting ledger books, the way Pierpont Morgan used to do them."

I stopped and asked a trader what the rupiah/dollar exchange rate was.

He told me, and then he looked at his screen. "Headed down," he said.

I glanced at Nin. "What would J. P. Morgan do in a situation like this?"

Nin's face darkened as blood flowed to it. His brow contracted and his upper lip tightened back from his teeth. "How long have you been in this business?" he asked me. "Soeharto is announcing a new budget tonight. With the rupiah at these levels, the entire country of Indonesia will go bankrupt unless he does something. Do you think he's going to just sit there and let the country crater? Come on."

"I'm not sure Soeharto can fix Indonesia," I said. "It's not a question of shooting Communists this time. He might have to shoot you."

"He needs me," Nin said.

"No—he needs your money," I said. "And he already has that."

I looked around the trading floor—the house that Sebastian had built. The only energy I could sense coming from people was their fear.

Fai and Peter were going to have to redefine the lower limits of their downside case. At the rate the markets were going, we might hit those limits tomorrow.

I looked at Nin. "Got any idea when these markets are going to find the bottom?" I asked. Of course, no one did. I just wanted to hear how he would try to answer the question.

"The day starts in Asia, and sentiment is bad here," said Nin. "The markets come back when London and New York wake up. It'll be better in ten hours."

We walked to the edge of the trading floor. "Craig Chin was killed today. Shot to death. I was with him when it happened."

Nin stared at me. "What are you talking about?"

"Craig Chin, from King George V, was shot to death by two guys while we were having lunch on Glenealy Street."

"From King George V?" Nin asked. "He was a friend of Jacqueline's. They used to study together."

"He's dead," I said.

"God, that's awful," Nin said. "How do you think New York is going to open?"

I turned and walked back through security to the elevator bank and pushed the button.

"I'm afraid this deal might be too hard," I said. "I'm sorry."

The elevator arrived. I walked into the elevator and turned. Nin was staring at me as the doors closed. He didn't say a word. But for the first time, I saw on his face an expression I remembered. It was one of Jacqueline's expressions, too.

I returned to the War Room and called Entrekin.

I considered telling him that the deal was dead. Just to put a rocket up his ass, like I had just done to Sebastian.

"Are you free for dinner?" he asked.

"No, but thanks," I said. "I'm going to be working with the guys for a while here and then I'll need another good night's rest. Maybe tomorrow."

"Richard told me you endured a terrible shock today," Entrekin said. "I want to extend my personal condolences to you."

"Thanks, Simon," I said. "I appreciate it."

"Let me know if there's anything that I can do, anything at all," he said.

It was a long haul that evening working on the model. Peter kept nodding off in his seat and Fai stared dully at us when I asked him a question, hardly able to speak. I kept wondering whether there was any point in continuing to push them so hard, with the odds against this deal mounting so rapidly. I decided there still was. It was partly selfish, as I found it soothing to lose myself in the long columns of numbers. There is a kind of Zen-like order and harmony in a smoothly functioning financial model—as unreal as it may be.

At seven thirty I got through to Walmsley, and gave him a briefing on the day. Several Asian currencies had hit new record lows again, and the Indonesian rupiah had hit its lowest level in almost thirty years.

I told Walmsley it looked like the firm's equity was close to worthless.

"Shit, that's no good," he said. "Those guys thought that their shares were worth a billion dollars a few months ago. They won't do a deal unless they make some real money on it."

"I know, Jim," I said. "I've got the guys working on recoding the model so we can see if paying out some of the bonds early helps improve value. The model will tell us whether or not to kill the deal."

"Well, what do you think?" Walmsley asked.

"It depends on what the model says. I'd say it's probably still worth doing," I said. "But who knows what these currencies will look like at the end of the week? At this rate, Southeast Asia is going bankrupt."

"Dusty, is this still worth doing?" Walmsley asked. "I mean, Houghton had the right idea when he identified TransPac as an acquisition opportunity at the beginning of the year, but maybe it's time to cut bait and move on."

"I hate to have to advise you to write off the ten million dollars in transaction costs we've already spent on this deal," I said. "But unless the model tells us that we can offer some extra money to Entrekin and his guys, this deal isn't going to get done. TransPac has been too badly hurt by these market declines."

"I don't give a shit about the ten million. No point throwing good money after bad," Walmsley said.

"I agree," I said. "I know Houghton wants TransPac badly, and to be fair to him, it doesn't make sense to turn out the lights without looking at the value of the changes we've been making to the model. I'll know first thing tomorrow morning, Hong Kong time."

"I guess that's right," Walmsley said. "Keep in touch."

"Sure thing," I said.

"Hey, and I'm really sorry about your friend," Walmsley said. "I was in an airplane crash outside Ames, Iowa twenty years ago. I was okay, but the pilot and one of the two guys I was traveling with got killed. The other guy broke both legs and his back."

"What did you do?"

"Well, in the first place I pulled everybody out of the plane," Walmsley said. "Then I walked to a farm house, asked to use the phone, and called an ambulance, and when the ambulance arrived I rode with Roberts to the hospital. Then I called the families and broke the news. I went back a week later and got the deal."

"Yeah, I'm going to see Craig's family tomorrow," I said. "If this deal is do-able, I'll get it done."

"I know you will," Walmsley said.

By ten o'clock that night it looked like Fai and Peter were about finished with the major recoding of the model.

"Let's call it a night," I said. "We'll re-group tomorrow at 6.30 a.m., do the cleanup and reformatting on the model, and start running sensitivities."

"Okay," McKee said.

I left them tidying up and got in a taxi and told the driver to take me back to the Peninsula.

CHAPTER FIFTEEN

NIN RANG SHORTLY AFTER I got back to the hotel.

"What can I do for you?" I said.

"Listen, Dusty, you sounded pretty discouraged a few hours ago," Nin said.

"Discouraged isn't the right word."

"I don't want you to do anything hasty."

"Don't worry. I've thought about it."

"Oh, you're not going to walk away from the deal?" Nin said, surprise in his voice. "Because that's the way you sounded—"

"The deal's about ninety-five percent dead, Sebastian," I said. "I'm only waiting to see what difference some changes to the model we've made might make. We'll know tomorrow morning, but I wouldn't get your hopes up. I'm being honest with you."

"Wait a minute," Nin cried. There was a silence on the phone. "Let me ask you a question—why did Coldstream get into the deal in the first place?"

"You know the answer to that," I said. I was kicking off my clothes, walking around the room, and pouring myself a cold vodka and soda.

"Sure," he said. "And my question to you is, have any of those things changed?"

I sipped my drink and looked across the harbor at the foreboding hills rising behind Kowloon. "No, but everything else has."

"Coldstream has always wanted my customers, my franchise, and my team and me—right?"

"Right," I said.

"Coldstream can still have all that," Nin said. His voice was urgent. "There's an important reason you should close this deal."

"Okay," I said, considering putting Nin on hold and ordering dinner from room service. "What is it? Tell me now."

"No, I need to show you," Nin said. "Why don't I come by and pick you up. Can you be ready in twenty minutes?"

I stared down at the room service menu resting on my knees. The prospect of a quiet night and an excellent meal was appealing. In the morning I could be on a flight back to New York.

"Okay," I said.

Nin picked me up in his late-model metallic blue Porsche, and we raced off up the Peak. Nin talked rapidly as he downshifted into the curves and stepped on the accelerator.

"The value of my firm to your firm lies in two areas. First, there's the securities TransPac holds from its various deals. Okay, so maybe that's gone down a lot. Second is TransPac's customer relationships across Asia."

"Yeah," I said, "and if I discover that TransPac is really a friend of the friendless, and does deals with people nobody else will touch, then I've got a real problem. In fact, I have to struggle to remember what the point of coming to Hong Kong was."

"Hey, Dusty, give me a break—the heart of the matter is really the value of our customer relationships. That's the soul of TransPac. And I can tell you, the soul is healthy. The hundreds of people we have working in sales and trading across Asia tell you that. I swear to you that those people have relationships around Asia that are without peer—and both sound and healthy."

"I'm glad to hear you say that, Sebastian," I said. "Because my view is a simple one. A bond is a promise. A promise to pay. A thirty-year bond is a thirty-year promise, longer than most marriages last. And I have found that bad people don't keep their promises. So, there's no point trying to buy a bond operation that relies on the promises of bad people. It's as simple as that."

The engine of Nin's Porsche whined as he suddenly downshifted and nosed toward the curb. I was expecting to be taken to a group of Asian businessmen, or possibly a group of Nin's bond trading and sales team.

We pulled through the gates of one of Hong Kong's finest apartment towers in the Mid-Levels, and we stepped out of the elevator into a magnificent multi-room penthouse with panoramic views of the harbor.

"This is my place," he said quietly.

The lights were already on, and Nin showed me into his living room. A saxophonist who sounded like Coltrane was playing "Every Time We Say Goodbye" over the speakers. A woman was seated on the sofa.

"Jacqueline," I said.

"Dusty."

Jacqueline rose from the sofa, the lights of Hong Kong gleaming through the windows behind her, and approached me.

She was still the image I retained in memory, only unimaginably better. The shy schoolgirl I had known now wore a beautifully cut décolleté frock suspended from her shoulders by thin straps. It was the simplest and most fascinating dress in the world.

Her lustrous black hair was also dressed with the utmost simplicity; only a master could have cut her hair with the faithfulness to such a single pure idea. As a school girl, Jacqueline had parted her hair on the top of her head, drawing back the long strands behind her ears. Now, her hair was parted on the left, and a cascade of lush sable seemed to flow just past each cheekbone and along the line of her chin. On one side, her hair draped gently on her shoulder. On the other side, it swung free, shining in the light, and setting off to maximum effect her lovely chin.

She lightly placed her hands on my shoulders and presented a perfumed cheek to kiss.

I kissed her cheek, my dazzled eyes catching her eyes at the distance of inches, and kissed her other cheek.

Her hands were still on my shoulders, her face was still close to mine, and she murmured, "I was so sorry to hear what happened to poor Craig today. I'm just heartbroken. Sebastian told me you were right there when it happened. You must be absolutely shattered. It's so sad and awful."

"Thank you," I said. "Please forgive me, but I can't talk about it."

"Oh, I can imagine," she said. "Words just fail me when I think of poor dear Craig. And you."

We sat down. "I'll be okay as long as I'm still in shock," I said.

Jacqueline watched Sebastian pour red wine into glasses for us. He set the bottle on the table in front of the sofa and walked out onto the balcony, where I saw his shadow slide along the windows to the right and disappear.

She turned her head with a sudden movement and looked at me. I couldn't help noticing her hair, how her earrings sparkled, her fine shoulders and elegant neck, and how her legs shifted as if she were rocketing down a *piste*.

"You poor darling," she said. She picked up the wine glasses and gave one to me.

I lifted my glass. "Cheers," I said.

She put her arm on the sofa behind me and turned toward me. "Now, tell me what you're doing in Hong Kong if you can," she said. "Sebastian is acting very mysteriously."

I couldn't help being intensely aware of her presence.

"I think I'm trying to do a deal that probably shouldn't get done," I said. "Except every hour or so I change my mind and try not to do a deal that perhaps should get done."

"I thought you were working with Sebastian and TransPac," Jacqueline said.

"I'm not sure who or what I'm working with anymore," I said.

"What a peculiar thought!"

"This is a peculiar deal," I said.

There was unmistakable amusement in her eyes. She set her glass on her thigh, close against her flat belly, and patted my hand. "You were always so gloomy," she said. "I can see some things haven't changed."

I can't remember what we first spoke about after we found our places on the sofa because my senses were overwhelmed by her presence, and by my growing realization the shy, reserved, girl I had known so many years ago existed only in my memory and had evolved into an exceptionally exciting and compelling woman.

"I thought it was such an odd thing when Sebastian told me that you were here in Hong Kong over the holidays," Jacqueline said. "I told him that surely you should be home with your family, but he said that you were working together on an important deal. Isn't that wonderful."

"Sort of," I said. "Are you visiting your parents?"

"Yes, I often come for a visit around Chinese New Year's, and spend Christmas with my in-laws in the States. But this year we decided to come to Hong Kong for Christmas. My husband Nathan flew back yesterday to go back to work."

Jacqueline had spoken with a cut-glass English accent when she was a girl. I had noticed that Sebastian's accent had become almost completely American, but Jacqueline's accent, although her vowels had opened up, still sounded more English than not. She had a Mid-Atlantic accent now—a foundation of English with an acceptable trace of the American accent.

I sat back against the sofa and stretched my legs next to the table. "I can't believe I'm seeing you," I said.

"Now," Jacqueline said, running her fingers along my shoulder, "tell me all about your wonderful family. I'm sure you have the most adorable wife and children. Boys? Girls?"

I could see Jacqueline had had a good life. Age had only enhanced her beauty. Her lips were full, now shaped slightly with a sensual curve that had been lacking in the plump lips I remembered, which used to remind me of little sections of pink grapefruit.

"I've got a girl and a boy," I said. "Eleven and eight. My wife is Australian. Or did Sebastian tell you?"

Jacqueline hesitated. "No, I don't think he did," she said.

The biggest change to her face was her eyebrows. When Jacqueline glanced away from me, I could see their mature shape, arched and somehow challenging, like a hawk. But when she looked directly at me, as she was now, I was transfixed by her warm brown eyes, which looked out from underneath her vaguely threatening eyebrows with extraordinary humanity and intensity.

"Now that I think of it," she said, "I'm absolutely certain he never mentioned it."

Jacqueline's eyes were incredibly mobile. She arched her eyebrows and her eyes widened.

"You know, you've grown up quite a bit since I last saw you," I said. "I'm glad to see laboratory coats aren't as boring as I remember them being either."

Jacqueline glanced down at herself. "This is vintage Emanuel Ungaro. I let Nathan toil these days. I haven't set foot in a laboratory in almost ten years."

"Sebastian told me a little bit about what you did at Stanford and Albert Einstein," I said. "You have serious intellectual horsepower inside your beautiful head. But I always knew that."

There was also a serious body inside that Ungaro.

"I lost track of you almost twenty years ago. What did you do after we stopped writing? Or, as I should say, after you *abruptly* terminated our correspondence!"

"I was busy making lots of stupid decisions back then," I said. "First, after graduating, I went to New York. Just up the railroad track from Princeton, so it was kind of the obvious thing to do. I took my Hasselblad and a backpack and found a little dingy apartment in the East Village, and I tried to make it as a photographer."

"At least that sounds interesting," Jacqueline said. "You used to always write about how you were planning to get your MBA. That seemed so dull."

"Well, that was what my dad had always wanted me to do, as you may remember. Get my Harvard MBA and become CEO of IBM," I said. "I eventually got my law degree, but first I spent two years in the East Village, and then I was in the US Army for six years."

"The US Army! That's the last place I would have expected you to end up," said Jacqueline. Her eyes seemed molten.

"I was just a trooper with the 82nd Airborne," I said. "I decided to get out when I was at Fort Bragg. I had been hanging out with a bunch of D Boys—members of Delta Force, the most elite unit in the US Special Forces—and one day they asked me if I wanted to go up for a HALO jump—High Altitude, Low Opening. You go up about thirty thousand feet and jump. You can't even open your parachute for the first fifteen thousand feet."

"What an awful idea," Jacqueline said. "I would have left the army, too."

"Well, I wasn't HALO qualified, I'd just done all the usual tactical jumps. But my friends talked me into going up with them on the jump, just for the ride, they said—they were going to jump and I would fly back down with the pilot and land at the airbase. We were in the cargo hold of a C-141, unpressurized, so I had an oxygen mask on too, and the jump master told me the safety regs required I put on the full jump harness and parachute. When we got to the jump location, they all grabbed me and threw me out the back of the plane—at thirty thousand feet—and then jumped with me. Oh, and this was a night jump, as well."

"When we landed, they gathered around me laughing and slapping my back and told me this was my official invitation to qualify for Delta Force."

"What did you do?"

"What did I do? I told them they were all a bunch of maniacs who should be in prison, and I got the fuck out of the US Army, that's what I did. I resigned that day. I had already been accepted to Columbia Law School, and so I left the Army, got my law degree and joined Coldstream."

Jacqueline was sitting very close to me, her knees drawn up on the couch.

"Well, it was silly of you to stop writing to me, just like that," she said.

I met her eyes. She looked at me steadily, raising her chin almost imperceptibly so that the light glowed on her cheekbones and reflected in her eyes.

"Well, I'll tell you what happened," I said. "I rang you, remember?"

"Yes," Jacqueline said. "It was very late at night, and you woke me up, and I asked you a very civil question, and then you got angry and hung up. Then you wrote me an awful, short letter and I never saw you again."

I cleared my throat. "That's right. I did. You asked me whether I still kept up with other old friends like this, and that offended me. As it happened, Craig Chin was staying with me that very week because he had flown to the New York area to interview at medical schools, and he was staying with me in Princeton. So, I felt indignant, and in a kind of iconoclastic, self-destructive frenzy I wrote a few sentences to you and mailed the letter."

"It was quite a polite letter," she said. "Brutal, but in a very polite way."

"That's the way I was brought up," I said.

"I must say, you made some peculiar decisions back then," she said. "I suppose I have you to blame for the fact I got married a year after Stanford to a guy who I thought was smart and earnest and sincere and good husband material. After you wrote and said goodbye, you seemed so authoritative and sure of yourself, I thought, 'Alright, then, Dusty must see something clearly that I'm not certain about yet, and so I'll accept his word for it. It's closed, over, finished.' And I guess I then went looking for a safe harbor, for somebody who would love me and be my partner for the rest of my life."

Jacqueline laughed briefly, bitterly. "And so I found him in a few months and within a few weeks allowed myself to be persuaded to marry him. He adored me so much, he said. He loved me eternally. Of course, he didn't know me at all. And we were divorced within two years, right after I graduated from medical school. Nathan is my second husband. I waited a long time after that first marriage."

She put a finger to my lips and smiled sadly. "One thing you did leave me with was the conviction destiny had chosen one man specially for me. But then you wrote me an angry letter and disappeared from my life."

"The reason I called you that night is because my grandparents, my dad's parents, had just had dinner with me," I said. "They were visiting from Amsterdam. And what they told me was that my mother wasn't my real mother. My real mother died in childbirth when I was born."

"You mean, the woman that I knew, your mother, the tall blonde—"

"Right," I said. "She was my father's second wife. My brother and sisters are my half-siblings. My mother is buried in a little cemetery in

Neuilly, near the Hôpital Américain where you and I were born. I try and visit her grave every time I go to Paris."

"Who was she?"

"Her name was Eva Schwichtenberg. Neither my grandparents nor my father could tell me much about her. She had no family. She had been in a concentration camp, the one at Dachau."

"So, she was Jewish?"

"I'm not sure," I said. "Dachau was mostly for political prisoners, so she may have been Jewish or she may have been ethnic German. I don't think I'll ever know. My grandparents told me over dinner. When I got home, I kind of didn't know what to do. I couldn't believe my parents hadn't ever told me, and I was really angry. But I was also so disoriented to think that this woman whom I had thought of as my mother all my life had nothing to do with me. It was such a relief. I felt such happiness. And of course, I was also curious to know more about my real mother— and I still am. That's the part I've never been able to do much about.

"All I can really do is go to the cemetery at Neuilly. So many records were destroyed during the war by the allied bombing of Germany it has proven impossible to learn anything more about my mother, Eva."

"I'm glad for you," Jacqueline said. "And I feel sorry for that young woman, your mother, who couldn't live, and never got to know her only son. She would have been delighted by you."

The beast with two backs appears first as an angel with two faces. Our lips were so close that the fragile and tender movement of our lips softly articulating words was very like kissing. Jacqueline's eyes shone just beyond mine like worlds of light. Angelic heads inclined toward one another.

I kissed her.

After a while I stood up and walked to the window and looked down on the harbor. My heart was pounding. Most of the lights had gone out in Hong Kong. Only the orange street lights illuminated the roads as they snaked among darkened office towers, around the waterfront, and up the mountain.

"We shouldn't have done that," I said. "I know that's kind of an obvious thing to say."

"Oh, don't be silly," Jacqueline said. "There's no harm in one little kiss between old friends. I enjoyed it."

She looked at me.

I turned away and looked at the view. "So did I, and that's the point."

I left the apartment shortly afterwards without seeing Sebastian. As I left, I started to kiss her on her cheek, but as soon as we were close and I looked into her eyes and breathed in the fragrance of her, I couldn't resist, and kissed her properly.

"I don't know what to think," I said.

"Please help Sebastian," she said. "He is surrounded by enemies."

On my way back to the hotel I rang Walmsley in New York.

"Jesus, what time is it there?" he asked. "It's the middle of the afternoon here."

"Yeah, it's late, Jim," I said. "I've been trying to work things out."

"It's a disaster out there today, Dusty," Walmsley said. "London opened straight down and New York hasn't been any better. Yields on government bonds are starting to go down all over the West, and investors are selling everything. Even the US stock market was down five percent today. If you can't sign the TransPac deal today or tomorrow, I think it's over."

"At this rate, Southeast Asia is going bankrupt," I said.

There was a silence on the phone.

"You can come home," Walmsley said.

"You mean walk out on TransPac?"

"Yeah. Leave Houghton to clean up. If we get the Hong Kong Monetary Authority involved now, they may be able to broker a deal to keep TransPac from collapsing."

"Give me another twenty-four hours," I said. "This could still be an opportunity for Coldstream to scoop up Nin and his bond-trading operation for next to nothing. In two years, we'd be laughing."

"I don't know," Walmsley said.

I took a deep breath, thinking of Jacqueline. "I owe it to Coldstream to stay," I said.

There was silence on the line.

"Okay," Walmsley said, at last. "Your call."

CHAPTER SIXTEEN

IT WAS HARD TO GET OUT of bed the next morning. I'd slept about three hours, and my brain felt heavy and inert. Craig Chin was dead, his body lying torn apart in the cold storage drawer of a police morgue. The doorbell rang, and a young man from room service appeared with a sumptuous breakfast, but the fruits and juices looked like smears of color on the tray as I tried to focus on them. I could hardly scribble my signature on the charge slip. My limbs were shaky with exhaustion.

As I sat in the armchair, my head hanging as I gazed through the windows at the winter sun glittering on the skyscrapers of Hong Kong, I began to feel warm and cheerful.

I had seen Jacqueline again. She was more beautiful than she was twenty years before. The stiff, rather cold beauty I remembered had been transformed into an incredible, charming woman—and I still loved her.

I poured myself a cup of coffee, rose and walked into the bathroom, and took a long hot shower. At first, I felt guilty—guilty about being so happy one day after Craig's death, not about seeing Jacqueline again. My God, I had kissed Jacqueline. I was delighted a kiss that had seemed frozen in time as an abandoned possibility of my early years had unexpectedly happened. I could still feel Jacqueline's hands on my shoulders, her body against mine, the smell of her hair and her perfume. At the same time, a terrible feeling of guilt and anxiety began to billow around inside me like squid ink. It was partly about Craig, yes, but also, I had to acknowledge my feelings of guilt about my marriage and what I had just done with a woman who was not my wife. But she was Jacqueline. Yet she was not my wife—however I regretted the truth, it was irrevocable.

I controlled the guilt with the thought that Jacqueline and I had simply been completing unfinished matters last night. Just tying up loose ends. Nothing to do with the future.

I had realized years ago that the phone call and the letter I wrote were just symptoms of a fundamental change that occurred the moment I realized that the woman I had grown up with was not my real mother. Suddenly, the psychological need that had dominated my adolescence— to win over this cold, unforgiving woman—vanished. There was nothing special about her; there was no need for me to surmount this particular obstacle; the meaning and purpose of my life, while still unknown to me, was now decisively decoupled from any requirement to achieve a fulfilling and loving relationship with the woman whom I had thought of as my mother.

The first consequence, although perhaps an accidental one, of this revelation was the phone call I made and its aftermath. Perhaps even as I rang Jacqueline, I had been unconsciously provoking her. When I was in college, long-distance phone calls were still expensive, and, certainly in the first one or two years when our pre-college friendships were still strong, it was a common practice to ring friends, even late at night, to talk. It was considered generous, and student lifestyles being as irregular as they were, a late-night phone call from a friend was welcome and hardly an inconvenience. However, by the time I rang Jacqueline to tell her what I had discovered, we were in the latter years in college, when high-school friendships had begun to fade, serious sexual relationships had begun, and late-night phone calls had lost their novelty. I wondered whether my decision to call Jacqueline when I did was determined, not just by the fact I was overwhelmed by the news I had never known my real mother and wanted to discuss with an old and trusted confidante, but by a subconscious instinct to push away the mother-surrogate, for as young as she was, there was no doubt that is what Jacqueline, at least in part, had meant to me—and who was no longer necessary.

I had always wondered why my feelings had been so wounded by Jacqueline's question. Even to myself I had conceded that the letter I wrote the following morning was an overreaction—and yet an overreaction I felt no desire to reverse, even as the years went by. Perhaps I had made the phone call with the farewell letter already almost in view, just beyond the horizon of my subconscious.

There was no need for further concern about entanglement with Jacqueline Nin. My guilt and anxiety about both Craig and Jacqueline began to lift. There was almost certainly nothing I could do about Craig, and Jacqueline's limited role in my past had been over for years. I must keep moving, ceaselessly, into the future as I had done all my life. Nevertheless, I was still going to do my best to help her brother.

When I finished showering and shaving, I went back and ate breakfast while tabbing through the scores of emails. Another bad day in the markets as Walmsley had told me a few hours before. Within Coldstream, anxious investment bankers were sending emails with inquiries and reports from Lithuania, Oklahoma, Egypt, the Czech Republic, Argentina, all struggling to save their deals in the sudden hurricane-whipped-up global markets.

I had my own deal to get done.

I got to the War Room half an hour late. The team looked completely exhausted, and they didn't care if I knew it.

"Hey, guys," I said, closing the door behind me.

McKee, Fai, and Peter were drinking tea. The computers were on, their screen savers blankly staring from the screens. McKee just looked at me.

"What's up?" I asked. "Did you finish up the changes to the model left over from last night?"

"Have you seen where the New York markets closed last night?" McKee said bitterly.

"Yes," I said. "Down again."

"Just wait until Tokyo and Hong Kong open this morning," McKee said. "I don't even want to think about what's going to happen. People are going to be jumping out of windows."

"Hey," I said. "We can't do anything about the market. The only thing we can affect is our own deal. Have you put any scenarios into the model since the changes were made?"

"No," said Fai.

"Okay," I said. "Let's get going."

We started by going back over market movements for the last twelve-, six-, three- and one-month intervals, and then looked at the last four weeks. Then we looked at the major holdings in the portfolio and came up with different combinations of redemptions at different percentages of cash received to total face value.

"Good God," said McKee. All eyes were on the valuation box at the lower left of the computer screen. "The new base case increases value by almost fifty percent over the old base case."

"That's a lot more than I expected," I said. "Are you sure that last night's changes were put through properly?"

Fai vigorously wagged his head. "Yes, I checked them and Peter checked them when I was through," he said. Peter nodded agreement.

I studied their weary faces. The good news on value had energized them, brightening their eyes, but their faces were lined and gray with fatigue. They smelled, too. Everybody needed to get their suits dry-cleaned. The problem on a deal like this is that people work like endurance athletes. Tension and fear make people sweat. Expensive wool suits and fine cotton shirts, silk neckties and calfskin leather shoes are for impressing clients and the other side in the setting of a negotiation, but the fancy stuff gets overloaded from the sweat and the wear and tear of a deal and starts to fall apart. Deal teams should wear camos when they're doing the real work; after a twenty-hour day we could just rip them off and have them hosed down.

I didn't like the big jump in value the model was showing; it felt wrong. "Okay, then tell me why repaying the bonds does so much to improve value?" I said, looking around. "It doesn't make sense."

Fai and Peter hunched together in front of the computer screen and began tabbing rapidly through the electronic worksheets that comprised the architecture of the model. They re-set scenario switches and tabbed back to observe the changes in the value, changed assumptions and watched the value change, and continued to explore forward and backward across the model.

"It's because of the way the model discounts future cash flows for volatility," Fai said. Peter nodded. "The more uncertain the cash flow, the higher the discount rate assigned. So once a bond drops below investment grade, which is where most of Nin's portfolio is already, every time volatility rises the model calculates a high level of risk and discounts the bond's future cash flows down to almost nothing. Getting the cash back, even at a steep discount to face value, takes volatility out of the model and makes a big improvement to the value of TransPac."

Fai was a PhD in Statistics. Peter had an MBA and five years of modeling experience.

McKee nodded. "That makes sense," he said.

"I can see a ten or twenty percent improvement," I said, beginning to doubt my judgment. I was exhausted, too. "Fifty percent surprises me."

"It's off a low base," said McKee. "We hammered the value in the old base case. Probably too hard."

"Okay," I said. Time to stop fighting my team. "Let's give Houghton a call and update him."

I dialed Houghton on the speaker phone so that the team could participate, and got put through by his secretary. Houghton was ecstatic when we explained the effect made by the changes to the model.

"Let's put the extra value on the table and sign," he said. "I think Entrekin and the boys are nervous enough now to accept the lower price. Hell, they'll be glad we can offer three hundred million."

"I don't think we should offer three hundred million, Rick," I said. "I get very nervous about last minute changes to mature models. They always create unpredictable effects on the model, and it takes a while to settle a model down afterwards. I'd rather we leave some margin for error."

"Dusty, this is no time to keep posturing for the purposes of negotiations," Houghton said. "I think we should offer everything we can."

"Rick, I agree this is the time to close this deal," I said. "But in my judgment they'll accept two hundred million. They're getting desperate."

"I think we should offer three hundred million."

"I think we should offer two hundred million," I said. "We need some margin for error."

"Are you saying the model is wrong?"

"We think the model is correct, but I'm not one hundred percent confident," I said.

"Well, that's not good enough," Houghton said. "On a deal like this, you have to get it right. Either the number is right or it's not."

"We think it's right," I said. "We've done all the checks we can."

"Offer them all of it—three hundred million," Houghton said.

"No," I said. "I report to the Executive Committee, and I'm going to offer them two hundred million."

Houghton hung up.

It was disappointing. After the good news, and a hard thirty hours of work by the team, they deserved a better response from Houghton. But there was nothing I could do about it.

"Let's drop the data from the model into some PowerPoint slides," I said briskly. "I'll call Entrekin and have him organize another directors' meeting for eleven o'clock this morning so that we can tell him and his boys the good news."

I left the War Room with my mobile phone and walked down the corridor.

"Hi," I said when she answered, her voice still breathy and low with sleep.

"Oh, hi," she said.

"You sound like you've been sleeping," I said. "Doesn't little Anaïs get you up at five thirty in the morning?"

"My mother looks after her. I needed a rest this morning."

"It was a late night," I said.

"It was nice late night," she said.

"It was very nice," I said.

"Maybe it was all worth it," she said.

"All what?"

"Everything between then and last night," she said.

I didn't want to think about it.

"When are we going to see each other?" I asked her.

"I just do things with my parents. See old family friends, go out to dinner," she said. "But I'm flexible; they'd understand."

"Look," I said. "I've got lots of work to do on this TransPac deal. I'd love to see you for lunch, or tonight, but I don't know when I'm going to be able to get away."

"How is it going?" she asked.

I hesitated.

"It was looking very bad until this morning," I said. "Now I think we might be able to go ahead."

"Why?"

"Oh, some modeling work we've been doing came out better than expected."

"You're so clever," she said.

"It's not me. It's my team, and it's the market," I said. "It just is what it is."

"You can't expect me to believe that," she said.

"It's just reality," I said. But I knew the model was based on twenty-year projected cash flows. It was best practice for investment banking, but it wasn't reality.

"I don't believe it just is what it is," she said.

"Well, nothing is certain," I said. She was as smart as I remembered. Last night I had been just too dazzled and overwhelmed by her presence to notice or care, but she was still every bit as intellectually extraordinary as she had always been.

"No, nothing is certain," she agreed. "But sometimes surprises are the best part."

"The very best," I said.

Entrekin was the first to arrive in the boardroom, shortly before eleven. His mouth was set in a prim line, and he studied my face as he walked into the room. Pelham from Corporate Finance, Cartwright from Equity Origination, and Jones from Asset Management were next. They took their seats around the table.

At ten minutes past eleven, Pelham shifted his bulk in his seat, and scowled. "Where's the brat?" he asked.

Entrekin touched one of the speed dial buttons on the speaker phone in the center of the table. After two rings, someone barked "Markets!" on the line.

"Is Sebastian there?" asked Entrekin, staring across the room.

"Sorry?" cried the voice. A roar from the trading floor filled the boardroom.

"Big morning," I commented.

"This is Simon Entrekin," said Entrekin, raising his voice. "I want to speak to Sebastian!"

"Okay, hold on—" and we were put on hold.

The silence in the room was almost a physical object.

A minute passed. There was a click and the roar filled the boardroom again. "Sorry, Simon," said Nin's voice. "You starting now?"

"Yes, we've been waiting"—Entrekin lifted his arm and consulted his wristwatch—"for almost fifteen minutes."

"Right," said Nin. "I'll be up in a second."

The roar was squelched like a genie disappearing back into a bottle.

"Right!" said Entrekin indignantly. "Alexander, why don't you and your team proceed. Sebastian can pick up the thread when he joins us."

Pelham, Cartwright and Jones nodded their agreement.

"Gentlemen," I began, "last night we made some changes to the model that helped us shape some strategies for raising cash for TransPac. Our view is that the most critical challenge facing the firm is no longer the value of the firm itself, but the survival of the firm."

I watched shock register on their faces.

"For TransPac to survive," I continued, "it has to convince the markets that it is stable. To do that, it's going to have to raise cash.

"We've done some work that shows how to do that. It means identifying the most liquid clients of TransPac, and going to them and convincing them to redeem their bonds. They'll only have to pay seventy or eighty cents on the dollar, and the ones we've identified still have large foreign currency reserves and can easily do it.

"Ted, can you go to the slide with the portfolio positions?"

I walked to the front of the boardroom and pointed to the screen. The slide listed the names of the five biggest bond positions in TransPac's ailing portfolio with the face amount of the debt and the estimated current market price.

"Okay," I said. "There's a quarter of a billion dollars of losses right there. If we could get two of those issuers to buy their bonds back, we'd be a long way toward fixing this thing."

"Why would they call the bonds?" asked Nin, who had just arrived.

I looked at him. "They'll only even think about it if they have the hard currency to do it. These guys seem to. Maybe you can talk them into buying them back because, first, they can do it for well below face value, meaning they've just been given free money by the markets, and second, because if they don't, they're going to continue to have their bonds out there being quoted at junk bond prices—and that will make their companies look like they belong on the trash heap. They lose face. Bad for business. Might even destabilize them."

"I see your point," said Nin. "But it won't be easy."

"You're not paid as much as you are to do what's easy," I said.

Nin glowered at me. "Don't patronize me. Why would we accept the bonds for less than we bought them for in the first place? That's a sure way to go bankrupt."

"This is about raising cash fast," I said. "If we can raise enough cash to pay back the funding lines that are most likely to get pulled in the next week or so and the short-term paper that's about to be rolled over, TransPac will survive long enough to manage out the losses. It's painful, but it's not as painful as riding the firm down to bankruptcy because we haven't raised the cash to pay back the banks."

Cartwright leaned forward in his chair, wagging his pencil, his bushy eyebrows working and his head red. "You should bloody well fix the mess you made, Sebastian—you little prick!"

"Get . . . to . . . it!" said Pelham, enunciating each syllable slowly and contemptuously.

"Fuck off," said Nin, not looking at them. "It's going to be bloody hard, Dusty. I reckon there's less than a dozen issuers who would even consider it. And it'll come down to price."

"That's fine," I said. "Look, there's an additional driver here. We were just trying to come up with a way to raise cash and help TransPac survive. But getting those bonds out of your portfolio helps value too."

McKee flashed up the slide showing the increase in value. I had had the guys only put back half the new value into the graph.

"See? If we can get some of this money back in the door, it increases value by almost two hundred million dollars."

The TransPac directors were electrified. They all stared at the screen, hungrily studying the bright lines.

Jones was the first to speak. "Well, dammit, let's get it done and close this deal! Is that what you're saying, Alexander?"

"Yes," said Entrekin, "are you saying you're willing to put that amount into the final sales agreement?"

"Yes," I said. "If Nin's issuers will redeem their bonds, and if we can confirm the value enhancement."

"Well, by God, that changes things a bit, doesn't it?" said Pelham, slamming his fleshy fist on the table. His face broke out into a broad grin, "Sebastian, old boy, get out there and get some money back into the door! You've tipped us all in it, but now's your chance to come good!"

"Quite right," said Jones, nodding at Sebastian. "If you save this deal, we can all let bygones be bygones."

Nin's face had darkened, and he seemed to be shuddering slightly with the effort to control himself.

"Ted, can we look at the slide with the top thirty issuers?" I said quickly. "Sebastian, let's quickly run through the companies most likely to buy back their debt."

We quickly decided against the Burmese companies—the trip to Rangoon and back would take too long. Most of the Indonesian companies were probably hopeless, sham companies set up by the ruling family; they would have no hard currency. That left a couple of Korean construction firms, some Philippine companies, and a bunch of mainland Chinese companies.

"We've got better things to do at the moment than get up to Seoul or Manila and back," I said. "Where are the Chinese issuers based?"

"A lot of them have their headquarters in Kowloon," said Nin.

"Take me to your favorite client," I said. "Let's go."

The meeting broke up, but McKee stopped me outside the boardroom. "Dusty, aren't you getting too involved?"

"What do you mean?"

McKee glanced both ways and shouldered closer to me. "If you go with TransPac to meet with their issuers, the market may start to think that Coldstream is already involved."

"I won't let Nin say who I am," I said.

"I didn't realize your Chinese was so good," McKee said.

"Good point," I said.

I looked at McKee carefully, and then I turned and walked to the end of the corridor. I stood before the window and gazed at the mountains rising behind the harbor.

I walked back and said to McKee, "I'll be doing due diligence, that's all. It's not unheard of for an acquirer to meet with the largest customers of a target company in a friendly acquisition. No one can hold Coldstream responsible for what's happening at TransPac."

McKee had a strange expression on his face. He looked almost frightened. "Look, Dusty, if we start telling Entrekin and his team what to do, and then we start going out and negotiating deals with TransPac's customers, the Hong Kong Monetary Authority might decide we're making management decisions here. Then they may take the view we're partly responsible for TransPac's losses. And then the Hong Kong authorities might get the US Federal Reserve to force us to pay up."

The HKMA ran a tight ship and had lots of credibility with the US Fed. Normally, Coldstream could count on its battalions of lobbyists, untold hundreds of millions of dollars in political donations, and the fact that several senior Treasury officials originated at Coldstream to ensure the Fed would face down a foreign regulatory agency. But not necessarily when global market losses were over a trillion dollars.

"Got it." I nodded. "I'm conducting due diligence, that's all."

"This is Asia," McKee said. "And these are the worst times possible. People are not going to be in the mood to make fine distinctions."

"Don't panic," I said. "It isn't professional."

"I hope to hell you know what you're doing," McKee said grimly.

I looked at him. The only thoughts that had come to me as I looked out the window at the harbor and the mountains were memories of Jacqueline Nin.

CHAPTER SEVENTEEN

WE DEPARTED FOR KOWLOON in a beautiful old Daimler limousine. Entrekin hadn't wanted to go, but I insisted.

"How can you expect to have any hope they'll cash you out to the tune of fifty million if you don't personally ask them?" I asked him. "It's got to come from you, you know that."

Entrekin reluctantly agreed. I wanted him along because, despite having lived for almost forty years in Hong Kong, he spoke almost no Chinese. I figured that if Nin had to translate everything for Entrekin, he and his clients were less likely to slip something past me.

Nin sat next to me, across from Entrekin, his face still dark with passion from the meeting. "How dare Pelham say those things. He's a fat fuck. A waste of space."

"You're just making noise," I said.

Entrekin's face was tight, and he seemed drawn into himself as he looked at Nin.

"Pelham's department is a joke," Nin said. "You know that, Simon. He's done only two acquisitions in the last year. His talk about his 'eighteen million' yesterday was almost all money I've made for him in my bond department."

Entrekin looked ill.

"Well, isn't that right, Simon?" Nin demanded.

"As you know, Sebastian, and as I've said this many times, TransPac is a firm that draws strength from its parts," began Entrekin. "And all the parts—"

"Oh, bullshit!" said Nin, staring out the window.

"The simple fact of the matter, Sebastian," I said, "is that your operation has added a lot of value in the past, and now it's taking away

128

a lot of value. If TransPac goes down, it won't be because of Pelham's department."

"Yeah, but Coldstream isn't negotiating to buy TransPac because of Pelham's department either, and he has no right to say what he did."

"Oh, he didn't mean anything particularly bad," I said. "It's just his sense of humor. His English schoolboy sense of humor. I think he was actually trying to establish some camaraderie between the two of you."

Entrekin nodded, and then glanced nervously out the window again.

"Well, it's a loutish sense of humor and I don't find it funny," said Nin.

"It's typical rough public-school manners," I said. "Pelham means well. You never know what wires get crossed when you get buggered sideways from the age of twelve at school, and then have to re-adjust to girls and marriage when you become an adult."

"You were with Jacqueline when you were fourteen," Nin said softly, and he looked out the window.

I ignored the comment. "Tell me about who we're going to see."

Nin glanced at Entrekin and then looked at me. "We're going to see Three Dragons Corporation. They're joint venture partners throughout Southeast Asia with Perkhidmatan Pendidikan, who import their food-processing equipment and their bicycles and scooters into Malaysia."

"This is the same Perkhidmatan Pendidikan who is a major shareholder of TransPac, presumably," I said.

"That's right," Nin said. "That's why I wanted to start with them. Three Dragons knows Pendidikan is considering selling to Coldstream Holdings, and if we can convince them that buying back their bonds is in their own interest, they should be willing to help Pendidikan sell out as well. Right, Simon?"

Entrekin closed his eyes and nodded.

"Okay," I said.

There were a lot of new roads in Hong Kong, and the trip took less time than I expected. I wasted time I should have used mentally preparing for the meeting by wondering how much the Daimler would be worth if the assets of TransPac were put to auction. It would hardly be worth the trouble of selling it, I thought sadly, running my eye over the burled walnut doors with their carefully matched, hand-sewn leather upholstery. It was a classic automobile in exquisite condition, but it wouldn't make much difference against a billion dollars in losses.

We were only three blocks from our destination when Nin said, "How do you want to run the meeting?"

"It's not my meeting," I said. "You and Simon do the talking. Explain to them that because of market conditions it may benefit them to redeem their bonds early. They may want to save face by redeeming them at 100 percent—"

Sebastian laughed shortly.

"Well, okay, they're trading at eighty percent," I said. "If they agree to buy their bonds for anything more than that, this trip will be worth it. Otherwise, we might as well sell their bonds into the market and raise cash."

"If anyone will do it, they'll do it," said Nin.

"I'm interested to see what kind of people your favorite clients are," I said. "I'm looking forward to meeting them."

Nin looked out the window.

The headquarters of the Three Dragons Corporation was a large glass and steel monolith with all the crude visual power of upended railroad tracks. The elevators were like freight elevators in the West, and the most prominent feature of the executive floor upon which we arrived were numerous photographs of anonymous Corporation executives standing beside the senior leadership of the Chinese Government, and sometimes beside foreign politicians.

We were ushered into a large room. Clustered at one end of the room were ugly chairs in Central European Communist modern with small lacquer and mother-of-pearl tables before each chair.

Mr. Zhu, the President of Three Dragons, was preceded by three aides who rushed through the door like bodyguards. Mr. Zhu himself was a man in his late sixties with a military bearing. We shook hands all around as Sebastian Nin made the introductions. Mr. Zhu looked

Entrekin and me directly in the eye as he shook our hands, nodding and smiling as he watched us.

His three aides were a mixed lot. A young one looked sensitive and intelligent; possibly an MBA graduate from the US. The other two puzzled me. In their early thirties, one was named Ng and I didn't get the name of the other. They were hard, rough-looking men.

The Chinese do business differently than the Japanese. The Japanese negotiate in packs of fifteen or more. Several smartly dressed, US-educated spokesmen will front up, and in fluent English, represent the group. There is often much discussion between the spokesmen and the rest of the group in Japanese, but only an experienced eye is likely to notice the elderly, often somewhat shabbily dressed Japanese man who will be sitting at the back, saying nothing. He is invariably the boss, and only by carefully watching his reactions during the course of the negotiation, which are often contradicted by what his English-speaking subordinates are actually saying, can one reach an agreement.

Zhu was clearly in charge of his side. He asked all the questions, and responded directly and bluntly, occasionally with salty humor.

It's hard to say how things got out of hand. The conversation suddenly became animated, and at first Nin kept translating in short bursts.

"Zhu says Coldstream trying to steal TransPac."

"Three Dragons don't want business from *gweilo* robbers who try to cheat its partners."

"Three Dragons don't need to save face. Three Dragons has much face."

As voices were raised, Nin stopped translating back into English for the benefit of Entrekin and myself. The aide named Ng seemed to take great exception to what Nin was saying.

Zhu had stopped speaking and was watching Ng. Blood had rushed into Ng's face, darkening it, and Ng was arguing in a hoarse, angry voice with Nin. Obviously Ng was no financial expert or corporate strategy type, and he didn't like whatever he was hearing.

Nin's voice was high, excited, indignant, futilely trying to interrupt Ng's angry voice.

Ng stood up abruptly, pointing his finger repeatedly at Nin. Then Ng stepped around the little table in front of his chair and stood over Nin.

Surprised, Nin showed no desire to get up from his chair, which protected him slightly, but I could see globules of spit, some flying, some floating in an arc against the dirty sunlight, cascading on Nin as Ng's shouting became louder and louder. Nin stood up reluctantly, his face set. His movements were awkward, tense.

Ng waved his hand directly in front of Nin's face, flicking, then chopping, his hand, fingers open, an inch from Nin's nose as if he were batting flies. I thought he was going to slap Nin. So did Nin; he stepped back against his chair. He leaned slightly backward, further away from Ng.

It happened very quickly.

Ng didn't hit him, but he made a strange clawing motion with his crooked fingers across Nin's belly, catching his necktie in his fingers and flipping it. I was watching the tie, absurdly looped up, as it floated in the air. Then Ng shoved Nin, a short sharp push of his outstretched hand against Nin's left shoulder.

"Hey," I said, standing up. The air burst with shouts.

Ng probably didn't hear what I said, but I stepped toward him and he saw me out of the corner of his eye. He spun around to face me. To my surprise he threw a left punch straight at my head.

Finance is a sedentary profession. Lots of traders and investment bankers would love to be ex-Special Forces or combat veterans, adding retrospective glamour to their safe, privileged lives. But all you are likely to need to know is what the Army teaches you in basic training about hand-to-hand combat, even if, like me, you ended up only serving for a few years in a combat unit that is deployed in the US and never hear a shot fired in anger.

Ng's punch started high. I watched it coming. I bent toward it, my shoulders curving to the left as I rotated my hips and leaned forward over my left leg, my weight shifting over the left knee. I didn't even have to move my head. His punch grazed my shoulder and, for an instant, his forearm rested on the seam of my suit coat. I was slightly crouched, inside and close to him, his arm flung out and over me. I could have been his wife.

Life is made up of all kinds of opportunities. Being prepared helps, but some types of opportunity can be forced, while the key to success in others is just recognizing the gift for what it is.

No fighter leads with a left hook. The most devastating of all punches, it requires being close to your opponent, and an opponent's options are just too complex to anticipate. You can never set up a left hook—you just have to know how to deliver one when you get that perfect chance. I found myself leaning into Ng's chest, my cheekbone nestled against his lapel, his arm thrown over my shoulder in a parody of protection. Clenching my bicep, I snapped my arm into a hard right angle, my left elbow pointing for a moment into my thigh just inches from the hip. I surged upwards, twisting to the right, rising and facing Ng as I continued to turn, my chest and shoulders twisting as my cheek brushed across the lapel of his coat.

For a split second, my left fist floated motionlessly as the elbow lifted. Then my left arm scythed up, spinning on the pivot of my spine, backed by the full weight of my upper body. The left hook had hardly snapped eight inches before I felt the unyielding, somehow sodden mass of his body compressing against my fist. Ng grunted, jolted backward, his head snapped forward and his body seeming to hover like a badly hung suit coat. I must have struck his liver or the bundle of nerves nestled at the wishbone of the rib cage.

We were so close I felt his sour breath burst against my cheek. I brought my right elbow to shoulder height and stepped left, pivoting again in the opposite direction. A hook is the most difficult punch to throw. I had been lucky with my left hook, but my right hook snapped around too wide, losing a bit of pace. Ng was still stunned, unresisting, but my fist connected with his jaw near his ear, instead of cracking into his chin. It was a lot of bone, and I felt something inside my fist slip as

Ng dropped out of sight. The sound of the tea service and the snapping of the wooden table was all I had time to register before I stepped back and Zhu's other guy came at me.

I knew two things as I turned to meet him: I was already winded, and he was probably a gunman, otherwise he couldn't have held a job, not in Hong Kong, using his fists the way he did. He came at me, shrieking, his hands high by his cheekbones and his elbows out, working like oars. His entire stomach and solar plexus was open.

But there was a body down and I was standing on a broken table or on one of Ng's limbs. Nin's chair was behind me, too, perhaps already upended. I didn't have time to look, but I was unsure of my footing and on the defensive.

The gunman came at me, attacking in a flurry of quick jabs and funny little hooks that started at his shoulders and wouldn't have made much difference if he'd hit me. I threw my elbow into one punch, hoping to jam one or two of his fingers, and blocked the other punch with my forearm. That one hurt. He threw another right and I blocked it again with my left elbow. I was thinking now.

I had already mashed my right hand hitting Ng in the head. My hand might already be broken and I couldn't afford to hit this guy in the chin with my right. I stayed too long on the left and he got an uppercut into me with his right. It hit me low, and I collapsed slightly over it, rolling to the left with it. It's almost impossible for a guy like the gunman to hit a fighter who can roll with a punch.

Thirty seconds of throwing punches feels like an hour of anything else. I was breathing heavily. I could hear Zhu screaming in Chinese, and I heard Entrekin saying, "Alexander, *please*, Alexander . . ." On the other hand, this guy was in close, and I was expecting a knee to my groin any moment. I also felt the rush of blood in the underside of my forearms, which felt tight and hard.

I was exultant, joyful.

The guy's hands and arms were still high, and I poked a quick left jab right through the big arc of his punches. My fist cracked straight on against his chin. Another badly thrown punch. His head snapped back and he froze, but my fist, instead of connecting with the glancing blow that would have transferred the shock to him, also absorbed a great deal of the force. I dropped suddenly and punched my injured right fist into his body, doubling him over.

I didn't know whether or not he was carrying his gun, so I played it safe. As I straightened, I brought my left knee into his face. He heaved up and backward, flopping back over another one of the little tables. I heard porcelain shattering as I looked around.

Zhu was shaking Entrekin by the coat. The last of Zhu's guys, the MBA, was trying to pull Ng clear of the toppled chairs and tables. Nin was urgently talking into Zhu's ear as Zhu shook Entrekin.

I pulled Zhu and Entrekin apart. "Come on," I said. We walked out briskly, and as Entrekin and Nin headed for the elevator bank, I closed the door of the boardroom. Downstairs our driver was smoking a cigarette with the security guard at the front desk. We flipped our security badges over the desk and walked out.

The Daimler started up and we pulled into traffic. I looked at Nin. "Sell the bonds," I said.

CHAPTER EIGHTEEN

As the Daimler rolled through traffic, Nin and I looked grimly at one another. Entrekin sat across from us, his face in his hands, occasionally kneading the bridge of his nose or running his long fingers, with his signet pinkie ring and no wedding band, through his thinning hair.

"Maybe Zhu's guy wasn't going to whack you," I said, "but I just hate to see people getting beaten up. It's always been something that makes me go crazy."

Entrekin shook his head and groaned. "I . . . I must say, I just couldn't—"

"I'd hate to think what you might be capable of doing," Nin said. "That was way over the top."

"You don't have to thank me for saving your sorry ass," I said. "Just in case you were thinking of going to the expense of sending flowers."

"It was probably my fault," said Nin, relenting. "Pendidikan told them about the lower price that Coldstream Holdings is talking about for their TransPac shares. They thought we were coming to them with the same kind of deal. They thought I was making them lose face."

"I couldn't do anything for my friend yesterday," I said. "Sometimes we have to accept the shit that happens."

Entrekin put his face in his hands.

"Simon?" I asked the top of Entrekin's head. "Is this going to screw things up with Pendidikan?"

He looked up, his face a picture of misery. "I spoke with him on the telephone after this morning's meeting," he said. "He was very pleased to hear Coldstream's offer had gone up. Now he's going to be very, very upset."

"I'm sorry," I said. Thinking of Craig's murder had suddenly turned my mood very black, just as the adrenaline rush faded. "I really thought Ng was going to sock Sebastian, and once I took Ng out, I had to deal with his friend. It got out of hand."

I recognized I was suddenly very depressed.

"Well, it's done," Entrekin said, "and at the end of the day, all Pendidikan really cares about is the money. He's going to have plenty of pressures on his other businesses as a result of falling markets, and he won't do anything that jeopardizes his chances of getting a big check from Coldstream."

"What about the Hong Kong police?" I said. "Are you going to be able to straighten this out with the authorities?"

Entrekin looked at Nin. "Oh, I expect so," he said a little breathlessly. "Yes, yes—I'll make a few phone calls when we get back. I may have to make a couple of visits tomorrow. Hong Kong doesn't quite operate the way it used to, of course. New faces. But it should be alright. They would never go public with it."

"They'd lose face if they did," said Nin, with a sour smile. "It works both ways."

"Terrific," I said.

We had crossed back onto Hong Kong Island.

I looked at Nin. "Are you still willing to try some of the other issuers on the list?"

"Don't worry about it," said Nin. "The link between Zhu and Pendidikan was a complication. I thought it would help, but obviously it didn't. But that won't be a factor with the other issuers. I know what to say now."

"Can you deal with the rest by yourself?" I asked.

"Sure," Nin said. "Absolutely. I'll start making phone calls when we get back."

We sat in silence until the Daimler arrived at TransPac headquarters. Entrekin and I went up to his office, letting Nin get out of the lift on the level of the trading floor.

Nin looked at us and nodded twice, quickly, as the lift door opened. "Talk to you later?"

Simon was silent.

"See you," I said.

We went into Entrekin's office. His beautiful secretary brought us mineral water, tea and cigars.

Simon caught me looking at her long sleek legs as she walked out and smiled wearily. "Lovely, isn't she?"

I reached for the cigar. Cohiba, the dictator's special. A fine cigar. I took my pen knife out of my pocket, wincing as my knuckles brushed the fabric of my trousers, and cut the end off.

Then I lit the cigar thinking how Craig would have indulged me, even though he loathed cigars.

"I say, your hands are a mess," said Entrekin, watching me burn the cigar.

My knuckles were swollen, and my right hand was turning purple. "Think how they feel," I said.

"Shocking afternoon," said Entrekin.

I blew a long blue tusk of smoke up toward the ceiling; the last rays of light from the sunset transfixed it.

Entrekin was watching me. "Alexander," he said hesitantly. "Are you sure you're going to be alright?"

"Why—because I'm getting into fistfights with all my new friends?"

"Yes."

"Simon, I want you to be honest with me," I said. "What kind of people does Nin do business with? I admit I shouldn't have knocked down two of Zhu's guys, but then I've never been in a meeting where a colleague looked like he was going to get the shit kicked out of him either. Who are these people?"

"Well, in the first place, you are aware of the relationship between Three Dragons and our shareholder." Entrekin shifted in his chair, clasped his hands in front of him, gazed contemplatively down at the cigar sticking out of his fingers, and then looked up at me, his eyes wide with candor.

"Had you ever met Zhu before?" I asked.

"Oh, yes. We had a sumptuous closing banquet when we completed the bond underwriting."

"Right," I said. "Who brought in the deal?"

"Oh, it was one of Sebastian's deals, of course. The introduction came through my relationship with Perkhidmatan Pendidikan."

"Do you have a procedure for deciding what deals to do and which ones you don't want to do?"

"What do you mean?" Entrekin said. "We make money by doing deals, not by not doing deals."

"A smell test," I said.

Entrekin pulled on his cigar. "Well," he said, "one must be careful not to impose one's own cultural expectations on Asia. It's easy for us Westerners to slander Asian entrepreneurs. And perhaps especially you Americans, with your Foreign Corrupt Practices Act, if you don't mind my saying so. It's a bit sanctimonious. Go back a couple hundred years, George Washington was the wealthiest man in America when he was elected President. Alexander Hamilton, Secretary of the Treasury, was a New York bond dealer. By what right do you point fingers at those who take risks and are building wealth in Asia today?"

Entrekin appraised me coolly, looking as confident as I had seen him since I met him.

"If we had a problem with truly talented Asian entrepreneurs, we wouldn't be looking at this deal," I said. "We're here because of your relationships and the relationships Nin has developed with his issuers. I just find it a bit disconcerting when I go to meet one of the most important new clients I might be acquiring and find myself in a fist fight."

A small smile appeared in the corner of Entrekin's mouth as he extracted his cigar. "Sebastian is fond of pointing out that Junius Morgan, J.P.'s father, originally went to London to try and negotiate between English bankers over the multitude of bonds on which the various American States had defaulted. That was a little more than a hundred years ago."

"Yes, I've noticed Sebastian has a thing about J.P. Morgan," I said. "He seems to think of himself as a bit of a J.P. Morgan."

"Well," said Entrekin, "he is correct, you know, in pointing to parallels in the process of capital formation. One hundred years ago, the State of Georgia was a third world government issuer with defaulted bonds. Very low class. Today, Three Dragons issues bonds that are trading at eighty percent of face value. What's the difference? Maybe the only difference is a hundred years. TransPac has the vision to see that. Somebody said one mustn't enquire too carefully into the making of sausages or bond deals."

"Bismarck said that. He said it about making sausages and laws."

"There you are—even more to the point," said Entrekin with his new, cool smile.

I was enjoying the cigar. I was in no hurry to leave, so I listened to Entrekin continue to hold forth on his views about how things get done in Asia.

A properly smoked cigar takes a long time to burn; mine was two-thirds gone when Nin called, breaking in on Simon's lecture. I pushed thoughts of Craig out of my mind; I could try to solve his murder—and most likely fail—or I could try and save TransPac, and perhaps prevent a global financial crisis.

Entrekin put him on the speaker phone. Nin's voice was excited. "We've got three issuers, and maybe we'll get four or five, to redeem their bonds. I'm only halfway down the list. It looks like we're going to pull this off."

"Good man," I said.

"This is excellent news," said Entrekin. "Extraordinary news. Well done!"

"Thanks," said Nin, almost gaily. "I'm going to get back to it," he said, and rang off.

Entrekin looked at me, smiling broadly. He extended his hand. "Well, I must say, Alexander, when James told me that he was sending his best man out, I hardly dared to believe that you would be as good as you have turned out to be. You Americans can be remarkably effective, on occasion, I must say."

"Thanks, Simon," I said. "The firm's American, I'm not. And a lot can go wrong between now and tomorrow."

"Well, let's move things forward as rapidly as possible then," Entrekin said.

"Okay with me," I said.

"And let's go out tonight and celebrate," Entrekin said. "Why don't we go up to my club?"

This was Entrekin's third invitation in three days. If we were going to do this deal, I should join the TransPac executive team to celebrate what looked like a breakthrough.

"That'll be nice," I said.

My only regret was I wouldn't be going to see Jacqueline.

Chapter Nineteen

I WENT DOWN TO THE WAR ROOM. McKee told me the markets had closed down again, steeply. After discussing the closing prices of the various currency, bond and equity markets, I thought about it for a moment.

"We're still okay," I said. "I only told those guys today that we had increased our price by two hundred million. We still had another hundred million to play with."

"Not anymore," said McKee.

"I know," I said. "But we can still stick to what I said we'd pay."

"Dusty," McKee said. "I've been thinking about what happened at Three Dragons today. I think maybe you're under too much strain."

"Ted, I couldn't do anything about it yesterday when my friend Craig Chin got blown away in front of me. I'm not going to defend what I did today, but all I can tell you is that I can't imagine reacting in any other way."

McKee shook his head. "I'm not criticizing you, Dusty. I can understand how you feel. It's just that there's a lot riding on your good judgment."

I left and went downstairs. I had arranged for Winston to pick me up and take me to the apartment of Craig's parents in Happy Valley.

Winston looked drawn and pale. He nudged into traffic and my mobile phone rang. It was Houghton.

"Dusty, we need to talk," he said.

"We can talk," I said. "But I can't come by right now."

"I want to tell Entrekin we've got an extra hundred million."

"Why?" I said. "Entrekin and the boys looked pretty happy about the two hundred million when I told them this morning."

"Yeah, that's good," he said. "But what if they get another offer from another acquirer? I think we should foreclose that possibility by offering everything we've got."

"If they're going to go to somebody else—and I'm not saying they won't, but it's going to be pretty tough finding somebody else willing to buy TransPac right now—wouldn't it be better to have the extra hundred million up our sleeves for a counterbid? If they shop themselves around at three hundred million, and somebody bites, we'll be out of ammo."

"I don't agree," Houghton said. "Are you sure you can't come by? Where are you right now?"

That pissed me off. I didn't report to Houghton. "I'm on my way to pay my respects to somebody's parents," I said. "It's just something I like to do when I'm in Hong Kong and a friend gets killed in front of me."

"Oh right," Houghton said.

"Anything else?"

"Well, Dusty, I don't know how to say this . . . Hate to have to bring it up, but do you think you're okay? *Compos mentis?*"

"It didn't take you long to hear about the punch up," I said.

"It doesn't take me long to hear about anything that happens in Hong Kong," Houghton said.

"Well, Sebastian Nin was attacked. I wasn't going to let him get beaten up."

"I can't imagine that that was the only alternative," Houghton said. "If I had been there instead of you, would there have been a fight?"

"Nin is your guy, Rick, the star you want for your operations," I said. "I would think you'd be happy that I prevented him for getting his head bashed in."

"This is no way to run a deal, Dusty."

"At least it hasn't taken me a year, Rick."

"Don't fuck my deal, Dusty!" Houghton shouted.

I hung up.

I spent a sad hour with the Chin family. Craig's aged parents spoke no English, and the Chinese show little emotion by Western standards.

But all of Craig's brothers and sisters were there, and they looked stricken. I couldn't be absolutely sure I wasn't responsible in some way. The worst thing was that, in the absence of a clear motive for Craig's killing, the worst kinds of suspicions hung over his memory. I was torn between the desire to be completely absolved of bringing Craig into a role that had proved fatal to him, while wondering what he might have been involved with personally that could have gotten him killed by a couple of professional gunmen, and wanting to shoulder the guilt for inadvertently tangling him in some web that hung over TransPac—and being sure Craig had died as an innocent man.

The conflicts within me, and the confusion and shame I could see in the faces of the Chin family, made the visit one of the toughest things I've ever done.

It was almost a relief to get back to TransPac, even though when I got back, I could see I was surrounded by skeptics who had begun to question my fitness.

I went back to the War Room. McKee and the guys were eating Chinese takeaway.

"Do you want some, Dusty?" Fai asked. "There is plenty."

"No, thanks." I checked my watch. It was just before five o'clock, too early to ring Walmsley.

My mobile phone rang. "Street speaking," I said.

"Houghton wants me to bring you home," Walmsley said. "I've just spent an hour on the phone with him, and he is extremely pissed off. He said you're getting into fist fights with major customers of TransPac who have links to the shareholders."

Houghton had called Walmsley at three in the morning, New York time.

"Yes, that's right," I said. "But it's not the whole story. What do you want me to do?"

"I'm not pulling you off the deal, Dusty," Walmsley said. "But Houghton is going to send a formal note to the Executive Committee. Can you shoot me an email explaining what happened, and giving us an update on where you've gotten to on the TransPac deal? I'll need it for my opening."

"Sure, Jim," I said. "I'll get right on it."

"And Dusty, for Christ's sake, stay out of trouble from now on," Walmsley said. "Houghton wants you fired. You know what that would mean for your long-term comp. I thought you should know that."

"I sure will," I said. "Thanks, Jim."

I felt my intestines clench and ache as I hung up. Entrekin had obviously telephoned Houghton as soon as I left his office and given him his version of what happened at Three Dragons. I doubted the account emphasized the physical danger to Nin. Entrekin had no doubt made it sound like I was out of control and couldn't be trusted to produce a fair value for TransPac. Now that I had found an extra two hundred million, Entrekin was trying to take the money and run. He knew Houghton wanted to do the deal almost as badly as he did. I had thirty or forty million in long-term compensation that would get gradually paid out to me once I went limited. Being sacked would put ninety percent of that at risk.

But Houghton obviously didn't understand the risks he was rushing to bring into Coldstream Holdings. He could only see as far as acquiring Nin's bond operation and growing his fiefdom in Asia as a springboard for becoming managing partner of Coldstream Holdings Global. Houghton was obviously a brutal, no-holds-barred political infighter; I knew him, but not well, and I had always thought he was a perfectly reasonable, straightforward guy. That showed how skillful he was politically.

Houghton reminded me of a certain French swordsman of the Renaissance, who, when he had defeated his opponent, would put the tip of his blade on the man's throat and promise to spare his life if he denied God. If his opponent refused, he would lean on the blade and kill him. But if his opponent denied God, the duelist killed him anyway, with the additional satisfaction of having condemned his opponent to eternity in hell.

If Houghton could succeed in getting me dismissed, the majority of the money I had made in the last ten years would be denied me. At Coldstream Holdings, most of a partner's compensation was tied up in a partnership account and reinvested in the firm until one retired. When a Coldstream partner decided to retire, he "went limited", and over five years the capital in his partnership account was paid out. But if a partner was dismissed for misconduct, all the wealth tied up in his partnership account was redistributed among the remaining partners. Because of the structure of Coldstream Holdings, I didn't have much other wealth besides my house, which still had a large mortgage.

In two days, I had gone from being a wealthy, highly regarded investment banker to being threatened with the status of a pariah, and stripped of most of my fortune. I'd be lucky if I could pay off my house if Houghton succeeded in getting rid of me. I knew how difficult it would be to find another position in New York after being fired for misconduct from Coldstream Holdings.

I couldn't believe what was happening to me.

I signed onto one of the computers in the cubicles and spent the next couple of hours composing an email report on the TransPac deal, which I sent to Walmsley just as Entrekin's secretary telephoned and said that Entrekin was ready to go to his club.

The more I thought about it, the more furious I became at the thought of Entrekin using his back channel to Houghton to try and get me kicked off the deal—and completely ruin my career and my life. Sam and the kids might have nothing to show for their loyalty and patience.

There was nothing to be done at the moment, except to go to Entrekin's celebration.

I got up and walked over to McKee. "Let's get downstairs and join Entrekin and his guys."

"Okay, Dusty," McKee said.

I had been thinking about whether to get Fai and Peter an invitation to Entrekin's club, but thought better of it. What they needed was sleep. "You guys go home and get an early night," I said. "We'll have our own private celebration on this deal after financial close. If we get there."

Entrekin had organized three Daimlers, and twelve of us squeezed into them and started up the Peak toward Entrekin's club. McKee and I were in the same one as Pelham and his second-in-command, a tight-lipped prematurely balding young man named Snelling. Pelham was already smoking a cigar in the back of the Daimler, and he kept tilting his head back and laughing big clouds of cigar smoke into Snelling's face and his dwindling streaks of hair.

"So, Dusty, I understand you had some trouble keeping your mitts to yourself today," Pelham greeted me. "You ought to let young Sebastian stick up for himself, and if he can't—to hell with him!"

I sat back without a word, watching Pelham blow smoke into his young subordinate's ear. Snelling pretended not to notice, and smiled weakly when he couldn't pretend, but by the end of the short trip, especially after the Daimler began whipping back and forth up the hairpin turns on the approach to the club, he looked green. It must have been a dirty job working for Pelham.

I wondered what Jacqueline was doing. Then I thought about Sam and the kids and what they were doing. It was four o'clock in the morning in Vermont so they were hopefully peacefully asleep.

We pulled up at a fine, old Colonial building and were greeted by Chinese attendants in starched uniforms, who surrounded the Daimler and opened the doors for us. Entrekin's Daimler pulled up behind us, and then the third one arrived, and after we had all collected, we passed through a magnificent vestibule into a grand hallway, and turned right into a vast old bar room.

"Alexander!" Entrekin said heartily. He took me by the arm and ushered me in. Pelham, holding the dark, slippery-looking stump of his cigar, accompanied us.

Entrekin and Pelham led the way under big slow-moving ceiling fans to a long table not far from a splendid mahogany bar that glowed in the mellow lights of the bar. Our group was trailing plumes of cigar and cigarette smoke as we circled like a corpulent snake around the table, and then with much scraping of chairs, shuffling of feet, and creaking as furniture received the weight of mens' bodies, we found our seats.

Entrekin's cheeks were already flushed. "Pink gins all around!" he exclaimed to the Chinese waiter. "And then we'll wash that down with vintage champagne."

Watching Entrekin and Pelham, it occurred to me that Entrekin didn't have enough backbone to take someone like me on by himself. He must be relying on someone for advice and support. Watching the two of them, I decided it was probably Pelham. The way I understood the history of TransPac, the original idea had been Entrekin's, and he had lined up most of the capital from Massoud and Pendidikan, whom he knew from his career working as a banker in the Gulf. TransPac had trundled along with the likes of Pelham and Jones, but it wasn't until Entrekin hired a dropout from a fourth-rate Caribbean medical school, who was a Hong Kong native and a speaker of Chinese, and who just happened to have spent a couple of years as a bond salesman in New York, that TransPac really took off. On his own, Entrekin had enough fire in his belly to run a sleepy, genteel third-rate outfit. Events had made him the managing director of the most powerful and influential investment bank in Asia. He needed support to live up to his unexpected role—and to take on Nin, who was the real brains of TransPac.

Entrekin would have needed to be persuaded to take me on, and in effect, to throw in his lot with Houghton, in the hope of dividing and conquering Coldstream Holdings. He didn't have the guts to think it up, or to do anything about it. It must have been Pelham.

The noise level started to rise as several rounds of drinks quickly disappeared. Hilarity quickly established itself. Even Nin was smiling, and I noticed for the first time that he had fine, white teeth against rich pink gums that were almost red, and slightly sharp incisors. He was guarded but cheerful, and I noticed he was handsome when he looked happy.

"Hey Dusty!" he called, lifting his pink gin. "Here's to the deal! The redemptions are in the bag."

Entrekin put a pinkie and a forefinger into the sides of his mouth and let out an appalling shriek of a whistle. Everyone stopped in mid-sentence in astonishment at the blast. It was extraordinary that such a loud noise had come out of Entrekin's thin frame.

"Gentlemen, fellow directors, colleagues, friends, new partners-to-be, we are gathered here this evening, amidst the storms of the market, to celebrate! Our distinguished guest Alexander Street has managed in three days to accomplish, in the worst markets in a generation, what the rest of us couldn't manage for the past twelve months while the going was still good—he's done the deal! And as a result, we'll all soon be working together! So, I propose a toast on this auspicious and memorable occasion, to Dusty and the deal!"

"Dusty and the deal!" roared the table.

I had the eerie feeling that I had just been listening to my obituary.

I put up my hand, pushed my chair back, and stood up. "Thank you, Simon. While it may be premature to toast me or the deal, it has been a pleasure for Ted and me to work with you and your team, including yourself, of course, but also Ralph, Grahame, Lew and Sebastian. So, I would like to use this auspicious occasion to propose a toast to the team!"

"To the team!" roared the table.

Several people had glanced at my hand as I raised my glass to propose a toast. I caught the expression on their faces. Laying my hands flat on the table in front of me, I inspected the torn skin and bruised fingers and knuckles. They were purple, and flecks of skin hung from various places. Little crusts had developed when they stopped bleeding.

Entrekin signaled for champagne, and bottles of old French champagne were popped around us and poured into bright flutes. More toasts were proposed, on increasingly light-hearted and then scatological themes.

"By God," roared Pelham. "What a week it's been! I just got back last weekend from a visit to a piggery in Australia that one of my clients is thinking of acquiring—and after that hellish experience I was actually looking forward to Monday. If I had only known!"

He looked around a table. "Has anyone been to a piggery? Horrid places. They're mostly underground—all these dark tunnels and passageways. The chap kept stopping before the next closed door and saying, 'Are you afraid of a little blood?' By God, it was ghastly! Rivers of black blood everywhere from the slaughtering. Not on the floor, you know, the blood spilled at the killing stations is all channeled into these gutters where it literally runs like rivers."

Cartwright's harsh laugh cut across the table. He leaned forward, his big yellow teeth bared in a grin. "Zounds, I once looked at floating a piggery in Thailand. Simon," he nodded toward Entrekin. "Remember that deal?"

Cartwright's fluffy eyebrows squirmed up and down. "They have workers at those places, these fellows who have the job of standing alongside the assembly line as these great big pigs come trundling down, unconscious"—his arm shot forward over the table—"and jabbing them in the neck to kill them. Blood spurts out like a hose when they do it, and they're just standing there, their arms black with blood, their faces and hair splattered with blood."

Cartwright laughed helplessly, shaking his head. "Can you imagine having that as your *profession*? Can you imagine having it on your curriculum vitae—Pig Jugular Slicer? Senior Pig Jugular Slicer? Imagine the interview!"

He slapped his hand on the table with another shout of laughter. A howl of laughter accompanied him from around the table.

I had not been favorably impressed by Entrekin's team before this, but now I had an inkling why Sebastian Nin had such contempt for them. They, and their deals, were truly bottom drawer.

"Grahame, Grahame—" chuckled Entrekin, leaning toward him. "Remember the Spike Man?" Entrekin addressed the table.

"At this Thai piggery, at the spot on the assembly line where they cut the heads off the pigs, there's a long ramp into a lower level, and the heads roll down this ramp, and the Spike Man is waiting at the bottom and he grabs the heads like this"—Entrekin's heavily starched, Egyptian cotton-clad arms, his hands bony and hectic, rose above the table grasping an imaginary pig's head along with his cigar and champagne flute—"and then *smashes* it down on a big steel spike in front of him and splits the skull!"

Entrekin's hands came down violently toward the table, flinging champagne from the flute and cigar ash from his cigar on Snelling, who sat to his left.

I was ashamed for Entrekin. Normally he managed to cut a more impressive figure than the rest of his team, with the exception of Sebastian Nin. Now, I could see the basis for the bond between Entrekin and his pals Pelham and the rest: at heart, they were coarse, small-time grifters.

Sebastian was cut from different cloth.

"Alexander," called Pelham, pointing at me with his cigar. "Did you know there's a difference between the pork from a male pig and female sow?"

"No, I didn't," I said.

"Well, there is," said Pelham. "Any pig man could tell you the difference."

"Really—" exclaimed Lew Jones.

"Yes," said Pelham. "Male pork has a distinct smell. Percy, what is the smell?"

Snelling looked up at the ceiling thoughtfully. "Heady," he said.

"It's because of some hormone in the meat that is excreted by the testicles, you know," said Pelham.

"The pituitary gland, actually," said Snelling.

"By both, most likely," snorted Pelham, pulling abruptly on his cigar. "I say, did I mention that when I went down to that Australian piggery, the managing director told me they had begun to export pig rectums to Asia? Apparently there's a big demand for them here. 'Imagine,' he said. 'We'd been throwing them out all these years!'"

Pelham barked out a laugh, almost choking with mirth. He wiped a tear from his eye. "If I were a shareholder in that piggery, I would thank God for the Chinese connoisseurs who buy pig rectums!"

"Hah!" Pelham said, fixing a red, fatty eye on me. "For that matter, thank God for the bloody Yanks!" He raised his glass and banged on the table. "To the bloody Yanks!"

"I'm not a Yank, actually," I said.

"The bloody Yanks!" roared the table.

"To the Septic Tanks!" roared Pelham.

"The Septic Tanks!"

Numerous calls rose for another round, someone began throwing peanuts, and shortly there were showers of peanuts cascading back and forth over the table. McKee and I stood up and walked to the bar where Nin joined us.

"Classy bunch, your colleagues," I commented. "Real aesthetes."

"Now, now Dusty," Nin grinned mirthlessly. "It's just Ralph's schoolboy sense of humor. Remember?"

"Glad to see you're learning to work and play well with others," I said.

Nin sneered. "Pelham would just as soon knife me as look at me. If he had any guts, that is. The only reason for the camaraderie, as you call it, is because you put another two hundred million on the table. If it was less than that, Pelham would be back to his old strategy of trying to carve it out of my hide."

Nin disappeared in the direction of the mens room.

"Just a second, Dusty," McKee said. His faced was a little flushed from drinking, and he looked agitated.

"Yes, Ted," I said.

McKee glanced around the room. "What are we trying to accomplish here?" he asked.

"You mean at this bar?" I asked.

He looked straight at me. "No, I'm talking about the TransPac deal, Dusty," he said. "I've been working on this deal for almost twelve months. I wanted to get it done as much as anyone. But in the last couple of days, I've seen TransPac in a new light. Even though you've been able to dream up a strategy to get some value back into this deal, I'm not sure we weren't better off yesterday when the deal looked dead.

"It's not the currency devaluations or the collapse in the bond and equity markets, as bad as they are. I was blown away by what happened today. Look at your hands! These guys have done bond deals for dictators, drug lords, the Chinese Army . . . We have no way of knowing how much money, if any, they're ever going to get back."

"Well, they're getting some of it back," I said. "Nin's got almost half a dozen issuers lined up to redeem their bonds at a discount."

"I'll believe it when I see it," said McKee. "The guy says a lot of things."

"So, what you're saying is we shouldn't be doing business with TransPac's customers anyway?" I said.

"That's what I'm thinking," McKee said. "And when I forget, I just look at your hands."

"They're okay," I said.

Nin returned to the bar, and ordered a round of single malts for us.

"Sebastian," I said. "What do you think about the idea that your issuers are a bunch of drug lords and fronts for the Chinese Army?"

"Who's saying it?" Nin said.

"Lots of people," I said.

"Tell me who," he said.

"No," I said.

"Then I'm not going to answer it," he said. "It's just cheap slander."

Pelham was bellowing something from the table, but I couldn't make it out. Men began to rise, pushing back their chairs, and then collected around the bar.

"Right," said Pelham, pressing forward and stopping in front of me. "It's time for the venerable tradition of bar diving."

"Never heard of it," I said. I looked at Nin. He shook his head.

"Well!" said Pelham, looking at Entrekin with a grin. "Here's the way it works, old chap. First, we get Kenny"—he nodded to the barman—"to turn off the fan for a moment and stick a bit of paper on one of the blades. Then he turns the fan on again, follow? Then everyone grabs each other's wrists like this." He squeezed one wrist in a fleshy, flushed fist and opened the fat fingers of his other hand as if to grasp someone else's wrist. "We stand across from one another, in two rows facing each other, holding on like this to make a stretcher, a hammock, a net." Pelham smacked the top of the bar with an open palm. "Then one of us blokes climbs up on the bar, and dives off into the stretcher the rest of us make with our arms. The object is to snatch the bit of paper off the fan as it goes around. The one who does it is the Celestial Bar Diver."

I looked up at the fan sweeping in great slow circles above our heads. The tip of the blades swept the air above the floor about a yard in front of the bar, so to snatch a bit of paper off the end would require a full leap out from the bar, probably followed by a fall of five or six feet into the mesh formed by the gripped arms of the group. In the summer the fans probably spun more quickly, but in the winter they moved at a stately pace designed to gently push the warm air rising to the ceiling back toward the revelers.

"No thanks, Charles," I said. "I'm not going to be jumping off a bar this evening."

I watched the expression on his face shift to a mask of perplexity. "Well, why not, Dusty? You're not yellow, are you?"

"I just don't jump off bars," I said.

Pelham's face changed again, this time mimicking the expression of a sad clown. He glanced over his shoulder at Entrekin.

I looked at Entrekin too, and I was startled to see what looked like admiration in his face as he met Pelham's drunken glare. Entrekin was standing, his posture stiff as usual, his elbows drawn in against his ribs and his champagne flute delicately balanced in his left hand. He seemed totally focused on Pelham, anticipating Pelham's every gesture with eagerness, as if Pelham possessed a physical prowess Entrekin could only experience vicariously.

In spite of myself, I found myself annoyed by Entrekin's attitude. Entrekin was a guy who had almost gone into shock when I had taken on Zhu's bodyguards in order to protect Nin, and yet here he was treating fat blow-hard Pelham as if he were a death-defying daredevil. It shouldn't have bothered me, but it did.

"Well, I can't be part of the landing net," I said, holding up my hands. "These aren't in any shape to hold someone else's arm, or to be held."

The grimaces almost made me smile.

"Right, that's okay. But nothing's stopping you from competing for the championship," said Pelham. "Kenny, turn off the fan, affix the birdie, and let's have a round of Laphroig to put some steel in our spines, some wings on our backs, and some fire in our bellies!"

At Pelham's insistence, Snelling was the first to climb onto the bar. He was glassy eyed, and he moved his head as he peered up at the blades of the fan sweeping the air above his head, and then down toward the double row of five men on a side, gripping one another's arms across the center, and then he looked down at the floor directly in front of the bar. For a moment he looked like he was going to topple backward off the bar.

"Oh, dear," he said, steadying himself with his hands out.

Pelham began a chant that was quickly picked up by the group. Bystanders from other parts of the bar and picked up their drinks and come around to watch, and they, too, began to chant, "Got to live, Got to die, Got to Go—Now Dive, Dive, Dive!"

Snelling looked bewildered, staring down at the crowd yelling "Dive, Dive, Dive!"

Pelham's throaty cry rose above the roar, "Dive, Percy, you bloody bastard!"

Snelling reacted with a start, stepping forward and lurching beyond the lip of the bar, waving wildly as the fan blade swept over him with the bit of paper. The blade narrowly missed striking Snelling's wrist and then he plummeted toward the floor, a high shriek escaping him as he collapsed into the arms of the waiting men.

Howls and laughter rose together as their arms momentarily sank with Snelling's body and then billowed up. He lay, sprawled on his side, like a mackerel in a net as it breaks the surface, a stunned expression of drunken terror on his face.

After he clambered down, a thin, medium-sized man from among the bystanders asked if he could have a go. He and his mates put fifty-pound notes on the bar, the bet respectively for and against his ability to snatch the birdie from the blade of the fan. He scrambled up on to the bar, and spent several minutes concentrating on tracking the movements of the fan blade, his hands moving unconsciously with the rhythm of the fan's motion. His short hair was brushed back from his square forehead, and his intent expression, his flushed cheeks, and his strong thin nose made him resemble a minor bird of prey, like a chicken hawk, alert and ready to attack.

Suddenly he sprang toward the fan, a well-timed jump, and his fingers seemed about to close on the paper just as the blade was swinging around, but he missed it and plummeted into the arms waiting below.

"Damn!" he cried, as he came up in the arms of the men, bobbing up as if deposited on shore by a wave amid the laughter.

Nin was standing to one side, his face a mask. I moved over to him and asked, "Are you going to bar dive?"

"Are you joking?" he said. "They wouldn't catch me."

Next, Pelham climbed onto the bar. There was a moment of tension as everyone surveyed his considerable bulk as he stood above the crowd on the bar. The men gripping arms shuffled their feet nervously and braced themselves as Pelham fixed his eyes on the birdie revolving in the air above him.

Pelham launched himself from the bar, a fleshy red hand pawing the air just as the blade swung over the bar, and for a split second, it looked as if he had closed his thick fingers on the paper, but then the blade continued its sweep, the paper still affixed to it, and Pelham hurtled down onto the waiting forearms below. A collective groaning sigh filled the air, and ten sets of bowed shoulders sank toward the floor under Pelham's weight, before Pelham seemed to heave back up, and with relieved laughter the men set him down on the floor.

"I say, that was bloody close!" exclaimed Pelham, coming up to the bar. "Drinks all around!"

Pelham looked at me. "The Yank! It's time for the bloody Yank to be inducted into the Venerable and Dishonorable Order of Bar Divers."

It was a stupid game, but it was their game, and I had been standing there gradually becoming aware I wanted to beat them at their own game. I wasn't going to hang back like Nin, I was going to force them to drop me, if that's what they wanted to do.

Beers were being served all around, and these were rapidly drunk as the men formed up again for another bar dive.

"I don't know, guys," I said. "I'm heavy. I don't know if you'll be able to hold me when I land."

"Aw, stuff," cried Pelham, gripping the wrist of Snelling, who stood directly across from him. "They held me with no trouble. Don't be a bloody coward."

"Muscle is heavier than fat," I said.

"There's no call for that!" bawled Pelham. "Get up there, you bloody Yank! Come on!"

"Dive, Dive, Dive!" The chant filled the barroom.

I put a foot on the brass railing, and stepping with my other foot on the bar quickly pulled myself up and turned around to face the crowd. Red, sweating faces turned up toward me, and Pelham's face had a huge grin as he bellowed, "Septic Tank, Septic Tank."

The chant was picked up by the crowd, but I blocked it out as I concentrated on tracking the sweep of the fan blades. I had noticed the other divers had made the mistake of trying to tear away the paper just as their hands were about to close on it. With the paper sweeping rapidly across, it was that last unnecessary gesture that had cost the previous two divers the prize. I decided to just let my hand sweep on its own arc, one that would intersect with the arc of the fan blade, and hope the paper would come off in my hand as the two arcs intersected and the fan blade swept away leaving the paper in my fingers.

The blade began to come around again, and I hardly heard the chanting as I stepped out and leaped toward the fan. I flung my arm toward the spot where the birdie would pass over me, and as my fingers closed and the blade passed in a blur above my head, I realized I was stretched full length in the air, ten feet above the floor, hurtling toward the forearms of the men from TransPac. It was too late to try and save myself should anything go wrong. I saw Pelham's and Jones's faces in a blur just before impact, and there was a sickening feeling as I felt the arms beneath me give way. There was the sound of hollow knocking and groans around and above me as I stopped with a lurch.

I had come to rest, still on their arms, on the floor. The impact of my fall on their forearms had pulled everyone's shoulders suddenly forward, and all but one pair had cracked heads together like coconuts. Nin and Jones were fine, perhaps because of Jones' long arms or Nin's agility and reflexes, but the top of Pelham's head had collided with the thin aristocratic nose of the young man across from him, who was now sitting on the floor, leaning back, and kind of crying and snuffling as blood ran through his fingers from his nose. He made a brave job of it; tear ducts almost always react from a blow to the nose, and he was quite composed, under the circumstances.

Arms slithered out from underneath me as the men disengaged from one another, and as I started to rise I saw the birdie in the fingers of my right hand.

I stood up and set it on the bar. A drop of the young man's blood had spattered it.

"I say, are you alright?" I asked, bending down and clapping Snelling on his shoulder.

He closed his eyes, squeezing tears down his cheeks, and nodded his head. "I believe so," he said indistinctly through his broken nose.

I pulled an Irish linen handkerchief out of my pocket. "Here you go, Percy. Use this."

I helped lay young Snelling on the table, and the barman Kenny put an ice pack on his nose. I noticed he had a lovely complexion and beautiful skin that had gone so white he looked almost like a corpse as he lay perfectly still, holding the ice pack to his nose with his eyes closed. Pelham's idea was to solemnly continue to drink around Snelling's prostrate form on the table.

It reminded me of a macabre wake. Then it reminded me of Craig.

I was tired. And thoroughly disgusted.

I decided to call it a night and went around shaking hands, saying I was sorry for bringing down the safety net, and wishing everyone a good night.

I got in the taxi, gave instructions to take me to the Peninsula, and got out my mobile phone. During the day I had kept thinking about my next telephone conversation with Samantha. Before too much time passed I wanted to tell her I had met Jacqueline. But I had another call to make first. The lead inspector had given me his mobile.

"Chief Inspector Lin."

"Hi Kenny, it's Dusty Street."

"Oh hi, Mr. Street. How are you?"

"We're both better than Craig. Do you have any leads?"

"No, I'm afraid not, Mr. Street."

"Call me Dusty."

"No leads, Dusty. We're working on it."

"Is there anything else you need from me?"

"No, Dusty, thanks."

I hung up and hit my speed dial.

Sam's cell phone rang and rang, and then it was clicked on and I could hear fumbling sounds followed by a sharp noise as the phone on the other end struck something, and then Sam's voice hurriedly saying, "Hello?"

As soon as Sam answered the phone, I knew it had been a mistake.

"Hi, darling, it's me," I said. "Are you on the ski slope?"

"Hi, darling, I thought it was you," Sam said. "Yes, we've just gotten off the lift and we're about to head down again."

"How's it going? How are you?" I asked. I felt like a speck of dust in a vast universe.

"Sorry, darling?" Sam said after a pause.

"I just asked how you are doing," I said.

"I'm fine, fine," she said. "It's hard to hear you. It's windy up here and reception isn't great. How are you?"

"Oh, I'm a little tired," I said.

"Ok, darling," she said. "Well, get some sleep. Can you get some sleep?"

"Yes, I'm heading back to the hotel now."

"Good. Have a nice long rest," she said. "Love you."

"I love you," I said.

There was a rustle and the phone went dead.

It was almost midnight, and the lights were being turned out on Hong Kong, but the big buildings were still visible as eerie dark shadows, rising above the taxi as we descended into the Mid-Levels.

"And I'm not sure I have any idea what I'm doing any more," I said into the phone. "I'm just not sure."

CHAPTER TWENTY

I WOKE UP AS THE DOOR of my suite chimed. It was past one o'clock in the morning. I remembered there was no peephole in my door as there have been for years in the doors of American hotels. Whoever was on the other side of the door hadn't said 'room service' or 'urgent message for Mr. Street' either.

The doorbell chimed again.

I rang reception.

"Good morning, Mr. Street."

"Is it?" I said. "You could lose your job for letting someone up to my room without permission."

"I'm very sorry, Mr. Street," said the voice, shocked. "She was so— I'm sorry. Would you like me to contact hotel security?"

"No, thanks," I said. "And relax."

I switched on the lights, put on a robe, walked across the suite, and opened the door.

"A beautiful woman gets to play by different rules," I said. "Come in."

"I'm sorry it's so late," Jacqueline said, sweeping by me. "I just had to come over when Sebastian told me you were hurt. I knew you wouldn't seek proper medical attention."

She was wearing another gorgeous dress, one that fell away in a steep angle from her naked shoulders and arms, wrapping tightly around her body until it began to float in folds from her hips. A chain of heavy golden links hung around her neck.

"I'm perfectly fine," I said.

Jacqueline looked into my eyes and then dropped hers in order to look at my hands.

"They look awful," she said, taking my hands in hers. She looked up at me. "I had no idea."

"Would you like something to drink?" I asked.

"No, thanks," she said, settling herself on one of the sofas.

"You look like you could use a glass of champagne," I said.

I ordered a bottle of champagne and asked her to let in the waiter when he arrived. I went into my bedroom and closed the door. I shaved, freshened up, and changed into slacks, socks and loafers, and a white shirt, which crackled in panels of the hotel's heaviest starch.

Jacqueline hadn't touched the champagne when I returned. I pulled the bottle from the bucket and poured myself a glass. I sat down on the sofa also, and looking at Jacqueline, I raised my glass. "Here's wishing you the bluest skies," I said.

"Sebastian told me what happened today," Jacqueline said, moving over next to me. "I couldn't believe it when I heard it."

"Oh, don't you start in on me," I said wearily. "I was just trying to look after Sebastian."

"Of course, you were! It was incredibly brave of you. I'm here to help you because you're so far from home, and I knew you wouldn't go to the doctor to make sure that you were okay."

"It doesn't matter," I said.

"I'm a doctor. Let me look at those hands of yours."

"They still work," I said, holding out my hands. "But I'm going to fire the manicurist who did this."

My right hand was slightly swollen, and several of the knuckles were an angry purplish red, the skin scraped and tattered. My left hand looked better, except where my wedding ring had been. I had taken it off when I returned to my hotel room earlier in the evening, because the skin had twisted around the ring when my punches landed. The place where my ring had been was still pure white, but the finger above and below it was purplish and swollen.

"Oh, Dusty," she sighed. "They look terrible. I suppose whoever you got mixed up with looks worse."

"I didn't stay around long enough to find out," I said.

"Can you move all your fingers?" she asked. She held my hands lightly in hers.

I raised my hands and wiggled my fingers. The outside of my right hand burned.

"Yes, no problem," I said.

"I wouldn't be surprised if you've broken something in this one," she said. Carefully she examined the hand, running her fingers lightly along the joints of the fingers, and then down the back of the hand along the frail bones that fan out from the wrist. She gently stroked the outside of my hand.

I winced.

She was watching my face. "That's what I thought," she said.

She set my hands carefully in her lap and reached for her bag. She brought out a glass sphere of mottled gold, laced in a net of gold braid. Jacqueline undid the knot, and loosening the golden net she opened the sphere with a careful twist. Inside was a deep red gel that had been lightly furrowed in shallow swirls, obviously by fingers. Fragrance rose from the open sphere.

"It's hard to believe, in this day and age, that you needed to defend my brother in a fight with your fists," she said.

"Sebastian needs to meet a nicer crowd," I said.

"It's just so primitive," Jacqueline said, starting to rub my hands with the ointment. "So barbaric. Please don't misunderstand me, Dusty. I'm so glad you were there to protect him. I don't think you're barbaric. But to think you had to fight somebody off who was attacking my brother . . ."

"There's no way of knowing what the guy would have done," I said, "since I decked him before he had a chance. Maybe he would have only slapped Sebastian or spat on him, or something. I don't think his life was in danger. I don't even think he was facing grievous bodily harm. But after what happened to Craig the day before, when I saw things escalate in that meeting with Sebastian, I just snapped. I was going to put a stop to it with everything I had."

"Well, I'm glad you did," Jacqueline said. "Regardless of the consequences. Whatever they may be."

"All I know is I wasn't going to see Sebastian get beaten up. I don't know if that's what was going to happen, but it sure looked like it. I hate to see people get physically abused. I can't stand it."

"It's okay," Jacqueline said soothingly. "You did the right thing. It's alright now."

Under the light strokes of her fingers, the gel became clearer and began to cover my hand like a glaze. The fragrance changed, too, and the spicy scent became warmer and more wine-like. I found myself feeling relaxed, but also sad in a sweet, unfamiliar way.

"Sebastian also said you had done something clever to save the deal. He said that you'd been able to increase the price by two hundred million dollars."

"Sebastian talks too much," I said. "And we'll see how clever the idea is. The markets are continuing to move against us."

"Didn't you go out tonight to celebrate? I thought it was a done deal," she said.

"You're well informed," I said. "But it's never a done deal until the ink is on the paper."

Neither of us spoke. I concentrated on the sensation of Jacqueline's touch. In the beginning, she touched my hand lightly, her fingers like feathers. While it was a pleasant sensation, it was also abstract, impersonal. Then her finger tips slowed as they passed along my skin, working between my fingers and along my palm. Her touch was still light, but there was something soft, elegiac about the passage of her fingers through mine.

For a moment I thought of Sam; her confident, practiced wife's touch was so different from the feel of Jacqueline's hands. Jacqueline's hands were exploring terrain both familiar and unfamiliar.

Jacqueline lifted my left hand and began to caress it with the ointment.

I looked at the purple streaks around the place where my ring had been when I punched Ng. The rest of the hand looked alright, but the knuckles were roughened and red. Jacqueline's elegant fingers moved up and down through my fingers, her beautiful hands interweaving with my flat, broad, battered hand.

"The hands that saved my brother Sebastian," Jacqueline said softly, cradling them.

I thought she might kiss them.

Instead, holding my hands in her left hand, she reached behind her head with her right hand and loosened her hair. It cascaded around her shoulders like hand-rubbed mahogany, like the place at the bottom of the glass where wine looks most like heart blood. Then she gathered her hair in her hand and, bending forward, began drying my hands with her hair.

It was an incredible sensation. It felt like something soft and pleasing, but permitted, and something wild and animal—utterly taboo. Her hair was as soft as a silk woven to please the touch, but also luxuriously heavy, like ermine. The fragrance from the ointment, mingled into my skin, combined with the smell of Jacqueline's hair and her person.

Perhaps I was tired. My hands trembled.

She wrapped my trembling hands more tightly and intimately into her fingers and the tresses of her heavy, shining hair. My heart was beating so hard I could feel my pulse throbbing in my neck and against my skull.

My heartbeat was loud in my ears, and I could hear both our breathing become slower, longer, more rhythmic.

Jacqueline intertwined her fingers in mine. Slowly she lowered our hands together, allowing our fingers to disengage from her hair, lowering our hands so I could feel my fingertips tracing down her neck, and then into the rising swell of her breasts. Our hands came to rest between her breasts, and I could feel the beat of her heart against my fingertips.

Gently I slipped my hands beneath her dress and cupped her heavy breasts, drawing her to me as she looked me straight in the eyes, and kissed her deeply.

That would have been the obvious next step, but I actually didn't do it. I did what girls do when they find themselves at a turning point just before they've decided they're ready to go over the falls.

"I'm sorry," I said, and gently but firmly disengaged my hands, resting my wrists against my thighs. "I can't do it."

Jacqueline looked startled, and then her eyes flashed as her cheeks colored.

I put a finger to her lips and then caressed her chin. "No name-calling," I said. "Boys get to say no, too."

She looked angrily at me, and with a hard, challenging smile said, "Not even 'poofter'?"

"No," I said, smiling and rolling my eyes. "You can do better."

"Okay, then how about 'spineless wimp'?"

"Nope."

Then I kissed her, and with my lips still grazing hers, I murmured, "Because as much as I want to make love with you, Jacqueline, right now, you are married and I'm married."

I kissed her deeply.

"Sorry, I just can't help it," I said, and kissed her again.

Then I sat back on the sofa a little farther.

She opened her beautiful eyes, pools of light, and looked calmly and steadily into my eyes. Not making it any easier.

"I'm not ready, Jacqueline," I said. "I probably shouldn't ever be ready."

Her eyes shone brightly, and then she looked down at my trousers, and, reaching, she sharply snapped on my upper trouser leg with her fingers.

"What do you call that?" she said. "You look ready to me."

I kissed her, but carefully, lightly. She averted her face. "Hmm? Who's doing the talking for you?" she demanded.

"I didn't say I didn't want to, I said I wasn't ready."

She slowly kissed me. "Hmmm?" she murmured. "Ready yet?"

I embraced her, then I stood up. "Sorry," I said.

She looked up at me, then dropped her eyes and looked directly in front of her, at my trousers. She laughed. "Sorry," she said, covering her mouth with her hand. "It's just too funny."

Jacqueline straightened her back, shifted her legs, and with a couple of smart tugs adjusted her dress. She stood up too, tilting her head back, her long fragrant hair hanging to the side over her shoulder, and with her eyes opened she kissed me on the mouth. "It's up to you," she said.

"Thank you," I said, walking her to the door. "My hands feel wonderful."

"My pleasure," she said, and left my suite.

I undressed and went to bed. As I walked back to my bedroom through the outer rooms of my suite, I suddenly seemed to see and feel my daughter Stephanie walking next to me, holding my hand in her small hand.

My shoulder still ached as I lay down but my hands felt light, purified. My body felt old and heavy, like dross, except for the newly forged, angelic instruments at my wrists.

Chapter Twenty-One

I woke up exhausted.

I checked my emails and made phone calls. The news was really bad.

Coldstream's trading desks had battened down the hatches for a prolonged global storm in the financial markets. The limited risk-taking going on was all on the downside, shorting selected securities that looked like they could be carved out from the herd, hunted down, and taken out.

Activity was coming to a halt, and liquidity was drying up with it. It was going to be extremely difficult, if not impossible, to implement any strategy now. The only good news was that the prices of TransPac bonds were up strongly in European and New York trading. The only way prices rise is when there's less supply than demand. It looked like my visit to see Dorfman had worked out as I planned—as I expected, he had broken his word and started scooping up TransPac bonds. I smiled to myself.

The bigger picture was temporarily promising, too. Piecing together my conversations that morning with bits and pieces I had picked up over the last couple of days from my friend at the State Department and elsewhere, it seemed clear the US was going to try and save the situation soon.

It wouldn't work, but it might buy time to close the TransPac deal.

As I sat in the armchair with my fifth cup of coffee, wondering what to do, I found my mind wandering from TransPac and the crisis in the market to Craig's death and wondering why he was killed, to Jacqueline and my life with Samantha and the kids.

I found myself wondering which relationship represented the deepest and most meaningful emotional structure in my life. On one hand, it was obvious my marriage was more significant than the platonic and episodic relationship Jacqueline and I had shared. Samantha and I had been married for many years and produced two wonderful children. We were intertwined with one another in all the myriad legal, financial, practical and habitual ways that develop between a husband and wife in a family.

And yet, there was something wonderful and mysterious about meeting Jacqueline again in Hong Kong. Jacqueline and I had known one another practically since we were children. We had been born in the same hospital at almost the same time. These details might have seemed irrelevant coincidences, except we had met again, at a time when we were fully capable of implementing any decision about our lives we decided mutually to agree upon.

My feelings at seeing Jacqueline again had surprised me with their strength, and I wondered if my emotions were some kind of proof of a lifelong significance for the relationship between the two of us. Despite the legal and social structures that bound me to Samantha, was it possible in some deeper, truer, sense that the real story of my life was a life-spanning love for Jacqueline?

I realized, however, that the sudden reappearance of Sebastian and Jacqueline Nin in my life was distracting me from the fact I was a very different person than the boy who had been their schoolmate in Hong Kong. The years since I left Hong Kong had been a period of constant evolution in my life as well as in their lives. It would be absurd to attempt to reestablish a relationship, however significant, from such an early time in our lives, especially when it meant betraying my wife and displacing the partner in my life as it was now. Which I was arguably already doing.

Maybe structure wasn't the issue, I thought. Perhaps what I was looking for was a sign of the authenticity of my relationships with Samantha or Jacqueline. I remembered the blow I had used to take down Zhu's thug. A left hook bursts out from a split-second conjunction of inspiration and opportunity. It can't be manipulated or preplanned but it creates its own structure and can transform a life.

It was too early to discern the authenticity of my renewed encounter with Jacqueline, but my marriage with Samantha had been very much like a left hook. Samantha and I had met in Milan, where I was working on what would have been the first cross-border acquisition of an Italian company since before World War Two. It was a friendly deal; I always do friendly deals. But it had become mired in regulations and restrictions, and mutually exclusive approvals and procedures designed to keep Italian companies under the control of the small clique who runs Italy.

Our acquisition team included an Australian, and one night he told me he was going to have a drink with a former schoolmate of his from rural Australia who happened to be traveling up the Italian peninsula on her way around the world. We met at a café on the Via Montecuccoli, and she stopped me cold from the moment I saw her sauntering up to our table, challenging and playful and fully aware of her own beauty. I asked her out several times, and each time we fought relentlessly, without asking or giving quarter. In the end, it didn't matter.

Sam went on to London, I returned to New York three months later, after we finally succeeded in finishing the merger, and when she made her way to New York after another year in London, we met up again and were married. I couldn't possibly have planned it to work out the way that it did. Sam and I didn't really know enough about one another to make such a solemn commitment. I wonder whether a man and a woman ever really do. We just met, in a special way, in a unique relationship to one another, at just the right moment in our lives. Like a left hook, becoming engaged required a complex choreography of numerous elements we had nothing to do with, which all had to work in complete harmony. And yet it had started with the intuitive recognition that this was the time, the person, and the situation that was right for all eternity. That's how it started.

Regardless of what had happened since, the commitment I'd made to Samantha was lifelong. I shook off thoughts of Jacqueline Nin and got ready to go into TransPac.

When I arrived at TransPac's offices I went to the trading floor and found Nin. He was conferring heatedly with some guys on the trading floor, but after a few moments walked over to me.

"Morning," he said.

"Tough day in New York," I said.

"Oh, we'll be alright," he said.

"What do you make of the price of TransPac bonds?" I asked.

"I know," he said. "Incredible. They're up almost 10%. Somebody must be buying."

"Have you heard from Dorfman or Brightling?" I asked. "Any response to the proposal you sent over?"

"Not yet," Nin said.

"Well, don't get too excited about the jump in the price of TransPac's bonds," I said. "The price action won't last. Our friends at Lobo Global must have decided on their own to start buying TransPac bonds in order to position themselves to get a piece of the action in the acquisition. They're doing it out of London and New York to try and ambush us."

"Bastards!" spat Nin.

"Relax," I said. "We gave them the idea, remember?"

"Yeah," said Nin, his expression puzzled. "I wondered about that when you were telling them."

"I was pretty sure Dorfman wouldn't be able to restrain himself," I said. "So he's waded into the market and bought up fifty million dollars' worth of TransPac's bonds, I'd guess."

"But why would you want to have to deal with Dorfman?"

"I don't care," I said. "If TransPac is still alive so I have to deal with Dorfman, I'll be ecstatic. What we need over the next day or so are some signals to the market that TransPac is still alive and kicking. Speculators are stalking the markets, smelling blood, trying to pick off the weakest companies. We've got to convince the hyenas TransPac is a survivor."

"And by tricking Dorfman into buying TransPac's bonds, you've engineered a rise in the price and sent a signal to the markets of our financial strength," Nin said.

"I didn't trick him," I said. "I asked for his cooperation."

"Knowing he'd try to screw you," Nin said.

I nodded. "This is only going to last a day or so, though. We've got to ratify the deal at the shareholders' meeting this afternoon, and then immediately get on with sailing TransPac through the storm. Second, the

US Fed is going to cut interest rates soon, probably tonight our time, and you should be positioning your guys to make a quick buck by selling as everyone else is buying. You'll make a few points and be able to raise some more cash. Don't get greedy. The goal is to raise cash—as much as possible—so TransPac can survive when the banks start pulling your funding lines, which they'll do starting sometime today the way it's going. It'll start with one or two banks, and if you can survive that, you may be able to convince the rest of them not to follow. If not, the game's up."

"Yeah," said Nin.

I walked over to one of the trading positions and looked over the trader's shoulder at the screen. He was monitoring the bond page of the Hong Kong office of one of the big US investment banks. Like insect movements, the digits kept flickering here and there on the screen amid the rows of bond prices. Steadily down.

In their restless search for advantage or slightly lower risk, the financial markets continuously innovate. The great trading banks have pored over the secrets of chaos theory in order to optimize their complex global investment portfolios. Chaos theory addresses the reality that, under certain conditions, a butterfly flapping its wings in Hong Kong can trigger a chain of events that produces a hurricane from New York to London. A perfect storm.

It helps explain how a currency devaluation in Thailand or a bond default in Indonesia can trigger a meltdown in the financial markets across Asia.

Perhaps chaos theory could explain why Jacqueline and I spun out into our separate lives, marriages, and families. Perhaps it had started because of something very small. As small as a phone call and the short note that followed.

"I should be going," I said to Nin, and walked toward the elevator.

Chaos is made comprehensible by identifying within the swirl of random events tiny patterns, fragments of meaning. These patterns are called fractals. Fractals are special kinds of patterns that replicate themselves: the shape of a cell that resembles the leaf that contains it, which resembles the shape of the tree itself.

Jacqueline and I were born within the same week in Paris. We had met, and been in love in a shy, tender way in Hong Kong. Now the winds of crisis had brought us together again.

Of course, there were other patterns. Legal and emotional and financial patterns like marriage, like my wife and Jacqueline's husband, like our children—living patterns with immortal souls entwined in our unmingled genes.

CHAPTER TWENTY-TWO

I RETURNED TO THE WAR ROOM. McKee came up to me, his face grim. "We need to talk," he said.

Fai and Peter were at their computers, not looking at me.

"What's up?"

"The guys have been through all the changes that they made to the model again, after a good night's sleep," McKee said.

"Uh oh," I said.

"Yeah," he said.

"How far down did the value go?" I asked. For some reason, it's never up.

"Well, the original improvement would have been more like fifteen percent," said McKee. "Not fifty."

"That was what I thought," I said. "It seemed strange."

"We'd probably still be in the game except that the markets closed down again in New York and London, and so that means it'll be another bad day out here in Asia. Even though the two hundred million was only based on a thirty percent increase, we're now below that, and more."

I felt a pit open in my stomach.

McKee was studying my face. "I know. It's bad," he said.

"We've been blown out of the water," I said.

"I'm sorry. I feel responsible," McKee said. "I shouldn't have talked you out of your skepticism."

I was studying the wall of the War Room, thinking about all the people who were depending on the higher value: Entrekin, Nin, Pelham and all the guys at TransPac, Walmsley, Houghton—and Jacqueline. It was a disaster, an embarrassing disaster. I wondered whether Houghton would press forward with his threat to fire me.

"Shit," I said. I looked at McKee. "Forget about all that. I was here the whole time, and I could have kept asking questions. It didn't make sense to me. I wanted the higher value to be true. It affected my judgment. Don't worry about who's responsible—I'm responsible. It's my fault. The point is, what do we do now?"

"The deal isn't over," McKee said.

"It looks to me like it's over," I said. "There's no way we'll be able to talk the TransPac guys into selling us their shares at the lowered price," I said.

"It may be fixable," McKee said.

"How?"

McKee cleared his throat. "Well, so far, only the four of us know about it."

"Yeah, so we've got a couple hours to confirm it really was a mistake, and then break it to Entrekin and his crew."

"No, it was a mistake, alright. I've confirmed it," said McKee. "What I mean is, you know, the value is based upon a whole lot of assumptions." McKee looked very uncomfortable, almost breaking out into a sweat, but he stared at me earnestly. "The model projects forward for twenty years, you know. Who are we to say where currency markets are going to be in even three years? Or three weeks?"

"So, you're saying we've been too conservative in our assumptions?"

McKee hesitated. "Well, I mean, I felt comfortable with our assumptions before, but, you know, maybe we're gutting too much value out of TransPac."

"So, you're suggesting we change some assumptions and get the value back up so we can stick to our offer of the extra two hundred million?"

"Well, not in so many words," said McKee, looking more uncomfortable. "But we've been doing this so fast, maybe we've gotten our assumptions out of line—maybe we're unrealistically pessimistic. I'm suggesting that now that we know for sure there was a mistake in the model after we made those changes, we review the assumptions and confirm we're happy with them, and that we're not unfairly penalizing TransPac by being too pessimistic."

McKee's suggestion was tempting. After yesterday, and especially after the celebration last night, we would look like fools if we switched the value back. Worse, we might appear to have been acting in bad faith. Finding unreasonably pessimistic assumptions we could change and getting the value back up to where Entrekin and the other shareholders would do a deal would be a painless way to get out of this mess.

I knew how Houghton would react. Houghton would do his damnedest to get me kicked off the deal—and sacked. I would be out of it, and when the deal fell apart, the version everyone would hear back in New York was I had come in and fucked it up. I was beginning to understand Houghton was gunning to succeed Walmsley as the head of the Management Committee. Running Asia had been a perfect stepping stone until the markets had started to fall apart several months before. In order to salvage his chances, what better scapegoat for at least part of what was going wrong in Houghton's fiefdom than demanding the head of one of Walmsley's guys?

"How long do you think it'll take?" I said.

"We can sit down right now and go through the assumptions," said McKee.

"The shareholders' meeting is at two this afternoon," I said. "We've got to know well before then so I can brief Entrekin if necessary. You know what we need to do? We need to get Nin down here to help us go through the bond portfolio to see if what we're doing makes sense under the changed assumptions."

McKee frowned. "You want Nin to know we've got a problem?"

"He's got more at stake than we do in getting it fixed," I said. It might not be true for McKee and the team, but as far as I was concerned, Nin and I were in the same boat. We were both facing the sudden end of our careers. We were both being threatened with the possibility we would be stripped of our reputations and the hard-earned equity we had built up in our partner's accounts.

"True," McKee shrugged. "But once he knows, what'll stop him from telling everybody?"

"He can tell anybody he wants to," I said. "But if word gets out before we've had a chance to fix it, his chances of realizing any cash for his TransPac shares will go to zero."

I picked up the phone and stopped with my hand in mid-air.

"You know what our real problem is, don't you?" I said to McKee.

"What?" said McKee, looking miserable.

"No one is going to believe we didn't do this deliberately," I said.

"What do you mean?"

"Well—by putting the higher value on the table, we got TransPac to jump into our arms when they might have had some other options," I said. "Those options aren't likely to be there now."

"If they ever were," said McKee.

"Perhaps," I agreed. "But even if they didn't have any other options, they'll think we set them up."

"It would have been an incredibly high-risk strategy to have done it deliberately," said McKee, rubbing his forehead morosely.

"This is a high-risk deal," I said, and rang Nin. "Can you come down here? It's an emergency," I said into the telephone.

"I've got one up here, too." Nin said. I could hardly hear him over the roar of the trading room in the background. "What's up?"

"There was a mistake in the model," I said.

"A mistake! What does that mean?"

"It means we don't have two hundred million to offer on top," I said. "And after the way New York closed, we're heading south to the point we won't have anything extra to put on the table."

"Bullshit!" Nin screamed. "What do you think you're doing? Are you telling me you have vaporized two hundred million dollars in less than twenty-four hours? You can't fuck me that way!"

"Listen," I said. "We're trying to see if we can get any value back into the model—"

"You're trying to fuck me, you prick!" screamed Nin. "Entrekin and Pelham and the rest are going to come after whatever is left and try to take it out of my share of the equity! You've fucked me, you lying bastard!"

"Calm down," I said. "Get down here and help me fix this."

"You double-crossing prick! You set me up!"

For a while I listened to the sound of his breathing on the phone. "Okay," he said, at last. "I'll send down Yun and Johnny, my two best quants, to help you go through the model. I'm busy. But I'm warning you, Dusty, if you fuck me—I'll kill you."

The line went dead.

A couple minutes later, two frightened analysts appeared at the door of the War Room. "How's it going in the markets?" I asked.

They shook their heads. "Not a good day."

We gathered around Fai's computer and began hurriedly running sensitivities by changing scenarios and looking at the difference it made to value.

As I stood over the computer screen, watching the columns of figures skid by as we desperately went over the key assumptions, I fully realized the excruciating nature of my dilemma.

Modeling mistakes are endemic to deals. Model construction is such a complex, detail-oriented job that human error is inevitable. That is why acquisition teams try to get a model "fully baked"—past the point of any major changes—well before the deal approaches financial close in order to have the model audited and catch any last errors that have crept into it.

The problem was that Entrekin and his team had been, and still were, living on false hopes. My arrival in Hong Kong had allowed those hopes to continue; they knew that their livelihoods were at terrible risk from the crashing markets, but they continued to hope that an outside force, Coldstream Holdings New York, would step in and reverse the devastation, at least as it affected their personal wealth and positions. The relief they had felt when they thought of me as their savior would now turn into equal, or possibly greater, anger when they could no longer delude themselves everything would be alright. They were about to lose almost everything that they had worked for, some of them for most of their careers. When I told them that the extra value had only been a modeling mistake, I was going to kick away the last prop supporting their dream castles.

They were going to go wild. It wasn't rational, but I would be the scapegoat for their loss of livelihoods and reputations, their accumulated wealth, and their dreams.

Houghton was a more complex case. He was too smart to believe the situation could have been righted by Coldstream Holdings alone, but he, too, had invested a substantial portion of his career and his personal prestige in Asia.

In order to reach the pinnacle of our profession, Head of the Executive Committee of Coldstream Holdings, he would have to demonstrate the ability to build a business that could prosper in good times and weather the bad times.

So, if I could prove to him that acquiring TransPac would be poison for his Hong Kong operations, Houghton would probably back off from the deal. But if he still thought TransPac would bring something to his business, and if the deal fell apart because of the appalling market conditions, then Houghton had every incentive—professional and personal—to shift the blame from his own shoulders to mine, and by extension, to Walmsley's. I had no illusions about Houghton: he was perfectly capable of destroying my career and reputation in order to rise one more step on the ladder of his own career.

Sebastian was going to suffer along with the rest of the TransPac partners if Coldstream did not acquire TransPac, but I believed he would be much better off. Even though it was his bond portfolio that had destroyed the value of TransPac, he had the aura of a market visionary who had built an impressive, even if ultimately flawed, business. Sebastian had invented a new market, a rare achievement that elevated him into a very select circle.

The nature of capital markets is such that, in order to learn his secrets, another house would hire Sebastian and as many of his team as they could. Then they would put controls in place designed to prevent the same debacle, and allow Sebastian to build an improved version of his new business for them. The shareholders of TransPac would be left with the losses Sebastian had caused as he was learning how to perfect his vision.

I told myself Jacqueline was irrelevant. Of course, I had enjoyed her admiration when she thought I had saved her brother's firm. It was deeply satisfying to show up in Hong Kong, years later, as a successful financier. It was obvious Sebastian would tell her almost immediately that it was my team and I who had made the fatal mistake, and that instead of saving the deal, we were the ones to turn the lights out on it. I told myself Jacqueline's opinion didn't matter, that what Jacqueline thought was the last thing worth thinking about at a time like this.

Within forty-five minutes, it was obvious there were no easy fixes. There were many assumptions that were very sensitive, true—but we had been using forecasts from the Coldstream trading desks for those assumptions. Changing those assumptions would be changing the rules we play by. I couldn't write a check on Coldstream Holdings only in order to save myself. I couldn't do it, but that's what it had come down to: buying my way out.

"Well, that's that," I said.

McKee gave me a long look. "What are you going to do?"

"I'm sick about it, but we're going to have to inform Entrekin we've made a mistake."

"Your call."

"Well, do you see any way out?" I asked.

McKee started to speak. "Well, I just . . ."

"I thought you didn't want to do this deal," I said. "Now you're willing to fuck around with the assumptions to get it done?"

"I just hate to go to that crowd and let them shit all over us," McKee said softly, "which is what they're going to do. I don't want to admit we've made a mistake like this—especially to butt-slime like them."

After the evening at Entrekin's club, I could imagine what it was going to be like. It was going to be bitter.

"I know what you mean. I'd rather hit my hand with a hammer for a week than admit to that idiot Pelham I've fucked up," I said. "But do we have the right to put hundreds of millions into TransPac by tinkering with the assumption set?"

The question answered itself. Or should have.

McKee looked at me. "I don't know the future," he said, "but I do know it won't look like what the model is projecting."

He was right, of course. However events actually played out, the reality of the next ten years would have a very different impact on the value of TransPac than what we showed in our model. The model was based upon the best estimates we had now, knowing what we knew now. Of course, it would work out differently. But that didn't mean that the value was wrong. There were lots of ways the future could play out and still confirm TransPac wasn't worth a nickel anymore—or was worth billions.

The model was only a highly sophisticated estimate. McKee was proposing we corrupt the process.

"I can't just change the assumptions without letting Walmsley know," I said. "You think TransPac might be worth more than the model says. Sure—but it could be worth less. Are you willing to defend a different assumption set?"

"There's no way to defend any particular set of assumptions," McKee said. "Have you checked Bloomberg in the two minutes? The situation is too chaotic. Who knows what's going to happen?"

"Okay," I said. "Then we stick with the best our team's been able to do. We rely on ourselves."

I picked up the phone and dialed Nin. "Sorry, Sebastian, we've been through the model with your guys—and we've definitely lost the two hundred million. We've explained the mistake to them, and they understand it. They can walk you through it if you want it confirmed."

"Stop fucking around, Dusty. What are you going to do about it?"

"Do? We're going to have to pull the offer," I said. "There's nothing else we can do. I've got to call Entrekin now and give him the bad news."

"Why don't you go fuck yourself while you're at it," he said, and hung up.

Only after I started to dial Entrekin's number did I realize that there hadn't been any background noise during my last call to Nin.

I spoke to Entrekin briefly and told him I had to see him immediately. I told him to round up his management team.

"Do you want me to come with you?" McKee asked. I could see from the look in his eye that it was the last thing he wanted to do.

"No, I'll break it to Simon myself," I said. "I've got to tell Walmsley about this too, and I'd better brief Houghton. If I were Entrekin, the first thing I would do is get on the horn to Houghton and Walmsley and scream at them, try and get them to stay in the deal at the new price we came up with yesterday—the price we've blown to hell this morning when we fixed the mistake in the model. What time is it in New York?"

McKee looked at his watch. "Two fifteen in the morning."

"I'll let him sleep a little longer," I said. "I'll call Houghton first."

Houghton didn't mince words when I explained the situation to him. "You're off the deal, Dusty."

"You're real sure that's what you want?" I said. "Think it over carefully, because you're going to get what you want."

"You heard me," he said.

"You're going to handle the TransPac Board meeting yourself?" I asked. "It's in one hour."

"Be there," he said. "But I'm going to be there, too. And I'm calling the shots."

Then I rang Walmsley. I listened to him curse softly and intensely for a while after I explained the situation.

"Look," he said. "Houghton doesn't have the authority to commit Coldstream to a deal. Only the Executive Committee can do that."

"Are you sure you have the votes to block him?" I asked.

"Of course," Walmsley said.

"You're real sure?" I asked.

"Yes, of course," he said. "Why?"

"Houghton's acting pretty confident," I said.

"He always sounds confident," Walmsley growled. "It's part of his schtick. He's too stupid to know when he should be confident or not."

"No, he's not stupid," I said. "But sometimes he wants things so badly he acts stupid. TransPac is one of those things."

"Well, you've got to keep him under control," Walmsley said.

After I rang off, I thought about the dilemma I was in. Walmsley didn't want to do the TransPac deal, but he wasn't going to fire me if it did get done. Houghton wanted TransPac so badly he was willing to do almost anything, including destroy me, to accomplish his goal. Walmsley wanted me to prevent Houghton from doing something reckless, but it was becoming increasingly obvious I was going to have to deal with Houghton for a long time to come—if I kept my job—while Walmsley was a year away from retiring and going limited. The sensible thing to do was to placate Houghton—if I still could.

CHAPTER TWENTY-THREE

IN THE WESTERN PART OF PARIS, between the stately Bois de Boulogne and the Avenue Charles de Gaulle, the great river of traffic that divides Neuilly, there is a little cemetery. Avenue Charles de Gaulle is one of the great arteries of transportation, not only of Paris, but the world: it is like Park Avenue in New York, Hyde Park Corner in London, Wilshire Boulevard in Los Angeles. Every hour, tens of thousands of people course along the Avenue Charles de Gaulle, their destinations leading them toward a myriad of chores and appointments, confrontations and obligations and whims.

The Rue des Graviers intersects the Avenue Charles de Gaulle, running quickly into the quiet streets of Neuilly, and then threads its way along a high, silent wall into the Bois. The silence behind the dressed stones of this wall seems to have a palpable presence when one enters the gates and walks under the pines that stand along the wall. The snarling of traffic that still carries on an errant breeze from the Avenue Charles de Gaulle as one walks along the tranquil footpath alongside the Rue des Graviers suddenly ceases as one approaches those gates, as if it is pushed back by the silence welling up from the cemetery.

It is this silence, this abundance of emptiness among the tombs and stones, that is the harvest of the barren, carefully tended field inside the wall.

Sometimes I come to the cemetery by walking along a very long street, the Rue Jacques Dulud, which is roughly parallel to the Avenue Charles de Gaulle and traces the northern wall of the cemetery. The silence wells up over the wall and stills the restless sounds of traffic from this approach as well. Just as the living districts of Neuilly are divided by Avenue Charles de Gaulle, the cemetery is divided by a long alley formed

183

by two very high hedges. This hedged alley runs in the same direction as the Rue Jacques Dulud, and therefore parallels Avenue Charles de Gaulle, the broad river of life and obligations and distractions outside the wall. This is where I come whenever I visit Paris. It is the closest I can be to my mother.

I walk along the alley between the hedgerows, and when I come to the seventh dirt path that intersects the alley and runs into the graves, I turn right and walk among the graves. The graves are lined up one after the other, like a parking lot, as one would expect of those who have come to rest after a lifetime of journeying along Avenue Charles de Gaulle and its tributaries. There are a few small tombs among the graves, but mostly the graves are constructed of panels of aged-scoured marble that rest above the ground like tables or desks, the coffins underneath and inside.

This is not the glamorous environs of La Recoleta, but it has not gone to rack and ruin either. I walk through the clutter of lapsed remembrance of forgotten lives, the stones and slabs that succeed in preserving, at most, the names and either endpoints of those whose remains were brought here, and I always wonder why no grass grows, why the dirt paths never seem to support the burden of any plant life. Perhaps the silence is like an ever-freshened stream of water, welling up from the graves and denying any life an enduring purchase on this soil, carrying away anything that could breathe, or absorb sunlight, or grow and change.

The grave of my mother is one of the few acts of generosity my father ever performed. It is one of those tables of marble, crowded in among all the others. It says simply "Eva Street, née Schwichtenberg" and gives the dates of her birth and death, the latter just two days after my birthday. My mother's name isn't an especially incongruous name in that cemetery. Many other tombs bear the names of Alsatians with their Germanic names; a city rejuvenated by Baron Haussmann is a perfectly fine place to bury a young woman named Schwichtenberg who died giving birth to her first and only child.

One of the reasons I return to that grave in Neuilly is because the words and dates carved into that slab of marble covering what is left of her body constitute the majority of what I know about my mother.

I wonder how many people in their relationships with their natural mothers ever experience the joy I experienced at the discovery that the woman who was married to my father was not my mother. But I have never experienced any corresponding moment of happiness in relation to my real mother; I know too little about her.

My parents met in Amsterdam after the war. My father has told me that he never knew anything about my mother's family; it may well be true. Apparently, she never referred to them. She told him that she had been in the women's camp at Dachau, but that was all she said. Whether her family were Jewish and she couldn't bear to discuss their fate, or whether they were German and as a political prisoner she had felt betrayed by them, I will probably never know. What I do know is that, as a young woman, my mother not only survived Dachau, but her spirit survived enough of the experience to still believe in the possibility of life and hope and happiness. That is why, as I tell myself, she would have married my father, who at that time in his life was probably still a plausible partner for such a dream.

Still a teenager, she emerged from that region of death and inhumanity, and a few years later she was ready to try to love; she was still able to pass on the gift of life.

I honor her memory.

Because I know next to nothing about her, my relationship to her is only the sum of random, seemingly chaotic moments of intuition. Whenever I feel a better nature coming over me, a thirst for the truth or for justice, I feel the presence of my mother—or at least I feel the emergence of that part of me I believe I inherited from her.

I can't know for certain what part of me I get from her, but I do have the example of my father, and I have been able to mark out the elements of my outlook and personality that are not his. So those moments when I feel close to my mother, the times when I commit myself to doing what is right and to accepting the consequences regardless of what they might be, seem authentic to me. They are, in many ways, the most important moments in my life. I'd like to think it's those moments when I am who I really am.

Chapter Twenty-Four

Entrekin's secretary was wearing a pale blue silk dress today. Her lustrous hair cascaded down her back, shining against the dress as she preceded me with long lithe strides into Entrekin's office.

"Alexander," Entrekin said. He rose from his desk and shook my hand. Sitting at the table to the side of his desk were Ralph Pelham, looking sternly from under his wavy gray hair; Grahame Cartwright, glowering from under the gray tufts of his eyebrows; and Llewellyn Jones, his thin face twisted into a sour expression. "Sebastian Nin said he couldn't join us. I'll brief him afterwards."

"Gentlemen, I'm not here with good news," I said. "In fact, I'm sorry to report that we made a serious mistake yesterday—"

"Christ, don't tell me that you've changed your mind about the price," screamed Entrekin. "Because I won't hear of it!"

I nodded my head.

"No, I won't have it!" cried Entrekin.

"You gave your word," bellowed Pelham. "It's a damned rascally thing to do!"

"I did nothing of the sort," I said.

"Oh, yes you did," shouted Pelham. He whirled and threw a pen onto the carpet and stamped his foot. "Bugger!"

"I thought we had a good idea," I said, "and when we tried it out in the model, it looked like it was better than that. In fact, it was only an okay idea and the market took away everything we got from it, and now we're back where we started from," I said. "There it is. That's the way it happened. It is what it is."

"Alexander, what exactly is the meaning of this mistake?" asked Entrekin, a faint note of hope in his voice. "How much of the two hundred million in extra value you told us about last night was attributable to this mistake as you call it?"

"Well, the markets continue to go down," I said. "A day and a half of dropping markets plus this mistake have reversed out the entire two hundred million."

Entrekin looked at me with a kind of nervous dignity. "And to think that yesterday, we thought you were so brilliant . . . and it was all because of a mistake."

Pelham glared at me. "I reckoned you were a bloody septic tank yesterday," he said. "And you are."

"I'm sorry about this, gentlemen," I said. "I can understand how disappointing this must be for you. But the offer we will present at your shareholders' meeting will be consistent with what I've just told you. See you at two o'clock."

I went back to the War Room.

Chapter Twenty-Five

"You're presenting to the TransPac shareholders, not Houghton," Walmsley said. "And I told Houghton to keep his fucking mouth shut in there."

"You're okay with me making the low offer?"

There was a silence.

"I'm okay with whatever you decide to do."

"Okay, Jim," I said.

I listened to the line click dead.

Walmsley had just got away from the TransPac deal as fast as he could. He was managing a global crisis that was beginning to affect the farthest reaches of Coldstream's operations around the world. He only had one more year as Chairman; he wasn't going to have to live with the TransPac acquisition if it got done, and he knew how to manage Coldstream just as it was if the TransPac acquisition didn't get done. I understood.

My phone rang again as I walked across the War Room.

It was Houghton.

"I'm not coming to the shareholders' meeting. If you're going to screw the pooch, do it by your goddamned self."

"Okay, Rick—your call," I said.

The line went dead.

Walmsley's decision to back me against Houghton meant I was now the man responsible for TransPac. Nobody else. I felt a chill on my neck.

"Is our proposal prepared for the TransPac shareholders' meeting?" I asked McKee.

"Dusty, I've been thinking about it," McKee said. "And I'm getting very worried about this deal."

"Take a number and get in line," I said. "I've been worried about this deal since I first took a look at it."

"Yeah, but I don't think we should make any proposal at all to the shareholders' meeting," McKee said. "I think we should throw in our cards now and get out of town."

"This morning you were trying to get two hundred million dollars back in to the model," I said. "You were willing to change assumptions to do it."

McKee looked uncomfortable. "That's not the way I remember it," he said quietly.

"What do you mean?"

"I don't change assumptions just to get a particular value," he said.

"But you were willing to," I said sharply.

"No, I wasn't," McKee said. "You must have misunderstood me."

"That's bullshit, Ted, and you know it."

"I am firmly against putting any kind of proposal on the table at the meeting this afternoon," he said stolidly.

"You wanted to do the deal pretty badly this morning. What's changed your mind since then?"

McKee's face turned red, he looked even more uncomfortable and glanced away.

"Have you talked to Walmsley?" I asked.

He looked at me.

"Yes, I have," he said.

"What did he say?"

McKee looked down again. "He said it was your call," he said reluctantly.

I looked at him. "Listen, Ted," I said, putting my hand on his shoulder, "you're shaken up. Give Rick Houghton a call. Ask him to get us in to see the Hong Kong Monetary Authority this afternoon if at all possible. I have a feeling we'd better go over there and talk to them about TransPac."

I didn't want Houghton posturing by not taking my phone call after what had just happened.

McKee looked startled. "You mean it?"

"Yes. We've got to talk to them. This is getting too big for us to handle."

Houghton and McKee had worked together for a year. I was pretty sure Houghton would take McKee's call. I sure didn't have time to go find Houghton.

"Are you going to tell them we're out?"

"I don't know," I said. I thought of Houghton. "But maybe."

"Great!" he said.

"We can always change our minds," I said. "When you talk to Houghton, just tell him I think it's time to brief the Hong Kong Monetary Authority. Don't say anything about the fact we might pull out."

The phone rang. It was Jacqueline. I had left a message for her earlier. Last night had demonstrated we could handle ourselves, and I wanted to establish our new relationship on secure ground for the future. We couldn't sleep together but I didn't want to give her up. She fascinated me more than ever.

"Hey," I said, walking outside the room into the corridor. "When am I going to see you?"

"I don't know, darling," she said. "I wonder whether there is any point."

I thought about it. "Angry about last night?"

"Dusty, I'm not angry. I feel sorry for you. You don't know what you want. And there is a hardness to you that you think is some kind of ethics, which is preventing you from being happy. Preventing us perhaps from being happy."

"Jacqueline," I said, "I don't understand. You have a husband and a daughter, and I have a wife and children too."

"You're thinking too far ahead," she said softly.

"Maybe, but I want to see you again. Soon. I don't know how much longer I'm going to be in Hong Kong."

"What do you mean?" she asked. "Are you going to leave right after you finish the acquisition of TransPac?"

"I don't know if we're going to acquire TransPac," I said.

I heard her gasp.

"Sebastian knows it," I said.

"Are you sure?" she said breathlessly.

"Your brother has never been stupid—far from it," I said. "I called him this morning and told him we weren't going to be able to pay as much as we thought yesterday. There's a shareholders' meeting this afternoon, and we're going to put a fairly unpalatable proposal to them."

"I don't understand what you're saying," Jacqueline said, "and it sounds so serious. You're frightening me. You must meet me tonight and explain it to me. But in the meantime, don't do anything final."

"I have a feeling Sebastian can look out for himself," I said. "He doesn't need me—or his big sister—to take care of him. And besides, he doesn't seem too eager to meet with me anyway. He's had two chances today."

"Oh—don't read too much into that!" said Jacqueline. "He's just under such tremendous pressure. Don't hold it against him."

"Right," I said.

"Be kind, Dusty," she murmured. "Try to do the right thing."

"I'm doing my best, Jacqueline," I said. "What time would you like to meet tonight?"

"Why don't you come by and meet my parents, say at eight, and then we can go out to dinner?"

"I'd like that," I said. "Where would you like to eat dinner?"

"Felix," she said. "It's my favorite. So cool and spare. And the food is delicious."

"Felix it is," I said. *Felix culpa*, I thought.

CHAPTER TWENTY-SIX

SEATED AROUND THE BOARDROOM TABLE were the same faces from two days before, plus two lawyers who were representing the other two shareholders who controlled forty-two percent of TransPac. The shareholders themselves were on video link from the Middle East and Kuala Lumpur respectively, fidgeting in the strange, fractured images transmitted back in the day by the delay across the video links of the time.

Proper arrangements were in place, and I looked at the grim faces above the glass of ice water, two sharp pencils, and a notepad on a leather blotter, emblazoned with the logo of TransPac in gold, that had been arranged at each place.

I took a seat next to McKee and looked across at Nin, who looked at me calmly and steadily.

As Chairman, Entrekin convened the meeting. "Good afternoon, gentlemen. The principal purpose of today's meeting is to consider the proposal by Coldstream New York to acquire TransPac. Of course, we are dealing in extremely adverse markets at the moment, and Coldstream's investment proposal has been changing daily. The Board papers we circulated at the beginning of the week are out of date, and Coldstream will be making their latest offer in their presentation today.

"Alexander, would you like to continue?"

"Thank you, Simon," I said. "It's no secret the deal we've all been working on for many months has almost come unstuck several times in the last week. Nevertheless, Coldstream continues to believe there is value in combining forces with TransPac in this part of the world—"

McKee shifted uneasily in his seat.

"—and so we have been trying to stay on top of the collapsing markets with a proposal to benefit all of you as shareholders of TransPac. Ted, would you like to start?"

McKee and his team had updated the presentation from the day before. Yesterday's declines in markets around the globe had been particularly steep, and on the graphs the last two days displayed as lines that abruptly nosed down like a plane hit by a surface-to-air missile. Then McKee flashed a series of PowerPoint slides that depicted the estimated declines in the Asian bond portfolio. Images of the value of TransPac produced several dramatic slides as well. It was a catastrophe.

The shareholder from the Middle East kept saying "Good God!" and swinging his shoulders back and forth, producing jerky, alarming images on the video link. Finally, McKee put up a slide showing a list of the top thirty banks providing trading lines to TransPac. Over two billion dollars in liquidity that could get frozen at any moment.

A heavy silence filled the room when McKee returned to his seat.

Nin grinned and looked around the table. "But wait, gents, that's the bad news. Now Dusty is going to tell us that despite the fact that we've blown ourselves up, Coldstream has a special deal for us!"

Everyone else looked stricken. Nin looked at me. "Right, Dusty? You and your mob have built a fancy model that tells us we're dopes and had better sell out to you at a fire-sale price. Is that it?"

"Have you checked your Bloomberg screen lately?" I asked. "All we're doing is putting market prices into our model."

"No, you're not," said Nin. "Your model isn't a one-period model—it's a twenty-year model. You're taking a view. You're making projections. You're assuming things. And—guess what—you've assumed we're fucked and have to sell out to you for pennies on the dollar. I think maybe you should take your model and shove it up your ass."

McKee growled something deep in his throat.

"Mr. Nin has a point! Mr. Nin has a point!" said the investor from the Middle East, his voice sounding tinny across the video link. "Simon, have you had an accountancy firm audit Coldstream's figures? Have we had an independent opinion expressed by another investment bank on the value of Coldstream's proposal?"

"We haven't had the time, Mr. Massoud," said Simon. "We did have an independent opinion expressed about their last written proposal."

The investor from Malaysia spoke up across his video link. "But that was a month ago! Does Coldstream still value TransPac at a billion dollars US?"

Pelham leaned forward. "We don't actually know what Coldstream's latest proposal is, do we, Simon?"

Entrekin glanced at me. "No, as a matter of fact, Alexander hasn't tabled his proposal yet. Alexander, would you like to do so?"

"Yes, thank you, Simon. Gentlemen, I would like to make a couple of observations. First, it is true that the views we have expressed on the value of TransPac are our own views. But after conducting months of due diligence on your firm, we think we are in a better position than anyone in the world to understand and value the impacts of the market collapse on your firm. In particular, nobody but Coldstream and Sebastian Nin and his team have a better ability to value your Asian bond portfolio."

"But Mr. Nin disagrees with you," said Mr. Massoud.

"Yes, he does," I said. "But his judgment also got TransPac into the position it is today. You've ridden the value up, and now you're riding the value down. You'll have to decide how much longer you place your confidence in Mr. Nin."

"But Alexander," said Entrekin. "You yourself stated less than an hour ago that Sebastian's ongoing control of his bond operations is key to Coldstream's plans."

"You're being so flattering, Simon. It's not like you," said Nin bitterly.

"That's true, Simon," I said. "But while we would keep him in control of his bond operations, we would impose Coldstream's standard of internal controls on him."

"Oh, you would, would you?" said Nin, waving his middle finger at me. "Control this internally, why don't you?"

The two foreign investors were both shouting, canceling one another out in a wave of static.

Entrekin cleared his throat. "What is Coldstream's proposal, Alexander?"

"We can still offer one hundred million US dollars," I said. "That's for the entire firm—"

Mr. Massoud was the first to react. "It's unacceptable! Totally unacceptable!"

Cartwright's bald head had gone bright red, and the tufts of his eyebrows looked like miniature cockatoos sitting in the red dirt of the outback near Broken Hill. "You are a thief, sir!"

"Bloody septic tank," growled Pelham.

I glanced at McKee. His face was gray with strain and rage. I smiled at him.

Entrekin was patting the air in front of him, trying to make himself heard, but his thin voice was lost in the uproar.

Nin stabbed the table in front of him with a fistful of sharp pencils, sending splinters and fragments everywhere. "Hold it!" he shouted. "Hold it!"

A stunned silence fell. The investor from Malaysia had called his lawyer on his cell phone and could be heard across the video link murmuring instructions to the man, who was sitting at the table, hunched into his phone, taking rapid notes.

"Listen to me!" commanded Nin, glaring around the table at his partners. "The only reason you have to listen to this shit is because you're not talking to anybody else. You've let Coldstream become the only bridegroom at the wedding." He looked at Pelham. "You're Mr. Mergers & Acquisitions, Ralph. That was pretty stupid, wasn't it? Ever heard of 'competition'? And what about you, Simon? Has Dusty been sucking your dick or something? What were you thinking—letting Coldstream be the only ones talking to us?"

"That's quite right!" said Mr. Massoud, his image shivering and blinking. "That's quite right!"

"You little turd—" McKee began, looking straight at Nin.

I touched his forearm with a finger and shook my head slightly.

Nin smiled and stood up. "Well, I've been devoting a little time to maximizing shareholder value." He stood up and walked to the door and opened it.

In walked Mr. Zhu from the Three Dragons Corporation, and both Dorfman and Brightling from Lobo Global. Before Nin could introduce them to his partners, Dorfman smiled and said brightly, "Goodbye, Dusty!"

CHAPTER TWENTY-SEVEN

NIN STALKED UP TO THE TABLE and leaned over it, placing both fists on the table and looking up and down the table. "I would like to introduce you to another consortium I have been in negotiations with, who have the capacity to make a counterbid to the proposal we have just heard from Coldstream New York."

Entrekin looked at Nin in stunned silence.

"Well, Alexander," he said, turning to me, "this is certainly an unexpected development. But it seems to me this Board is obligated to hear the proposal of this other bidder."

"Absolutely, Simon," I said. "If you can ascertain that these gentlemen are prepared to make a bona fide offer to the Board, then my colleague and I will have to excuse ourselves so that you and your co-directors can consider their proposal."

"It's bona fide, alright," said Nin. "Between them, these parties own three hundred million dollars' worth of TransPac bonds, and they are prepared to make an investment proposal to the Board to take new equity in our firm."

Murmurs of approval raced around the table.

Entrekin looked at me, a startled expression on his face. He seemed to have trouble focusing his eyes on me. "Why, yes, Alexander, as you say . . . it's entirely proper that I ask you to excuse yourselves to permit us to consider the offer of these . . . these gentlemen. Sebastian, you will have to introduce them to the Board, of course."

I knew how Dorfman operated. Maybe I had done too good a job, letting a little blood leak into the water to awaken his killer instincts, because he seemed to have accepted whatever smooth line of persuasion Sebastian Nin, that superlative bond salesman, had fed him.

Dorfman was typically much smarter than that, and he could only have agreed to launch a full takeover if he had let his emotions overwhelm his judgment. Most people's instinct is for survival, and they are likely to turn too cowardly in a chaotic situation like the week's collapsing markets. But Dorfman was a killer, and his emotions ran the other way—when he smelled weakness and crippled prey, his bloodlust and greed were likely to push him into acts of total recklessness. It had paid off many times in his career, but to me this was the one time that Dorfman had to get himself under control. The stability of global capital markets could be at stake, especially if Lobo Global collapsed after getting sucked into paying too much for TransPac just as the banks pulled its funding—and they'd do the same to Lobo Global. That could easily destabilize Lobo Global's US parent, an enormous Chicago-based energy trading firm and power developer. It might just be the torpedo that brought down the New York Stock Exchange.

"Just a second, Simon," I said, putting up a hand. "We'll be on our way, but first—Bill, Sebastian—you guys have got to think about what you're doing. Bill, you're not in this for the long haul, you're in this to make a quick buck. Trust me, you and Sebastian are the worst possible combination for each other in this market. You can't listen to each other—you're just egging each other on."

Dorfman's eyes danced. "Dusty, I've known you for a long time, and I'd never pegged you for a sore loser. Come on, guy, take it like a man! You've had your chance."

"Bill, this is serious," I said. "You're never going to get the support of Lobo Global's Board of Directors to back TransPac up if you've got this deal wrong. They'll cut it loose and you'll have to explain a big loss on your bond position. But that's not the worst of it—if TransPac goes bankrupt, it could trigger a depression across Asia. Hundreds of millions of people would be pushed back into poverty. Thousands could commit suicide."

Dorfman grimaced and looked at the wall above my head. "Cut the shit, Dusty. Put up the money or get out."

"Coldstream can stand behind its judgment if things go wrong," I said. "We could pay out every last funding line if we had to."

Nin sneered. "If you've got so much money, why are you showing so little of it to our shareholders?"

"Because there's a good chance that whoever owns TransPac is going to have to pay out a good chunk of the unsecured short-term paper and the bank funding lines provided to TransPac by your banks," I said. My voice rose. "Bill, this isn't just about making a fast fifty or even two hundred fifty million. You can't save TransPac if it starts to go under. Don't listen to Nin. You could lose everything you've put into those bonds. And there's a lot more at stake, too, Bill. If TransPac goes down, the global markets are so fragile it might trigger another depression like the collapse of the Credit Anstalt in 1929."

"But buying those bonds was your idea," said Dorfman. "Funny how your tune changes when somebody outsmarts you."

I decided to try one last time. "Bill, no one knows this asset better than we do. We've been over the portfolio with a microscope and we're paying what we think it's worth. What makes you think you've got a better handle on its value?"

Bill stared at me.

"The lives of hundreds of millions of people could be at risk here—if not literally their lives, certainly their happiness, their health, their hopes for their children," I said. "This isn't just about money, Bill. It's not just about winning."

A kind of tremor went around the table. I looked at the sudden change in faces, looks of incomprehension, and hard, surprised glee. Laughter rolled around the table.

"Oh—yes, it is," shouted Bill. "It sure is, Dusty. Winning is *all* that matters—except when you turn out to be the loser. Like you just have. Don't try and bullshit us!"

Nin leaned forward. "You're pathetic, Street—get the fuck out of here."

Entrekin cleared his throat. "Alexander, with respect, these are really matters for Board deliberation. You have had your opportunity to present Coldstream's proposal to the Board. But I really must ask that you leave to the Board the question of whether the alternative proposal is appropriate or not."

It was clear which way this was going. I couldn't let Coldstream pay more for the equity of TransPac because I had a strong hunch we'd be putting up a lot more shortly—probably at least a billion and maybe more—when the liquidity crunch came. Nin and his friends thought they could afford to pay more for the equity because they didn't see the danger, or they didn't want to believe it.

They were going to put up their last dollars to buy TransPac and then have nothing left when TransPac's banks demanded repayment of TransPac's funding lines. But the Board, in shock at how little value was left in TransPac, didn't want to believe it either. For Entrekin and his colleagues, it meant the illusion of salvaging a bit more of their personal wealth, which had been ravaged in the past weeks beyond any level they could have imagined in their worst, most paranoid nightmares. They were going to sell to the highest bidder, even if it meant that TransPac might get driven into bankruptcy.

Everyone was looking at me.

I shook my head, ignoring Entrekin. "Sebastian, all I can say is that you'd better get this right," I said. I nodded to Mr. Zhu, who had been studiously ignoring me since he had entered the boardroom, and to Dorfman. "Your new friends aren't going to be happy if they lose money as a result of following your investment advice."

"Thanks for the free advice, loser," said Nin. "Your advice is worth exactly what it costs."

Entrekin looked at me with a tight-lipped smile. "Thank you for joining us, Alexander, and for all your work. Now goodbye."

"Thanks, Simon, and good luck," I said. "Our offer is good until close of business today, i.e. five o'clock Hong Kong time."

"Don't wait by the telephone," sneered Nin.

I turned to Entrekin. "Simon, if your Board chooses to reject our offer, I want to afford TransPac and its new shareholders every opportunity to make a go of the investment. The Coldstream announcement will probably cause further panic unless you and your new investors announce your new arrangements before we make our announcement. So I'm going to hold off as long as I can. Please advise me as soon as conveniently possible regarding the response of your Board to our proposal—"

Dorfman barked a laugh.

"—and also, if necessary, when you are ready for us to make our announcement that Coldstream New York is no longer in discussions with TransPac about a strategic investment."

"Certainly, Alexander, yes . . . I'll have someone get in touch," said Entrekin.

I rose. "Thank you, gentlemen, and good afternoon."

Dorfman winked at me as I passed him. McKee and I walked out, and I closed the door of the boardroom gently behind us.

Chapter Twenty-Eight

McKee cursed intensely and angrily as we walked down the corridor toward the elevator.

"Calm down, Ted," I said. "Don't let those guys get to you."

"I've got to talk to you, Dusty," said Ted, reaching for my arm.

"Can it wait a minute, Ted?"

"No, it can't," he said.

I looked at him, and I could see that he was barely holding himself in control.

"I'm not mad at those bastards," McKee said through clenched teeth. "I'm pissed off at you—how could you let Coldstream stay exposed by not taking our deal off the table after the way they treated us in there?" McKee leaned into me. "What the FUCK do you think you're doing, Dusty?"

"What are you talking about, Ted?" I said evenly.

"Look, Dusty," McKee said, so quietly it was almost a murmur. "TransPac is dead. We need to get out of here before the carcass starts to stink. Nothing else matters anymore—we have got to get the fuck out of here!"

"Ted, you need to get a grip on yourself," I said. "I think there's still a way to do this. We'll have to see."

McKee walked up to me and grabbed my elbow. "Dusty—what are you thinking? I've never seen you act like this before."

I lifted his hand from my elbow. "You don't know me as well as you think you do."

"I'm learning fast. I heard you used to go to school with Nin," he said. "At King George V, here in Hong Kong."

I looked at McKee, studying his expression.

"Yes, I did," I said. "So what?"

"I'm not sure," McKee said. "I've been trying to figure out if you're throwing the deal his way, or if you're doing everything you can to keep him from winning."

"Or maybe I'm doing my job for Coldstream," I said. "Ted, you're a good man in the due diligence room—better stay there on the next deal. Getting too close to the deal itself has been bad for your nerves."

"Why can't you pull the plug on this deal?"

"We're going to talk to the Hong Kong Monetary Authority. The way TransPac and their new best friends are going to be at one another's throats, we won't have to make the final call until later tonight I think."

McKee shook his head. "I don't get it. What are we waiting for? You want Coldstream Holdings sucked down with TransPac?"

"It's my equity, Ted," I said, pulling rank. "I'm a partner."

"Maybe you should go limited."

It was a slap in the face. He was telling me to retire. I was in my late thirties.

"I'm going to forget you said that," I said. "Let's go meet up with Rick and pay a visit to the Hong Kong Monetary Authority."

I called Houghton twice in the car but he didn't answer. I hadn't actually seen Houghton since yesterday, and I was immediately struck by how the tension had gone out of his expression and posture as we walked up to him just outside the Hong Kong Monetary Authority building that afternoon. His shoulders had settled from right around his ears and his eyes no longer anxiously squinted, framed by a set jaw.

He wasn't faking it either, if anything he tried to hide it by glaring at me, but all the angles had gone out of his lean body, and he stood waiting somehow rounded and reposed. Had he given up—and if so, on what? The TransPac deal? On saving the Coldstream business in Hong Kong? This was no time for that.

"So what happened?" he said, pointedly not shaking my hand.

"How does it look?" I asked. "Except that Dorfman and Zhu from Three Dragons submitted a counterbid to the Board. Then Entrekin kicked us out."

"What? Lobo and Three Dragons—how'd they get together?"

"Nin put them together."

"The guy's a genius," said Houghton, his face red. "Or a magician. See why we have to fucking acquire him and his team? The guy's a fucking wizard."

I looked at McKee. "He's a deal maker, that's for sure," I said.

Houghton had a couple inches on me and he leaned his red face so close I could smell his sour breath, acrid with cigar smoke. "I knew you intended to blow up this deal, you asshole, but I didn't think you were so stupid you'd let Nin steal it from underneath your nose. I'm going to have your balls nailed to the entrance of 10 Hanover Street."

10 Hanover Street, just off Wall Street, was the global headquarters of Coldstream Holdings.

"I'd be flattered by the recognition," I said, "but if I were you, I'd focus on what we're going to tell the HKMA in five minutes."

The three of us were alone in the lift.

"Do you want me to tell you more about the counteroffer?"

"I know what I'm going to tell Tang," Houghton said stonily.

"I gave it my best shot," I said. "Maybe one day you'll recognize it."

Houghton shook a cigarette out of a pack. "It'll never happen—and besides, you'll be long gone by then."

We stepped out of the elevator with McKee, who was pale and subdued.

Houghton drew on his cigarette as we waited a few seconds after giving our names at reception. The waiting room was packed with anxious executives, all of whom clearly knew Houghton, but he just shook his head and drew us over by the restrooms to stand by ourselves.

"Did you even consider," he asked quietly, "that Dorfman, Zhu and Nin know something we don't?"

"Nope. I'm more worried than anything else about being proved right too soon."

"What do you mean?"

"TransPac's on the brink, Rick," I murmured. "Their banks are going to start pulling their lines any hour, and then the place will implode."

McKee said, "Yeah, and it'll serve those bastards right."

Houghton looked curiously at McKee, and then reflected in silence while he smoked his cigarette.

In less than a minute we were ushered in to see Mr. Tang, the CEO of the Hong Kong Monetary Authority. He knew Houghton well and was very cordial, despite the tremendous strain he was under. He was joined by several staff members.

Houghton assured him of Coldstream's ongoing commitment to Hong Kong, despite the current crisis in the markets. Then we advised him of the status of our negotiations with TransPac and the sudden intervention of Three Dragons and Lobo Global.

I told him that while we were waiting to hear from TransPac's board by five o'clock that afternoon, we were not expecting to make the investment. Mr. Tang wanted to know if TransPac was likely to require support, and I briefed him on the state of their portfolio. "Once we have received a final response from their Board, if TransPac is willing to release us from our confidentiality obligations, we have a financial valuation model that would assist the authority in coming to its own conclusions about whether to support TransPac," I said.

Mr. Tang smiled slightly. "We can require TransPac to release you from your confidentiality obligations immediately," he said.

"I'm aware of that," I said, bowing slightly. "Coldstream would be happy to make everything we have available to the authority in these difficult circumstances."

"Would Coldstream be willing to participate in a consortium to rescue TransPac should that become necessary?" asked Mr. Tang.

"We would definitely consider it," said Houghton, before I had a chance to respond. "Call me any time."

"One last question," said Mr. Tang. "What is the status of those concerning investors in TransPac unsecured debt?"

"They're completely cleared," said Houghton. "TransPac's balance sheet is clean as a whistle."

"Given that it's gutshot," I said. "Who were the concerning investors?"

A dignified smile appeared on Mr. Tang's face and he nodded towards Houghton.

"I'll tell you later," said Houghton. "They're history."

I glanced at McKee but he was too cowed to speak.

We left Mr. Tang's offices and Houghton gave us a lift back to Transpac in his chauffeured car, but Houghton dismissed my questions about the investors in TransPac's short-term paper Tang had mentioned. "They were a couple pimples on the ass of TransPac," he said. "They're irrelevant. At least you didn't announce to Tang we're out yet. That was the smartest thing you've done in days."

"I guess we'll know by five," I said. "I'm pretty sure we know now."

McKee and I left the car and entered the foyer of TransPac's building.

"What's the story on those investors in TransPac's paper?"

McKee shrugged. "There were about a dozen entities that were regular buyers of TransPac's unsecured short-term paper, and the HKMA flagged the arrangements as suspicious."

"Why suspicious?"

"They were organizations known to be affiliated with unacceptable persons."

"Who were they?"

McKee quietly listed their names.

Chinese mafia, Communist Chinese front organizations, drug lords. More importantly, they were the same names Winston had told me when he drove me to meet Craig Chin's family. He'd said Craig had become good friends with Rick Houghton's wife and often accompanied her to gallery openings and social events when her husband didn't have the time or the interest. He said that what Craig had wanted to tell me just before he'd been killed was that Rick Houghton had told him those men were big clients of Sebastian Nin. The next morning I'd checked the list of bond issuers and realized that Winston—or Craig—had got it wrong. None of those men or the entities publicly associated with them had issued any bonds through Sebastian's operation, so I forgot about it—until now.

"Right," I said. "How much was involved?"

"It varied," said McKee. "But around a quarter of a billion."

"A quarter of a billion? Those are people who had better get paid back," I said. "When were they paid out?"

McKee looked uncomfortable. "They're not."

"But I just heard Houghton tell—"

"Yeah, but what he meant was that he has a commitment from Entrekin to pay them out before the acquisition closed."

I was thunderstruck. You don't want to owe a quarter of a billion dollars you can't pay back to Communists and drug lords. The second thing that occurred to me was this situation had nothing to do with Sebastian Nin. This was a problem on the liability side of TransPac's balance sheet, and Sebastian's responsibility was the bond operation, which was on the asset side of TransPac's balance sheet.

"Why didn't you tell me about this before?"

McKee shrugged. "It didn't seem like a priority this past week— and besides, Houghton had signed off on it. As far as due diligence is concerned, I had the necessary authorization."

"Get me the print-out of those entities and their positions in TransPac paper," I said, looking closely at McKee.

My mobile rang. It was Craig's oldest brother.

"Listen, Dusty," he said. "I don't know what's going on but you must be very careful."

"Why, what have you heard?"

"I can't say more because I don't know. Sebastian Nin is involved, but I don't know how. Maybe he is the target, maybe he is somehow part of a plan."

"Thanks," I said. "I think it's to do with some new friends he's been making."

"I would suggest you fly back to New York as soon as possible."

"Thanks," I said. "That seems to be the way it's heading anyway. I'll stick it out a bit longer."

McKee handed me the list Fai printed out, and I called TransPac's money market trading desk.

"Yes!" screamed a trader. The roar in the background sounded like a tidal wave was breaking over the trading floor.

I read the first account and asked for the current balance outstanding.

"Paid out!" he screamed.

"What?" I shouted, making sure he could hear me over the din.

"Redeemed! It's gone!"

It was true for all the other accounts I read out to him as well.

Nin's team had raised four hundred million dollars in cash yesterday by selling back bonds issued by their clients on the asset side of TransPac at a discount—and on the liability side of the balance sheet over two hundred million dollars had been used to pay out just a dozen investors in TransPac short-term paper. Winston had told me they were borrowers, in other words, the clients of Sebastian Nin, but he only knew what Craig Chin had told him. Craig didn't understand anything about investment banking. He was right about the men and their relationship with TransPac, but they weren't bond issuers, until earlier today they were owners of TransPac short-term unsecured debt. They had nothing to do with Sebastian Nin.

CHAPTER TWENTY-NINE

My mobile phone rang.

"Alexander?" said Entrekin. "Would you be able to meet with us as soon as possible to discuss Coldstream's proposal?"

The sound of his voice made me furious.

"You want me to come back to the shareholders' meeting?" I asked, controlling myself.

"Oh, no, no," said Entrekin hurriedly. "I haven't had time to explain. Just the four of us—myself, Pelham, Jones, and Cartwright. We're in my office. Can you come immediately?"

"Yes," I said. "See you soon."

Entrekin's assistant was gone by the time I arrived at his office. Entrekin himself was standing waiting for me, looking into the corridor from his assistant's office. He was holding a cigar joylessly, and as the elevator doors opened, he was taking a nervous puff.

"Alexander!" he said, hurrying forward. He took my hand with his thin, cold hand. "We've been thinking of a way we can still work together," he said breathlessly as we walked into his office. Pelham, Jones, and Cartwright were seated at the table by the window. They watched expressionlessly as I walked in.

"Good afternoon, gentlemen," I said. The first question I wanted to ask him was who authorized the payments of two hundred and fifty million dollars yesterday. But I didn't need Craig's brother to remind me that the situation was very dangerous, and I didn't want to reveal what I knew until I had a better understanding of who was responsible. One thing I was now certain about, it wasn't Sebastian Nin.

"Alexander," began Entrekin, "the four of us have been working on a concept we'd like to discuss with you in the wake of today's meeting."

"Certainly," I said. "I'm always ready to do business."

"Excellent, excellent," said Entrekin, returning to his chair with a swift, spidery motion. "As you may recall, you and I had a conversation in which you described, quite justly, your investment proposal as 'controversial.' It was 'controversial' in the sense that my partners and I feel that it disproportionately punishes good performance and rewards malefactors."

"Yes, I remember the conversation," I said.

Entrekin cleared his throat. "Well, we, the four of us, have devised a proposal for you. You have a financial valuation model that suggests that the value of TransPac is less than two hundred million. This, of course, came as a great shock and disappointment to us and to our other equity investors when we first heard it two days ago. Particularly because we view the decline in the value of our firm as almost entirely due to losses in the bond portfolio of Sebastian Nin. Now, Sebastian Nin's new investment consortium are willing to pay three hundred million for TransPac, partly in new money and partly by converting the TransPac three year bonds they hold into thirty year bonds. That doesn't seem like such an enormous difference between the two proposals, not in the grand scheme of things. Not for a firm with assets of five billion dollars. Not for the tremendous franchise and prestige of TransPac—"

Classic Dorfman. He'd bought those bonds at a steep discount, and now was planning to get paid the full three hundred million face value of the bonds—and with TransPac itself thrown in. On the surface, it seemed like a mind-blowingly great deal. "Okay, Simon," I said. "I hear you."

Entrekin started again, but it was the same old proposal. Kick Nin out, and share the rest of the money among the other directors. The only new twist was that Entrekin proposed suing Nin preemptively, in order to drain his resources more quickly and make it less likely that he could win a lawsuit against TransPac for stripping him of his equity and throwing him on the street.

Entrekin, pausing as he came to end of his little speech, looked around at his partners. "We are willing to approve Coldstream's investment on the basis that Nin is out."

I smiled. "That's a very creative and constructive proposal, Simon. I would like to thank you and your partners for giving me the opportunity to consider it," I said.

I looked around. "Obviously Sebastian Nin's new consortium of Three Dragons and Lobo Global made a proposal to you that was unsatisfactory in other ways. Why would you turn down their money?"

"Well, as a matter of fact," said Entrekin, "it was unsatisfactory. Sebastian wanted to become, in effect, managing director of all of Trans-Pac," He cleared his throat and spots of red appeared in his cheeks. "It was clear to each of us that we would be relegated to secondary positions or driven out of the firm altogether."

"The four of you have just over fifty percent of the votes, don't you?" I asked.

"That's correct, on a fully-diluted basis," said Cartwright. "A small, fatal slip by young Mr. Nin. He can't force his proposal, even with the two other shareholders on his side."

"Because you've all decided to stick together?"

"We have."

"And you think you can ram your proposal through because you have just over half of the votes?"

"Yes, we do," said Entrekin slowly.

"Well, I'm afraid it won't work. Coldstream wants that bond operation, and we'll need Nin with it. All I can suggest, gentlemen, is that you find a way to kiss and make up with Sebastian Nin."

"But he's made an utter hash of it!" exploded Pelham. "He's a double-crossing incompetent and very likely he's a thief! You don't think all that money he's lost has just disappeared, do you? He's lined his pockets at our expense!"

"That little shit has destroyed everything I've worked for here in the last fifteen years," said Jones.

"He must go," growled Cartwright. "I can't bear the sight of him one day longer."

"I don't think he's stolen any money," I said wearily. "Our financial valuation model shows that bad judgment in the portfolio was more than enough of a factor to account for the losses. Whether you like it or not, gentlemen." I continued, "you're married to one another. Marriages tend to break up when they get too hard or when the mystery goes out of them. You might want to, but you can't get a divorce now. Sticking together through this is the only way you'll get anything at all."

"Alexander," said Entrekin, "your ingenious metaphors aside, this is really about money. If Coldstream Holdings would match the price being offered by Nin's consortium, I could convince the other shareholders to vote with us."

"Well, thank you, Simon," I said, "but our proposal is about to lapse. And it is very, very late in the day for you to be fighting among yourselves."

"Alexander!" said Entrekin. "This is extraordinary! I don't like the tone of what you seem to be implying. What are you thinking?"

"I've told you—I'm thinking that a successful firm is like a marriage," I said. "It only works when both sides are committed. Coldstream can't pour money into something that is coming apart. You either patch things up with Sebastian Nin or Coldstream is out. I'm sorry."

Pelham cleared his throat. Normally his face would get very red when he was emotional. Now it looked quite white and mottled, like suet. "I must say, I must say," he began uncertainly, "I am beginning to get concerned that we may be watching all the value slip out of the firm." He shuddered suddenly. "Our shares may be worth nothing in a trice!"

My smile was tired, I knew. "You're not much of a negotiator, Ralph. You're not supposed to show your cards to the other guy. But what you're saying is exactly the same conclusion we've been coming to. TransPac may have one more day, but it probably doesn't. If we don't do the deal today, the firm will collapse, and your shares will be worth nothing. You'll have the clothes on your back and whatever you've been able to save elsewhere."

Entrekin turned his head slowly. He had been looking out the window. He looked at me with a strange calm. "Everything I have is tied up in my shares in the firm," he said. "I always believed it was the best investment I could have."

"Better do a deal with Sebastian," I said.

"You're not putting me out on the street, you bloody Yank," hissed Pelham.

"I'm not a Yank," I said.

I went back to my hotel. Five o'clock came and went. I tried to reach Walmsley but his line was engaged and I left a message with his answering service.

He was up early. What a life.

Then I made some phone calls and at six I rang McKee to tell him our offer had expired. I woke him up.

"Sorry, Dusty," he said. "I feel asleep in a chair next to the window. I'm pretty tired."

"Take your suit and shoes off and get into bed," I said. "Get a proper sleep."

"Right," he said sleepily.

I put in a call to Entrekin, but he was still in the board meeting. I showered and changed into a dark blue suit. As I was tying my necktie, the phone rang.

"Hey, Dusty," said Walmsley. "I heard from Houghton the TransPac deal is almost dead. Sebastian Nin beat you to the punch and brought in another investor group. Houghton's pretty disappointed."

"Yeah, we all are," I said. I knew Houghton had been hiding his true feelings in order to ambush me later.

"Well, Ted isn't," said Walmsley. "But Houghton is. Any chance of keeping it alive?"

"It's out of our hands, Jim," I said. I considered telling him about the cash used yesterday to pay out the TransPac paper. The money was gone, but so was the problem. At this point it seemed irrelevant—Walmsley wasn't interested in details at this point. I was glad we hadn't done the

TransPac deal. "It depends on the other offer. And what Sebastian Nin decides to do."

"Well, why don't you stand by, Dusty, and see if you can still pull something off at the last second," said Walmsley. "Rick Houghton chewed my ear off just now telling me how great it would be to have Nin's bond operation."

"He meant Nin's black hole," I said. "And it wasn't the only one."

"Just stay on top of things in case there's a last chance, okay?" Walmsley asked. He didn't seem to hear what I said.

"Sure, Jim," I said, "but unless Nin decides on his own that he wants to play ball with us, there isn't much hope. He's already busy trying to screw Entrekin and the rest of his old mates to the wall."

"He sounds like a prince," Walmsley said.

"He was always a princeling," I said. "Perhaps that's partly how all this happened."

I got a call a while later from the lawyers to let me know they'd prepared a final draft announcement of our withdrawal from the deal. I reviewed it, made some changes, and told them to send it on to Houghton and Walmsley. Later I got back emails from them okaying the announcement.

I had ordered one of the hotel's Rollers and at seven thirty I went downstairs, met my driver, and set off for the Peak to meet the Nins.

CHAPTER THIRTY

THE ROLLER WOUND UP THE ROAD toward the Peak like a big trout swimming through a stream. I always get an eerie sensation in Rollers, not being able to feel the road beneath or hear any sound from outside. It feels to me like I'm sitting in a theater watching a movie image reel by on all sides.

I found myself looking at the golden lights of Hong Kong, spiraling slowly as we threaded below and between the buildings. The Peak was shrouded in low clouds, and I felt alone, hidden, and strangely powerful.

As we mounted higher, leaving the Mid-Levels behind, the driver turned onto quiet, tree-lined roads that I hadn't been on in twenty years. I was in a pretty bad state, having averaged about three hours of sleep a night, and now that the TransPac deal was dead, the nervous energy that had been keeping me going was ebbing. I felt shaky and mentally disconnected.

In the calm of the Rolls Royce, I could almost see myself as a boy twenty-five years before, peddling up those streets under the tree branches, as the lights of the residences spun by from behind the foliage of their manicured gardens. The mist outside the car window was cold, and many of the trees were bare, but I thought I could smell the scent of frangipani and bougainvillea that had perfumed the summer nights of my youth, and from somewhere back in my memory, the moist warmth of a Hong Kong summer night, nuzzling my bare legs as I peddled my bicycle, came back to me.

My youthful relationship with Jacqueline wasn't a romance, but we did feel that through one another the world was opening up its possibilities. But we certainly had nothing other than the vaguest intuition that by becoming one flesh we might become a universe. I had drawn Jacqueline into my monologues, my introspection, my teeming speculations and fantasies about the world.

She had been a listener, and together we had cast off all contact with the reality surrounding us. In a disciplined, polite, well-brought up young virgin I found a kind, accepting substitute for the cold, loveless mother with whom I had grown up. I was accustomed to fierce arctic winds. Even a platonic relationship with the intellectual, well-behaved girl who Jacqueline was then proved to be a faint, scented tropical breeze that was enough to stir me, raise my emotional temperature, and begin to thaw my heart. But our relationship had never been a romance; it had been more like the relationship between a brother and a sister. That was all.

We pulled up at the small Colonial house in which the Nins had lived for over forty years. The house was freestanding in a tiny garden with a brick footpath lined by a mature boxwood hedge. It was an almost unimaginable privilege to live in a house in Hong Kong, but Jacqueline's father had bought it at a time of rising tension with China after the Korean War and Dien Bien Phu, and he had never been tempted to sell either during subsequent periods of tension, or by the many millions he would have made in more optimistic times.

The vestibule light was on, and it was Jacqueline who greeted me at the door when I rang. She wore a cocktail dress of deep blue that made her figure look sumptuous. When she was a girl, her wide shoulders had been athletic, slightly over-muscled, but in maturity they were elegantly fine and rounded, and her white throat dropped toward lavish décolletage. Her beauty seemed to hint at, even to promise, everything in the world rare, precious, luxurious and full of pleasure.

We looked at one another warily. Then her warm eyes with her peregrine brows fixed on me, drawing me toward her, and we kissed. After removing my shoes, I followed her down the hall to the sitting room at the back of the house, where tall windows looked out on Hong Kong and the harbor.

Dr. Nin was wearing a jacket and tie, and his trousers still had a knife-edge crease, as they always had done. He greeted me Western-style with a handshake, but I bowed slightly as I shook hands. Mrs. Nin was elegant as she stepped from beside her husband and said, "Good evening, Dusty." She still pronounced it "Doosty".

I presented them with the two bottles of Vintage Veuve Cliquot I had brought, and a maid took them from me and disappeared.

When we were all settled, I looked around the room. It was the same mixture I remembered: French furniture, a piano, a Persian carpet, and Chinese lacquer furniture, screens, and paintings. Silver-framed photos of Jacqueline and Sebastian as adults stood on a lacquer sideboard in the place their school photographs were once displayed, and a photo of an infant girl stood next to them.

I accepted a whiskey from Dr. Nin, and a butler brought in flutes of champagne for Mrs. Nin and Jacqueline.

"To old friends," said Dr. Nin, and we drank to that.

"I think Sebastian is still in meetings," said Dr. Nin without being asked. He had aged well, and his iron-gray hair was still thick, although his temples and forehead were higher than when I had last seen him. He looked wise and content. A handful of wrinkles appeared above his eyes for just an instant, and then he said, "Ah, well, he has his work to do. It's been a very difficult week for him. He has so much responsibility."

I nodded and smiled. "That's very true. I'm out here, of course, because my firm has been considering an investment in TransPac. But it looks like they received a better offer from another party."

"Well, that's too bad," said Dr. Nin. "It would have been nice to be involved together again."

He nodded to me. "You were a good boy if you don't mind my referring to you that way. Jacqueline had started to attract attention from boys about a year before she met you, even before she was interested in boys as I recall."

Dr. Nin looked fondly at Jacqueline. "I can remember Jacqueline so clearly when she was young girl. She used to speak with a lisp when she just learned to talk."

Jacqueline wrinkled her nose in a gesture I suddenly remembered.

"But you were my favorite boyfriend of hers until then, and for quite a few years after that," said Dr. Nin.

"Thank you," I said.

"Of course, Sebastian has to think of others," said Mrs. Nin briskly, returning to the subject. "He has to make the best choice for everyone for whom he's responsible. That's just the way he is."

"Yes, that's quite right, Mrs. Nin," I said. "At the end of the day, business is business. I don't mind losing the deal. Sebastian has to make the best decision he can."

Dr. Nin and Mrs. Nin nodded their heads simultaneously. "Yes," Dr. Nin said. "Sebastian has shown a remarkable talent for business at TransPac. The papers say that he has developed a whole new type of market here in Asia. We're so proud of him."

"It's true," I said. "Sebastian has created a market that didn't exist before."

"Yes," said Mrs. Nin, smiling fondly. "I'm just so amazed that my little Sebastian has been able to make such big changes. He's really doing great things for Asia he tells me. This new market of his could improve the lives of billions of people in Asia."

She sipped from her champagne. "He has always had a strong view about things. Even as a young boy, he always had his independent position. At the time you knew him."

"Yes," I smiled pleasantly.

Jacqueline smiled nervously. "Of course, Dusty, even if you decide not to invest in TransPac, you're not going to do anything that would make things difficult for Sebastian."

"Certainly not," I said, sipping the whiskey.

I looked out the windows between Dr. and Mrs. Nin. A new development of low apartments had been built on the slope below them, partially obscuring the view toward Happy Valley, but the long view down the Peak, across the harbor, and of Kowloon and the mountains to the north, was still spectacular.

"Didn't we invite you to come with us to Phuket?" asked Dr. Nin suddenly. "I can't remember for certain, but I seem to recall we talked about inviting you to join us for two weeks on our family holiday in Thailand. I think that was the summer your family was leaving Hong Kong."

"Yes, we invited Dusty," said Mrs. Nin to her husband. "You called his father but he said no. They wanted to send him away to spend the summer with his grandparents in Sweden."

Ironically, to relatives to whom I wasn't even related, I now knew.

"I remember it, too," said Jacqueline. "You left in the middle of the summer, by yourself, before your parents left Hong Kong. Just before we were about to go on the holiday we always took in Phuket."

That was how our letter writing began. I had forgotten. Blocked it out. I received a letter from Jacqueline at my grandparents' vacation house in Sweden. Rocky coastline, big mosquitoes, the smell of hot mud in the afternoon, and at night, the stale smell of a house of old people. The letter had said my dad called your dad and invited you to join us on our family holiday, two weeks in Phuket, but your father called back and said that your parents had discussed it, and since we had already said our goodbyes, it was best to send you as planned back to Sweden. I had spent the entire summer with my grandparents, whom I hardly knew—and never saw again.

I looked at the Nins and smiled, shaking my head. Sitting in their living room, the beautiful lights of Hong Kong shining through the darkness outside the windows, I felt the despair I had felt that day, in exile in Sweden, reading that letter. *Said our goodbyes!*

I wondered how my parents could have dared make that decision. Had they had no idea of the complexity of the alternatives lying hidden in the future? Had they not understood their posterity, their own destiny, was intertwined in that decision? It occurred to me then that they had disapproved of Jacqueline. Didn't want their lines intermingled with those of a Eurasian girl. Or perhaps they had viewed the first love of my life for some reason as expressing a regrettable tendency, still shallow, a tender seedling that must be uprooted as thoroughly and as quickly as possible. They couldn't have known those roots were already so deep— they could only see the fragile young plant on the surface, too young and tentative to be fruitful yet. No sign yet of the abundant fruit that might one day have hung from strengthened boughs. And yet, perhaps it hadn't mattered after all. Jacqueline and I did not have a romance. We were children. As I sat with the Nins in their house, for the first time in almost thirty years, it seemed at least possible my parents had only delayed the inevitable. Perhaps it really didn't matter what the model said.

But I knew I was lying to myself, or trying to.

"This may sound funny," I said, "but you were always so much more civilized than my family. I remember coming up here when I was a boy and feeling the peace and kindness you had created in your family."

"That's very nice of you to say," said Mrs. Nin.

"We have always been happy here," said Dr. Nin. "Hong Kong is home for us. Of course, now Jacqueline lives in San Francisco. But that sometimes happens when you marry. Isn't that right, Estelle?"

Mrs. Nin smiled slightly at her husband, and glanced at Jacqueline. "At least we can see our granddaughter a few times a year," she said.

Dr. Nin sipped his whiskey. "I remember Jacqueline so well when she was Anaïs's age," he said. "Always clever, always energetic, with such bright eyes. She never actually walked anywhere, she sorted of danced across the floor as soon as she learned to walk, on her toes, you know?"

We all looked at Jacqueline; she smiled obligingly.

"I remember Jacqueline riding horses," I said, "and how she used to concentrate, frowning slightly under her helmet as her horse approached the jump."

I also remembered the look of her muscled legs and bottom in her jodhpurs as she rose in her saddle just before her horse leaped. She was thinner then, and her face was fresh with an unwritten future, not truly beautiful yet in the way it was now. Of course, back then I thought she was beautiful, but since then her face had acquired character that taught me all over again, at my age, what true beauty really was.

As I thought about watching Jacqueline cantering her horse, I remembered the sight of the energy of the horse rolling up through its hindquarters and across its back, rippling along and into Jacqueline's body, up and through Jacqueline as she rose in her seat until, like the glistening foam on the lip of an ocean wave, her breasts lifted in the autumn air before her and then plunged downward into the next canter as her head and shoulders smoothly completed the complementary arc.

Mrs. Nin smiled a little wanly. "Little Jacqueline used to follow me around the house and say she didn't want to ever marry. She didn't want to be a mommy and sit in a little house."

I looked at Jacqueline. "You used to tell me you would never have children. You used to call babies 'parasites' inside their pregnant mother. You must feel differently now that you have Anaïs."

"Did I say that? How awful!" Jacqueline drank her champagne. "All I ever wanted was to lead a special life. I didn't want to be boxed in. I had a wonderful family, and we lived in our beautiful little house on the Peak, and I had my friends and my horses, and I just wanted to lead an exciting, wonderful life. That's all. I just thought I deserved more than just to be somebody's wife."

She looked at Mrs. Nin. "Of course, Maman, I thought you were very glamorous too, but I wanted to be like you but also to fly to Paris and New York and Río. And I knew you couldn't do it because of us kids, and because of Papa's job."

She smiled at me. "Of course, I adore my little Anaïs. She's the most important thing in my life—after, of course, my parents and Sebastian."

"Is Anaïs asleep already?" I asked.

"I don't know," said Jacqueline. She looked at her mother.

Mrs. Nin nodded. "She's caught a bit of a cold since she's been here," she said. "I had her given a little baby aspirin when she went down tonight."

"Really," said Jacqueline.

"It's alright," said Mrs. Nin. "She'll be fine."

My mobile phone rang. I frowned. "I'm sorry," I said, and answered. "Alexander?"

It was Entrekin. I excused myself and walked out onto the terrace. "Yes, what can I do for you, Simon?"

"Sebastian refuses to be reasonable," said Entrekin. His voice was bitter. "Pelham has gone over to his side."

"So Sebastian has over fifty percent of the votes," I said. "He's over the top."

"Yes, and now Sebastian's consortium has lowered their offer," said

Entrekin. "They're saying that they want us to take half the bonds in payment. That reduces the price by one hundred fifty million! They're saying that they have to because of the way the markets closed today. But it's really because they think they're the only ones left. But their offer is now lower than your offer was!"

"But not as low as our offer would be now," I said sadly. "Without Nin we won't proceed."

"Nin and Pelham will be fine!" said Entrekin. "They'll continue to run the firm. I'm being forced out, along with all the other loyal directors!"

"I can't throw Coldstream's money at your problem, Simon," I said. "The only way we could have invested is if you'd kept your team together. I'm sorry."

I rang Walmsley in New York and left a message. I walked back into the living room. All three looked at me expectantly. "It looks like Sebastian is going to be running TransPac." I said. "He and his friends have won control."

The most beautiful smiles suddenly broke out on the faces of the Nins.

The phone rang. Mrs. Nin jumped up, ran across the room, and answered it. "'Allo?" she said anxiously. A joyous smile beamed from her face. "Sebastian, darling!" she began, and continued in Chinese. Dr. Nin and Jacqueline listened intently.

We left shortly after the good news had arrived. I affectionately took my leave of Jacqueline's parents; it had been good to see them again.

The Rolls Royce started off. We looked at one another in the dim fleeting lights that filtered through the windows, and I kissed Jacqueline. She embraced me with a savage grip, biting my lips as she kissed me.

Jacqueline placed her hand on my thigh, and her palm moved up my leg as the Roller began a rapid descent down the Peak, swinging us back and forth on the seat.

My mobile phone rang.

"What's up?" Walmsley asked.

"Entrekin called me and wants us to match the other price," I said.

"What do you think?" asked Walmsley.

"I don't think we should," I said.

"I've had Entrekin on the phone sniveling to me," growled Walmsley. "And Rick Houghton wants this deal if there's any way we can still do it."

"The problem is that they're all at one another's throats at TransPac," I said. "There's nothing to buy while they're trying to kill each other."

I could see Jacqueline's eyes widen, the lights reflecting in her irises in the darkness of the Rolls Royce.

"Say, Dusty," said Walmsley. "I've heard around the traps you used to go to school with Nin."

"That's right," I said. "Does it matter?"

"The last thing the markets need right now is for TransPac to go down the tubes," said Walmsley. "I know you're not letting personal considerations affect your judgment."

"Am I supposed to be blocking Nin or helping him?"

"I sure as hell can't tell," Walmsley said. "It looks like he's come out on top. But maybe that's just the way it happened."

"Jim, I wanted to win this deal for Coldstream at the right price. I also hoped we could prevent a bankruptcy that would worsen this crisis in the Asian financial markets," I said. "I don't know if we can. There's no point throwing the last couple hundred million into TransPac just as it goes under."

"That's sure as hell right," said Walmsley. "I'm sorry I brought it up."

"That's okay," I said. "I've got to go to dinner with Nin's sister now."

Walmsley' laughter came down the telephone line. "I'd forgotten your sick sense of humor," he said, and rang off.

Chapter Thirty-One

We entered the Peninsula, went up the lift to Felix, and were seated at a table in the corner, next to one another rather than across the table, with our backs to the restaurant looking out on a magnificent view of Hong Kong at night.

I pulled my mobile phone out my suit and turned it off. "The deal is over, as far as I'm concerned," I said to Jacqueline. "And I hope your brother gets to enjoy the spoils, although I doubt he will."

"He's smarter than you think," she said, with a small smile.

"We'll see. And as a matter of fact, I don't care anymore," I said, admiring her face in the candlelight as I patted my pocket where my phone was nestled. "I remember telling Craig Chin a few years after we stopped writing that I was completely over you, that I had moved on with my life, and that I was looking forward to marrying someone else who looked, acted, sounded, tasted, and smelled just like you."

"Unfortunately for you," said Jacqueline with a smile, "I'm unique."

"As a matter of fact, the wife I did marry, Samantha, is almost your physical opposite—a blonde, blue-eyed Australian," I said. "So, what I wonder is whether our lives continued to evolve naturally, or did we make a fundamental mistake years ago that sent us both down the wrong roads for twenty years?"

The waiter came and Jacqueline asked for a glass of champagne and I ordered a vodka martini.

"I want to ask you a question," I said, when our drinks arrived.

She was watching my lips. "Ask me anything," she murmured.

"When did you arrive in Hong Kong?"

She looked up sharply, into my eyes, almost through them. "What do you mean?"

224

"I need to know when you arrived," I said. "When we met last night, you implied you'd been here since Christmas, although you didn't actually say it. I'd just like to understand exactly how long you've been here."

"Does it matter?"

"Yes, possibly," I said. "Possibly not. But don't worry—it's not public information. The airlines don't give out passenger details for privacy reasons, so I would have no way of knowing unless you decide to tell me."

Her eyes searched my face, and then they dropped and through her long lashes her gaze rested on my lips. "Oh, you're just saying that," she murmured. "You investment bankers have all kinds of sources."

I permitted myself the faintest smile at the corner of my lips.

"See? I knew it," she said. "You're testing me."

It sometimes amazes me how some people assume another person has so little control over their actions or expressions. Perhaps they project their own lack of control onto others. Perhaps it's me—maybe I strike some people as somebody who can't quite control myself. Or perhaps it's the Achilles heel of being a beautiful woman—you sometimes overestimate your ability to move men against their better judgment.

She took a breath and smiled at me. "I arrived five days ago from San Francisco. Cathay Pacific. Are you happy? Do you trust me now?"

"Sebastian must have moved quickly," I said.

"There's plenty of flights from San Francisco to Hong Kong," Jacqueline said casually. "And, of course, my passport is always current."

"Your husband didn't mind?"

"He knows how I feel about my brother," Jacqueline said calmly.

"It was a bit of a risk Sebastian took." I smiled. "What if you and I hadn't gotten along? If he thinks I might be persuaded to help him because of you, it must have crossed his mind that I might spike the deal if it turned out I still hated you or something like that."

A strange, amused, sexy expression appeared on Jacqueline's face. She rested her forearms on my shoulders and pulled me close to her face. Her eyes on my lips, she cocked her head slightly so that her heavy, scented hair swung slightly away from her cheekbones and she said softly, "Was it such a risk? Is that what you think?" and she kissed me slowly and with an abandon I returned from the very depths of my heart.

We ordered our dinner choices, but I cannot remember what they were.

"You're too philosophical," said Jacqueline. "No wonder Sebastian outmaneuvered you." She patted the back of my hand.

"Now, just concentrate on picking something very nice from the wine list."

"Right," I said.

"Put those strong opinions I remember so well to some practical use."

"I don't have strong opinions anymore," I said. "I had strong opinions when I didn't know anything."

The sommelier arrived and I asked him to bring out an old burgundy from my favorite vineyard. Might as well spend money before Houghton succeeded in stripping it from me.

"Let me ask you a question," I said. "Is it possible we were always meant for each other? Could that be, if we went away and married others and had children?"

"Sure, it's possible," she said. "If we want it to be."

"No, that's not what I mean," I insisted. "I'm not talking about what I want, or even what you want. I'm talking about what really is, what is meant to be."

Jacqueline shook her head impatiently and frowned. "Your life can be anything you want it to be. You know that. It's what you do."

"But what about my wife and children?" I said. "How could something terrible for them be meant to be for me, and for us?"

Jacqueline looked down at her hands.

I watched the way her thick glossy hair swayed by her cheekbones.

"Look at it this way," she said. "Maybe this is something that will improve your marriage. Make you a more daring person. A better lover. Give you some zest for life."

"Maybe I already have zest for life," I said.

"That's absolute rot," Jacqueline said. "From what I've seen, Dusty, you're in danger of turning into a first-class bore. You say you love your wife and children? You never see them, do you? You probably think you love your job, but you've just stuffed up this deal you were sent to Hong Kong to get done. Probably because you've become too damned pedantic and overscrupulous. And yet the only subjects you've talked about with any feeling for the last several days are returns, profit, and cash flows. You're turning into stone."

"Stones don't feel the way I feel about you," I said. I hadn't really told her how I had been secretly feeling about her—and now about her parents—and even—for days—about Sebastian.

"Talk is cheap, darling," Jacqueline said, patting the back of my hand again. In the same reproving spirit, her knee nudged mine under the table, giving it a sharp push. Sitting next to one another, rather than across from one another, was turning out to have its advantages.

"Yes, and since it looks like I've already been fucked by Sebastian . . ."

She cocked an eyebrow at me. "That's very naughty," she said primly, "and a very poor reason to have an affair."

"Can you think of a good one?" I said.

"The issue for me has always been about being free to make my own choices in life," Jacqueline said, suddenly serious. "When I was a young woman, I expressed my independence by not sleeping with men—"

"That would be the last time I saw you."

"Exactly. But at this stage in my life, I express my freedom by sleeping with whom I choose."

"How do you manage intimate relationships with several people at once?"

"Well, I don't manage several at once for one thing," said Jacqueline. "I simply do what I choose, which is a different thing entirely. But God manages relationships with lots of people simultaneously—with husbands and wives and their brothers and sisters and former lovers— they may despise one another, but God maintains his relationships with each of them and continues to love them. So why can't we?"

"Do you still believe in God?" I asked, surprised.

"You once asked me that question in a letter a long time ago." she said. "Do you remember?"

"No, I don't," I said.

"Well, I wrote back and answered you the way my parents would have wanted me to. Later, I sometimes wondered whether I had been untrue to myself when I replied to your question that way, but I decided I had said the right thing, because at the time I still *wanted* to believe in God, I just couldn't. Even though my intellect already knew the right answer, my feelings still persisted in the belief the world would be a better place if there were a God. It's like, at the same age, the thought of life without your parents gives you a sense of horror and emptiness. That is how I still felt about God back then when you wrote and asked me the question."

"But if you don't think that way anymore, why did you point out God can have relationships with lots of people?"

She smiled. "Because I think that you might."

"And you would be right," I said.

"Look at that frown on your face!" Jacqueline exclaimed. "You have this uncanny ability to make everything so complicated! Sex is a good thing, especially for men like you, who are in danger of turning into old bores!" She smiled. "I think men require sexuality in order to be motivated to take an interest in other people. Women, maybe because of our maternal instincts, can arrive at sexuality in a relationship at the end of the process, after they've realized how interesting the man really is. They don't necessarily always start with it like men do. Women already have an interest, at least a curiosity, about others. Many men would be solitary creatures without their sexual drives. It's certainly true of my husband and many of the men I've been with."

"Well, perhaps," I said. "For me sexuality and what I would call real love were disconnected when I was young. Real love, if the way I felt about you then was love, came first, and sexuality came afterwards and superseded my belief in love. In fact, losing my virginity was like giving up on love," I said. "It was like walking deliberately to the edge of a cliff, arms wide, and toppling over at the first puff of wind."

If I had been being truthful, I would have added that when I met Samantha, I learned to believe in love again. Love had just turned out to be much more painful, and much more disillusioning than I had imagined.

"How dramatic! Who was the puff of wind?" asked Jacqueline, sipping her wine. Her eyes were glowing under her fierce, elegant brows.

"The older sister of a friend," I replied, looking out over the lights of Hong Kong and thinking back. "It didn't happen at Princeton, or in New York on a weekend. My parents' marriage was breaking up, pieces dropping off everywhere and spinning toward the ground. And then Dad announced his business was virtually bankrupt.

"I had gone back to Cairo for the summer and after that I just had to get away. I couldn't face the drama at home. I ended up on Mykonos, and she came in on a sailboat with some friends on a cruise around the Ionic Sea. We ran into each other in town, and she invited me back and I rowed her out to their sailboat. I stayed for a barbecue off the stern, and then her friends went into town to go drinking and dancing. We stayed and smoked hash and looked at the stars. Then we drank retsina and made love."

"How romantic."

"It sounds like it, doesn't it? I remember thinking how perfect it was, and wishing I was with somebody I loved under those stars. As a matter of fact, I wished I was with you."

I looked at Jacqueline. "It's funny. For a long while afterwards, I felt like I had actually somehow spoiled the perfection of that Ionic night between the sea and the stars."

"I wish I had been with you that night too," said Jacqueline. "I don't think we would have spoiled the night."

"That night or any night since," I said.

Jacqueline smiled. "Well, losing my virginity was the single most carefully considered decision I have ever made, probably including my two marriages—I think I was in a pretty irrational state of mind when I agreed to them. When I chose to relinquish my virginity, I was stone-cold sober, although it probably wouldn't have been as bad if I'd had a couple of drinks.

"But to this day, if I want to feel wild and free, I'll drink. Emotionally, I can be more abandoned that way. But when I want to have the best sex, I'm careful what I drink. I can't get to orgasm when I'm drunk."

"It's a pity we're having such a great bottle of wine," I said. "Talk about a dilemma."

"This is still my first glass," she replied.

Talking with Jacqueline made me wonder all over again how on earth my parents could have been so worried Jacqueline and I, at the age of thirteen, were going to have sex with one another and run off and ruin our lives. Why had my parents even thought to compare their thirteen-year-old son to a Vietcong insurgent? What made them worry about the innocent daughter of a traditional Hong Kong family? It seemed to me they didn't trust me because they were already cheating on one another, or considering it. I've always found it very interesting to see whether someone is willing to trust others. Their ability to trust others is often related to their capacity for being trustworthy. The thought shook me.

"Shall we order dessert?" I asked.

"Not for me, thanks."

"Would you like a glass of port or cognac?"

"No, thank you. I like port, but tonight I'll resist."

"A cup of coffee or tea?"

"No, thank you."

"Would you like to go out to a club or a bar?"

"I think not."

"Shall I take you to your parents' house, or shall we go to my suite?"

"It depends."

"On what does it depend?"

"It depends on your intentions." she said. "I have no intention of going back to your suite only to be insulted by having you make inappropriate and unattractive propositions to me."

"I don't recall doing any such thing before," I said.

"Unfortunately, it's a bit of an unpleasant habit of yours," she said.

"Such as . . ."

"Such as being forced to sit and listen to you chronicle and categorize the long lists of your scruples," said Jacqueline. "No woman who knew what she was doing would willingly go to a man's hotel room and subject herself to that experience twice."

"Hmm." It was time to dispel the guilt I had begun to feel licking around my ankles like a miasma. "I have too much respect for you to even consider such an insult."

"You've developed a bad reputation with me," she said. "I'm not sure you're honest enough to make love with me tonight. So we're going to have to play truth or dare."

I turned and signaled for the bill.

"Okay," I said. "Who asks the question?"

"I do, and the question you must answer, or otherwise accept the dare for, is 'Are we going to sleep together tonight?'"

"I don't know."

"Just as I thought—that's not only the wrong answer, that's not an answer at all. Either you answer the question, or I choose the dare."

"Very well," I said. "What's the dare?"

Jacqueline made a small movement and suddenly her breasts were naked in the candlelight. "Kiss me where I tell you to," she said.

I glanced around. Nobody could see what Jacqueline had done. We were sitting facing the windows with our backs to the other diners. Jacqueline's arms blocked the view of her breasts from the sides. Only the reflection in the window revealed her state.

"Kiss me here and here," she instructed.

I lowered my head and complied.

"Now, kiss me here," she said, resting her finger on her lips.

We saw the waiter approaching in the reflection of the window. Jacqueline arranged herself before the waiter appeared with the receipt. We rose from the table.

"That was the dare. I also have an answer for you," I said. "Let's go."

"And the answer is . . . ?"

I put out my hand and helped her stand up in her high heels and step away from the table. "Talk is cheap," I smiled.

I felt a strange clarity as we left the restaurant. Jacqueline would have been cynical about what part of me was doing the thinking, but at that moment I suddenly felt my mind concentrating entirely on Jacqueline and me.

Everything else, and everybody else, were barely intelligible shadows in my consciousness. We were the only ones in the lift, and as we kissed while descending to my floor, I found myself also thinking about Jacqueline's idea that love made us like God, capable of loving different people simultaneously, or anyway like gods, of being more than we would otherwise be.

I'm not proud of it, but that's how I felt.

Chapter Thirty-Two

When we entered my room we were intertwined, scarcely able to walk and with little intention of remaining upright for much longer. I noticed the message light flashing on my phone as we walked into the sitting room, but I ignored it, and we passed through to the bedroom.

"I would like a glass of champagne," Jacqueline breathed into my mouth as we kissed.

"Jacqueline, I want to ask you a question," I said.

I felt her fingers against the back of my head, and my nostrils were full of the fragrance of her perfume, and I put my arms around her taut back muscles and pressed her to me, her breasts and the rhythm of her deep, confident kiss reminding me of how much I might have had all those years ago, the luxury that could have been mine, intoxicating me with a sensation of the intensity and the pleasure of life available to the two of us, only Jacqueline and me, because we were special, daring and beautiful, and because we deserved each other.

I knew it wasn't true. Something about the sensation, about how I felt deep down inside even with the blood coursing through my veins as my heart pounded and my senses, sated with Jacqueline's presence but urgently craving more, somehow all of it startled a response that welled up from deep inside me, up through the excitement and through the waves of feeling that broke over me as Jacqueline and I embraced. I knew what we were doing was not taking place beyond good and evil.

I took a bottle of champagne from the minibar and opened it. I poured a glass for Jacqueline, who was sitting on the bed. I had begun to unzip the back of Jacqueline's dress before, and she sat back, bracing herself with one hand on the bedspread, her legs crossed, breasts almost falling from her dress, and drank the champagne.

"That was perfect," she said, giving me the glass. I walked back to the dresser.

"Another glass?"

"Come here," she said. She wrenched my belt open. "Let's see what you've got." Just as I felt her fingers tugging at the zipper, the doorbell rang.

She looked up at me, alarm in her beautiful eyes.

"Forget it," I said.

The doorbell rang, twice quickly.

"I'm going to have to deal with this," I said. I closed the bedroom door, and adjusting my clothes as I walked, went to the door and opened it.

Ted McKee was standing there, a wild look in his eye.

"What can I do for you, Ted?"

"Jesus Christ, Dusty! All hell has been breaking loose!"

"What's going on?"

"I've left four messages on your mobile—"

"I must have turned it off."

"I've been coming up here every twenty minutes to see if you'd gotten back—"

"I was having dinner in the hotel, up at Felix. How'd you know I was here this time?"

"You'd switched the light from 'Make up the room' to 'Do not disturb.'"

Despite myself, I grinned. "Very observant. Why don't you come in and tell me what's going on?"

McKee looked at the message light still flashing on the telephone in the sitting room. "That must be me, Jim Walmsley, and Rick Houghton."

I was conscious of the fact Jacqueline was in the next room, able to hear everything that was being said.

"Let's give Jim a call," said McKee. "We can use the speaker phone."

"No," I said sharply. "Call him on the phone using the handset and have him patch me in on my mobile phone." I pulled my mobile out of my pocket and switched it on. "It'll be harder to eavesdrop on us that way."

McKee looked swiftly around the room, his glance settling on the open windows. Vibrations can be picked up electronically from window glass and interpreted back into speech. "Right," he said. "I'll just call Rick Houghton first—he's downstairs."

A couple of minutes later Houghton burst through the door.

I nodded to him.

"Where the hell have you been?" he demanded.

"Having dinner," I said.

"What the hell happened to your mobile phone?" he said.

I had never seen him this angry. "It was turned off," I said. "Sorry."

"Right," said Houghton grimly. "You have some explaining to do, Dusty."

Walmsley was angry when he came on the line, too, but I calmed him down enough so he could explain to me what had been happening: the price of TransPac's bonds had suddenly started to drop in late trading in London, and when New York opened they had plummeted.

"It doesn't make any sense," I said.

"Alright," Houghton said, talking into his mobile but glaring at me, "let's get something straight here. Jim and I want to know what your interest is in this deal, Dusty. Isn't that right, Jim?"

"Well, Dusty, we need to understand a little better where you've been coming from on this deal," Walmsley said reluctantly. There was no sign in his voice of his previous anger. What was in his voice was regret.

I was taken aback. "What are you talking about, guys? I've been trying to get this deal done for TransPac."

Houghton stepped toward me, his angry eyes leveled on me, and spoke low and distinctly into his mobile phone. There was something absurd about it, but the menace in his voice as it directly entered my ear through my own mobile phone was unmistakable. "So Nin pulls a last minute bid out of his ass that he gets funded by a guy you introduce him to, and the Chairman of TransPac begs you to make a counteroffer, and you refuse to make the counteroffer, turn off your mobile, and then disappear to guarantee you can't be reached. That's how you run a deal you're trying to close?"

It looked bad, no question about it. I had sent Walmsley and Houghton the final version of the announcement that Coldstream was pulling out of the deal, but it was up to them when, and if to release it. I knew that. I could have also said everything I knew about the quarter of a billion that had gone out the door this morning but something stopped me. For one thing, I would have looked like a wild-eyed conspiracy theorist. Secondly, something told me not to reveal how much I knew about the real inner workings of TransPac.

"Look, Rick," I said. "What you have to understand is that after today's close in the markets, TransPac is gutshot. There's no value left and the banks are about to pull the plug. Nin's offer is no good, or if it does get funded, it'll blow up in the faces of Lobo Global and Three Dragons. The only thing that will save them is that there's probably no time to fund."

Walmsley broke in. "Dusty, you were telling me yesterday you had found extra value in TransPac, and then you pulled the value off the table and refused to increase the offer for TransPac after Nin's group made their offer. We need to understand what was going through your mind. We have to understand your decisions."

The only person, besides me, who knew this much about what our team had been doing was McKee. I turned and looked at him. He was holding the handset of my hotel phone. He impassively returned my glance, staring through me. McKee must have realized Houghton wanted to acquire TransPac come hell or high water. Rather than take the heat while I couldn't be reached, McKee had decided to cast his lot with Houghton. It was his third one hundred and eighty degree turn on the issue of whether or not to acquire TransPac in twelve hours.

Jacqueline was in the next room, and if she had a cell phone, she'd be able to call her brother and report to him exactly what was going on and being said. She wouldn't know who we were talking to, of course, and she was only getting part of the conversation. But it was still a shit of a situation.

"Jim, Rick, I've already explained the extra value was a mistake," I said. "I had an idea, and at first it looked like it had dumped some extra value back into TransPac, but the next morning when we checked the new coding—Jim, it was after that that I rang you—we realized it was a mistake. My idea—"

Houghton broke in furiously. He hadn't lost all of his discipline; he spoke in a hissing whisper to ensure that he wasn't overheard in case my suite was being electronically monitored. "That's enough, Dusty. You're bullshitting us as if it was all your idea. Ted thought of it, and you're trying to take credit for the idea and to strangle it at the same time. That's the worst thing a boss can do to his subordinate and I just hate to see it happen. I never thought I'd see the day when you, of all people, would try to pull that shit."

I turned and looked at McKee. He stared right back at me, his chin lifting defiantly as he held the telephone.

There was only one way to cut quickly through the lies. It was a risk, because McKee was a clever, although limited, investment banker, but I had to accept the risk.

"Okay, Ted," I said low and calmly into my mobile, looking at him. "Why don't you explain to Rick and Jim the logic behind your idea, since you've told Rick it's your idea?"

McKee began to talk, in his orderly way, about the way the model discounted future cash flows using a discount rate that reflected the high risk of the portfolio, and in his methodical, structured way he did a great job of explaining why he had decided to try to get extra value back into TransPac by getting some of TransPac's biggest customers to prepay their bonds early. It was a masterly discussion of the intricacies of the model's architecture and the way it had affected the financial valuation of TransPac.

When he had finished, Houghton nodded to him and looked at me. "Well?" he said quietly.

Walmsley cleared his throat over the phone.

"There's only one problem with Ted's account," I said. "He's a good man for due diligence, but he doesn't understand how deals get done. He just gave you a brilliant description of the way the valuation changed, but that had nothing to do with my idea. The valuation impact was a fluke—my original idea was to build up a few hundred million dollars in cash fast, so that TransPac could pay down the first bank lines when the banks got nervous, and hopefully stop the banks from rolling up the rest of their funding lines. That will also give you an idea about the condition TransPac was in when I arrived . . . on its last legs. Nin's team actually raised four hundred million by yesterday but it's all gone now."

I thought about mentioning where two hundred fifty million of the cash had gone and looked at McKee, who knew as well as I did. McKee blinked and looked quickly at Houghton. Houghton frowned furiously and looked back at me.

"I . . . I don't know what to say," Houghton said.

"Ted's just focusing on the part of the deal he understands, Rick," I said. "The numbers. He did a great job of describing the model, but he was too busy taking credit for my idea to remember the original objective."

"It's . . . it's not the way it happened," said McKee.

"I think we'll deal with you later, Ted," Walmsley said. "Now, Dusty, what can you tell us about what's happening to TransPac's bonds? What the hell is going on?"

"Hard to say," I said. "It's very strange. Why would their prices be falling just as TransPac is about to close a deal with Lobo Global and Three Dragons?"

"We've got to do something," said Houghton. "We've got to figure it out. Otherwise the rest of the market will assume TransPac is dead and it will go into a liquidity crisis before we have time to lodge our counter-bid."

"The price of the bonds is moving in exactly the opposite direction it should be going," I said. "When Entrekin called me that last time, he told me Nin had succeeded in getting Pelham to cross over to his side, and along with the institutional investors, Nin has more than fifty percent and he was able to seal the deal with Three Dragons and Lobo Global. That should make the price of the bonds go up, especially since Three Dragons and Lobo hold three hundred million dollars worth of those bonds. It doesn't make sense."

"Well, our guys in London have picked up the rumor that TransPac is making mass layoffs and downsizing to try and stay afloat," said Walmsley.

"That's bullshit," I said. "Completely false. I know that for a fact. There were no plans to cut staff this afternoon. There are none in our acquisition business plan."

McKee nodded, looking miserable.

"Could Nin be doing it with his new shareholders?" asked Houghton. "I wouldn't put it past the son of a bitch."

Houghton turned and walked slowly to the sofa and sat down, holding the phone to his ear, staring sightlessly in front of him as he waited for me to respond.

"No, it's too destabilizing an action to take in this market," I said. "He wouldn't do it."

"Well, what the fuck is going on then?" Houghton said, almost despairingly.

"The way to think this through is to figure out who benefits," I said. "The short answer is nobody. This is going to start a bank run on TransPac as soon as the market opens here."

"Lines are already being pulled in New York, we hear," said Walmsley.

"Right—so TransPac is doomed," I said.

"Who would have done it?" asked McKee.

"Nin wouldn't have done it—he'll lose everything he's worked for. His new friends are going to lose some serious money. Most of the hundred million plus Lobo Global spent over the last couple of days will go up in smoke. Entrekin wouldn't have done it either; he loves the place. But the other guys who got screwed just might have. Cartwright and Jones. After they realized Nin had screwed them and would be forcing them out, they must have called their mates in London and spread the rumors.

They'd be bringing down the whole house of cards, but they wouldn't care because they had nothing to lose. And they could get back at Nin and Pelham for double-crossing them."

"Stupid fucks," said Walmsley. "This could bring down the entire Asian market."

"We'll have to get the Hong Kong Monetary Authority involved," I said. "They need to be ready to intervene when this market opens."

"Alright, that's your job, Rick," said Walmsley. "You've got to get in touch with Tang and alert him to the situation."

"What about our announcement! We need to announce that Coldstream is ending negotiations with TransPac," said McKee nervously.

"Use your head, Ted," said Walmsley crossly. "It's too late now. Why would we do that before the Hong Kong Monetary Authority was ready to intervene? If we just issued our announcement, the Monetary Authority wouldn't have time to stabilize the situation. Then the panic would be our fault, instead of the fault of those fools at TransPac and Lobo Global."

"Do you want me to go over to the Monetary Authority with Rick?" I asked.

"No, I want to keep Coldstream out of this as much as possible," Walmsley said. "Rick, you're the local guy and you can deal with the Monetary Authority by yourself. I don't want a big Coldstream delegation there."

"If Tang wants any help on valuing the assets as he's making his decisions about saving TransPac, you can just call me, Rick, and I'll swing into action."

Houghton looked sheepishly at me. "Thanks, Dusty," he said.

Walmsley spoke again. "Ted, why don't you get some sleep?" he said. "You're off the deal, and I want you out of Hong Kong on the first flight."

McKee hung up the phone and left.

"Are we squared away?" Walmsley asked. Houghton and I looked at each other.

"We're good to go, Jim," I said.

We rang off and Houghton and I lowered our phones.

"I'm sorry about all that," Houghton said.

I extended my hand. "No problem. We're all just trying to do our jobs," I said.

When Houghton had had a little sleep and got a chance to put all the pieces together properly, he would realize the TransPac acquisition was whistled dead at five o'clock the day before. The only thing left to do after that, which was what I had been trying to do, was to ensure TransPac's collapse didn't put Asia back a generation.

Houghton left, and I closed the door of my suite and walked back across the sitting room to the closed bedroom door. It wasn't clear what good it would have done Nin to have his sister reporting our part of the conversation to him, but I wanted to know how much Jacqueline had overheard.

I opened the door.

Jacqueline was curled up on the bed, the bedspread pulled up to her bare shoulder, her lush hair cascading over a forearm, asleep.

All the tension and paranoia I had felt vanished in an instant. Jacqueline wasn't a player, I thought, looking tenderly at her as the covers rose and fell gently with her breathing. She wasn't some ruthless seductress playing for hundreds of millions. She was a loyal sister, trying to do what she could for her brother in a tough situation. I suddenly felt totally exhausted.

I closed the door and went back into the sitting room. I took off my shoes and my necktie, cut a cigar, put my feet up on the ottoman and burned the cigar as I looked out on the darkened vista of Hong Kong. By that time of the morning, almost all the lights are turned off, leaving just the orange sodium lights of the expressways and the aircraft warning lights on the tops of the buildings. At that time of the night, Hong Kong looms indistinctly in the darkness, its famous office towers, just barely visible, hulking beneath the invisible Peak.

The cigar was half burned when I heard a trilling noise on the other side of the bedroom door. I was exhausted, and I didn't react at first. When I heard it again, I hauled myself out of the armchair and moved wearily across the sitting room. The trilling continued.

As I opened the door, Jacqueline was sitting up in bed, holding the bedspread to herself, saying "Hello?" into her mobile phone.

"Sebastian!" she cried. "What's wrong?"

"Oh no! . . . Are you alright? You poor darling! Yes, of course! Where are you? Yes, I'll be right down!"

Jacqueline leaped out of bed and hurriedly began to dress. "Someone tried to shoot Sebastian!"

"What?"

"He's covered in blood!"

"Covered in blood! How could he speak? Where is he?"

"Down at the Kowloon police station. The blood isn't his; it's from the other guy."

"He shot the other guy?" I asked.

"I don't know. I don't think so," Jacqueline said, her eyes wide.

I had my shoes and necktie back on. "I'm coming with you."

Jacqueline hesitated for a moment. "Okay," she said.

CHAPTER THIRTY-THREE

THERE WAS NO TIME TO ORGANIZE better transportation, so we caught a taxi downstairs. Jacqueline sat tensely in the taxi, urging on the driver in Chinese, hitting the back of the seat with her fist.

We hurtled along the almost empty roads, bathed in orange light, the doors of the old taxi rattling and wind whistling and hissing through the door jambs and along the windows.

The taxi plunged into the ugliness of Kowloon, rushing up empty boulevards and taking sharp, skidding turns across empty intersections. Twenty minutes later, we pulled up in front of a big blank building with the blue and white police checkerboard emblems lit up over huge doors. Jacqueline thrust some money at the driver, snapped something at him in Chinese, and pushed the door open.

I hurried behind her as she ran up the steps and accosted the first uniformed person she saw. In a flurry of Chinese, pointing in a couple of directions, she learned what she wanted.

"Come on," she said, hardly looking over her shoulder at me.

We went up a lift to the next floor and got out. Behind a counter like a shabby bank teller station was a uniformed police clerk. Police officers loitered in the area on the other side of the counter, talking and looking at papers.

Jacqueline spoke to the clerk. We were apparently directed to sign in and did so. I provided as little information as possible, giving only my first initial and the Peninsula Hotel as my address. It wouldn't look good.

A police officer appeared from a door and motioned for us to follow him down a hallway to left. Jacqueline in a demanding tone asked him something and the officer answered her briefly.

"What did he say?" I asked.

"He said that Sebastian isn't hurt. He was being held as a material witness but is now free to go."

The officer opened a room with a key and motioned for us to go in. Sebastian was sitting in a plastic chair next to a small table. An empty tea cup was on the table, and next to it, his nervous hand was tapping a skittish, insistent rhythm against the table.

Jacqueline rushed in. "Darling, are you hurt?" she cried, her heels clicking across the linoleum floor.

Sebastian looked small and somehow wrecked in his chair. His skin was gray, and there were dark circles under his eyes. Big dark splotches on his shirt, the size of outstretched hands, looked like blood. As we walked closer, I could see that the hair on the left side of his head looked stuck together with dried blood, and there was a smear along the left side of his jaw where blood had been partially wiped away.

Sebastian himself looked at us dully. There was a flicker in his eyes as he saw me, but his expression didn't change.

Jacqueline embraced him. He managed to get his hands up to her upper arm, but otherwise he hardly moved. When she stepped back from him, his face still wore the same expression it had before.

"They shot Pelham." He waved his hand in front of himself. "This is all his," he said, with a silly grin.

Jacqueline pulled a chair over and sat down next to Sebastian, placing an arm around his shoulders, with her other hand holding his hand.

"Darling, are you hurt anywhere?"

Sebastian shook his head. "I'm fine," he said. The grin appeared again. "I feel good."

"Sebastian, you're in shock," I said. "We need to get you to a doctor. At the least, you need a sedative and some rest.

"Darling, tell me, how did it happen?"

"I don't know," he said. "Pelham and I went out after we signed the papers. He wanted to go to his favorite nightclubs and stare at naked girls. Pelham was a classy guy, first class, number one. Just after two o'clock in the morning, we came out of one and were looking for a taxi when a car pulled up in front of us. Two Chinese guys jumped out and ran up to us with pistols. I thought they were pointed at me. Without a word, they started firing. They shot Pelham many times. He was so drunk he didn't know what was happening. It all happened so fast.

"God, there was a lot of blood," said Nin, looking down. "The police took my jacket. It was soaked with his blood." He held up his free hand. "I think I got most of it off. It's only under my fingernails now."

He looked at Jacqueline. "He kind of fell against me, you know. He was groaning, or sighing. Not for long. We both fell to the sidewalk under his weight."

It seemed strange. "Could you tell if they wanted to shoot you? Did you do anything that saved you?" I asked.

Sebastian looked dully at me. "I don't know," he said. "I don't think so. It all happened so fast. I've never seen a gun pointed at me before. I thought they were pointing at me."

"How many times was Pelham hit?" I asked.

"The police said eight times."

"Was there anyone else one around?"

"No," said Sebastian.

"No, they didn't intend to kill you," I said. "That should be some comfort to you. Otherwise, they'd have done it. But you'd better figure out what message it was that they meant to send you."

"I don't have any idea who did this," Sebastian said. "Or why."

"Were you keeping in touch with your London office last night?" I asked.

"No," he said. "I was busy negotiating the sale of TransPac to its new owners, and then Pelham and I took off to celebrate."

"Don't worry," Jacqueline was murmuring to Sebastian, her lips close to his ear. She stroked his hair. "Everything is going to be alright, darling."

Slowly, over the course of several minutes, Nin's expression began to change as his features gathered into a frown, and finally into a deep scowl. He stared down at the floor for some time before he looked up at me. The look in his eye chilled me.

"What happened in London last night?" he said slowly and distinctly.

"You need rest, Sebastian," I said.

"Go fuck yourself. I asked you a question."

Jacqueline tried to soothe him, but Sebastian angrily tossed his head as he continued to glare at me. "Well?"

I shrugged. "The market's dumping TransPac bonds. Someone put the rumor out that TransPac was about to make mass layoffs in a last-ditch effort to downsize and avoid bankruptcy."

Sebastian's face suddenly went dark. The change from the grayish color was a shock to see, and probably wasn't healthy. "That's a lie!" he cried. "We've just stitched up a deal with Three Dragons and Lobo Global, and TransPac is safe! Everything is perfectly fine! And it's mine!"

"What's left of it is yours," I agreed. "But those rumors and the dropping bond price will cause a bank run on TransPac's lines of credit this morning. I'm afraid TransPac is going to fall over today."

Jacqueline spun her head and looked at me in shock. Brother and sister stared at me for an instant. An identical look of fury crossed their faces.

"You did this," said Sebastian.

"No, I didn't. I'm afraid it looks like the rumors came from TransPac itself."

"What do you mean?" demanded Sebastian.

"You know the deal you did last night, I don't. But if you screwed the other TransPac directors to the wall, you wouldn't have left them much incentive to see TransPac get safely through the crisis."

"Entrekin would never have done it," said Nin. "TransPac was his child, his hope and dream."

"No, that's probably right."

"And Pelham was with me all night. Anyway, he had every reason to want TransPac to stay afloat. I got him a great deal. He'll never see a penny of it now."

"You may not either," I said. "For different reasons, thank God."

"Don't be horrible!" said Jacqueline to me with a furious glare. "How could you have let this happen?"

"That leaves Cartwright and Jones," said Nin. "They could have done it. They had nothing to lose."

"That's your fault, Sebastian," I said.

"Oh, don't blame this on me, you fucking asshole."

"Oh darling," said Jacqueline, and hugged her brother. Then she sat up suddenly. "Did those awful men have Pelham killed?"

Nin looked at me.

"No, I don't think so," I said. "I'm not sure exactly what happened, but my guess is one or more of the people who were ruined by the deal Sebastian did with his new friends called their contacts in the London market and spread the rumors that TransPac was about to go bankrupt.

"We found out about those rumors at Coldstream London and New York, and they called me. That's how I know. I don't think Three Dragons would have had any idea that something like this could happen. They're a bunch of Red Army guys who don't know how global capital markets work, and they wouldn't have had access to the market rumors or been able to see the price of TransPac bonds falling anyway. But Lobo Global would have. They would have picked it up and called their Hong Kong office. Dorfman would have gotten through to Three Dragons and explained what was happening. Then—I'm not sure at this point—it looks like Three Dragons took matters into their own hands.

"As you know, an 'economic crime' involving much less than a million dollars can earn a person a bullet in the back of the head from the Chinese Communist justice system on the mainland. Three Dragons and Lobo Global stand to lose almost all of the hundred million they invested just a couple of days ago in TransPac bonds. I think Three Dragons figured they'd been double-crossed and decided to start administering quick justice."

"Why didn't they"—Jacqueline shuddered—"try to shoot Sebastian?"

"I'm not sure," I said. "Maybe because they're smart enough to realize he's worth more to them alive than dead if they are to have any hope of getting some of their money back."

Sebastian stood up. "I don't believe a word of this. For all I know, you and Entrekin cooked this up between yourselves and put the hit on Pelham."

"Don't be absurd, Sebastian," I said.

"Come on, Jackie, let's go," Sebastian said. "I've got to get to my desk and start getting a hold of people."

"You're in no condition to do that," I said.

Sebastian stepped close to me and put up a finger on my chest. "I'm going to kill you," he said.

"Better bring help," I said.

I walked with them as they left the room and walked back down the hallway. We signed out at the counter, where Sebastian was given a plastic bag with his wallet, mobile phone, fountain pen, PDA, and other paraphernalia he had had in his bloodstained suit coat, which the police were going to keep as material evidence of the murder.

We went down the lift silently and outside the station building. Gray dawn light uncertainly illuminated the streets and low buildings of Kowloon. We walked up to a taxi stand and Nin got in, moving haltingly with Jacqueline's assistance.

Jacqueline started to get into the taxi. A long graceful leg was still outside, her foot resting on the pavement. Then she turned and looked up at me. She looked tired in the early morning light, her magnificent eyes burning.

"Goodbye, Dusty."

I saw tears welling in her eyes.

"This time forever."

I closed the door for Jacqueline and watched her taxi disappear into traffic.

CHAPTER THIRTY-FOUR

I CAUGHT ANOTHER TAXI BACK to the Peninsula, calling Houghton and Walmsley on the way. Arrangements were in place for the Hong Kong Monetary Authority to acquire TransPac when it became clear the international banks were going to suck all the liquidity out of TransPac. As it turned out, it didn't take long.

I went back to the hotel, showered, shaved, and changed into fresh clothes. I went over to TransPac and went looking for Entrekin. I couldn't find him. I heard Nin was still at his post on the trading floor, trying to save TransPac single-handedly. The guy had guts.

I went to the trading floor a little after nine thirty. Banks were calling up and demanding payment of their interbank lines, but with all their exotic bonds worth a fraction of what they had been trading for a month ago, TransPac didn't have the cash. It was clear TransPac was going bankrupt unless the Hong Kong Monetary Authority intervened.

Nin seemed outwardly calm. He obviously had had a change of clothes at the office, and he'd shaved. When I saw him, he was out on the trading floor among his people, doing everything he could as the disaster took shape. When banks would call up demanding repayment of their funding lines, he had the call transferred into his office and took it behind the closed door.

This was the last stand of TransPac. I sat down at one of the trading positions as Nin's troops were overwhelmed by the markets. One by one his traders put down their headsets and sat motionlessly, some with their eyes closed, some staring blankly into space. A few were crying, their heads down on their desks.

Within an hour, Nin was moving mechanically and he had a set stare in his eye. Even he knew it was hopeless. The magnitude of the currency crisis had wiped out TransPac's assets and left more than a billion US dollars' worth of bank lines that would have to be repaid by an acquirer.

A very pretty young woman came up to Nin and told him that the head of treasury from a major international bank was on the line.

"I don't want to talk to him," Nin said. "I've spoken to him five times this morning."

"He insists," she said.

"Fuck him."

"He said if you don't talk to him, he's calling the *Financial Times*."

Nin took the call, savagely stabbing with his finger the button for one of the lines on the console. "Yeah, what?"

Nin rolled his eyes as he listened. "Listen, I told you, I know what people are saying, but we are right at close on a major transaction that will deal with all those concerns. We're about to be acquired by a major New York institution."

"Hey, you can't say that," I said.

He waved me away. "Yes, very major, AAA, within the next twenty-four hours—"

"You can't *say* that," I said, raising my voice.

Nin whirled and cupped the phone. "Try and stop me!" he screamed in my face.

"It's not true!" I shouted. "I can't let you say those things."

Nin was saying. "Listen, Chuck, I gotta go. Yes, they'll be guaranteeing our lines. They'll take you out if you insist. But why would you?"

"Sebastian, you lied to the guy," I said.

"Oh, fuck off. Like you're the one to point it out."

"They'll have you on tape, you know that, with a time stamp. You need to stop—you no longer know what you're saying or doing. It's just not worth it, Sebastian. You could go to jail for staying that kind of stuff at this point."

Sebastian looked at me. "Who knows what's true."

"It's over," I said. I turned away and went back to the War Room to help the guys finish cleaning up.

Before I left, I went back down to the trading floor and found Sebastian staring out a window. The announcement had come across Bloomberg and Reuters that the Hong Kong Monetary Authority had acquired TransPac for one Hong Kong dollar. All shareholders had been wiped out to the last cent. Negotiations would begin shortly with the banks who had provided funding lines to TransPac. They didn't have a chance of being paid out in full unless the Monetary Authority decided to stand behind TransPac's obligations; it looked like TransPac would be dismembered.

Sebastian could see my reflection in the window as I approached him. He turned slowly, looking at me dully.

Craig Chin had gotten something else wrong. Sebastian hadn't been attracted to me when we were young: he was competitive with me. He still was, after all these years. I wasn't sure I had won this time, but Sebastian had certainly lost.

"I'm leaving tomorrow morning," I said. "Let's talk things over at dinner tonight. Just the two of us."

What else had Craig got wrong? Was it really Sebastian who had sent the Australian woman to meet me in the health club, or was it Entrekin? Or somebody else? I decided to reach out to Winston one last time; there might be something else, and he might be willing to tell me.

Nin chose the restaurant. Its décor was traditional Chinese, with lots of lacquer and gilt, and picture frames studded with semi-precious stones.

"Best food in Hong Kong," said Sebastian.

I nodded. My suggestion of dinner had been a test; if Sebastian had been surprised but eventually agreed, I would have guessed we still had a chance of parting on good terms. When he agreed instantly and without arguing, I guessed he'd decided I had just handed him an opportunity he hadn't expected on a silver platter.

The place had a funny air about it. It seemed seedy, despite the gilt and the jade. It felt like the kind of place where anything could happen.

Nin ordered single malts and rapidly instructed the waiter in Chinese what to bring us from the menu.

"To old friends," he toasted.

"To old friends," I repeated.

"Thank you for bringing me together with Jacqueline again."

"Oh, sure," he said. His face was expressionless.

"It's strange to think how life turned out."

"Yeah, you never know when you're going to run into a lying, double-crossing son of a bitch again," said Sebastian.

"True, but I've decided you're not all bad," I said. More importantly, I had come to realize, I had accounts to settle with Houghton.

Nin glowered at me.

"Nobody could have done that deal," I said. "Not with you guys at one another's throats."

Nin looked at me, reddening.

"It was too hard," I said.

"What about Jacqueline?"

I sighed. After a while, I said, "What about Jacqueline? She's someone else's wife."

"That didn't stop you from fucking around with her," he said.

There was nothing to say.

"I knew you were chicken shit," he said.

Nin stared at me.

"Sebastian, I had to cut TransPac loose from Coldstream, but I'm not cutting you loose," I said. "I'll do whatever I can to help you. I think you can still get a good job in New York."

"I've never wanted anything to do with you, and I don't now." He looked down. "What the hell. It was a beautiful thing. You didn't deserve to buy it. You didn't have the vision."

We ate in glum silence. The food was good enough, and we had several whiskeys before I noticed Sebastian's cheeks were flushed.

I remembered Jacqueline never drank when we were young. We had had a glass of champagne together once and her cheeks went bright red; she said she felt like she was burning. She explained to me later that some Asians could not metabolize alcohol. Maybe it was something she had outgrown.

Sebastian's eyes were shining. "I should have fucked *your* sister!" he cried. "I should have fucked you the way you fucked me!"

"Sebastian, I didn't sleep with Jacqueline."

"You want me to start believing you this late in life? Forget it," Nin said slowly and deliberately, "you bastard."

I couldn't hold it against him, really. After Jacqueline and I had picked him up at four o'clock in the morning at the police station, he had the right to think anything he wanted to about me. And Nin had gone from being worth more than a hundred million dollars US to bankrupt in a few months. It was too much to take.

"One more round," he said, turning in his seat and waving at the waiter.

"Not a good idea," I said.

He spoke rapid Cantonese to the waiter and then turned to me with a smile. "I insist."

The drinks appeared, bright red liqueurs.

"Tiananmen tanks," he said.

"I need to go to the men's room," I said. "Pardon me."

From the men's room I called the hotel and told them to send a sedan to the restaurant. The concierge said "Where?" after I gave the name of the restaurant.

I couldn't tell if my accent was thick, or if he was surprised. Then I rang the restaurant and asked to speak to Mr. Sebastian Nin. I put the call on hold and slipped the phone back into my suit pocket.

As I returned to the table, the waiter approached and whispered something to Nin. "I have to take a phone call," he said thickly.

I sat down. The two drinks were untouched. I switched them.

Nin returned with a thoughtful frown on his face.

He sat down, raised his drink, and said "Let bygones be bygones."

We drank. "Shall we get the bill?" I asked.

"It's my pleasure," he said, signaling the waiter.

He looked at me keenly once or twice after he handed his TransPac credit card to the waiter.

The last time that card will be valid, I thought. If it still is.

Nin looked up again with a surprised expression as he signed the bill, and suddenly he pitched forward on the table.

I could see the waiter looking at us, uncertain what to do. The maitre d' barked something at him and the waiter hurried over as two men burst out of the kitchen and stood over Nin, looking down on his back stretched across our table.

I stood up and allowed a pleasant smile to appear on my face. I nodded briskly to the men and walked outside, where one of the hotel's lovely old Rolls Royce Silver Shadows had just arrived for me.

CHAPTER THIRTY-FIVE

THE NEXT MORNING, on my way to meet with Houghton at the Hong Kong offices of Coldstream, I thought back to the last time I spoke with Jacqueline, twenty years before we met again in Hong Kong.

When my family left Hong Kong, we moved to Paris and finally to Cairo in the years before I went to university. Jacqueline and I continued to write to each other. We continued to write until our senior year in university and, occasionally, to telephone each other, sometimes late at night. The last time I spoke to her, under tremendous strain after my father's company was forced into bankruptcy, largely in consequence of the bitter divorce being litigated by my parents—and having just found out from my grandparents that my real mother had died giving birth to me—I rang Jacqueline late at night. I was a mixture of the deepest anxiety about our family's financial future and my own rapidly dimming prospects, while also filled with an abundance of the wildest elation and joy at learning the woman who had raised me was not my mother. I was unfathomable to myself.

I woke her up. Her voice was sleepy and irritated. "Do you stay in touch with anybody else like this?" she asked.

As it happened, Craig Chin, our mutual friend from our old school in Hong Kong, was staying in my apartment for a week-long visit while he interviewed with Cornell Medical school. For a moment I considered mentioning it.

"I'm sorry I called," I said. "Goodbye."

Then I wrote her that letter and I didn't speak to her again until Sebastian brought us together in Hong Kong. Jacqueline had probably been right that night on the telephone. What was difficult to understand was why I had reacted the way I had done.

Perhaps that, too, was a decision my parents had made for me, like the time they declined the Nins' invitation to bring me to Phuket. The harshness I had learned from them, the willingness to hurt those you love, the rigid defense of a position that has no merit, perhaps they were lurking like sea monsters below the waves as I trimmed my sails and charted a course that for many years took me so far, far away from Jacqueline. Perhaps these were some of the lessons with which I left my childhood.

But perhaps I actually didn't love Jacqueline the way I had thought for twenty-five years. How could I have hung up on her, and written Jacqueline that letter in the language of my parents if I had truly loved her? I was too young back then to know myself or understand my feelings—and she was too. Perhaps I was too young to love back then. I was probably right all those years to resist looking her up. It would have been easy to do—I could have found her with very little trouble. Craig and I had stayed friends, and all I had to do was ask. The fact he thought she was in Seattle instead of San Francisco was probably a slip of the tongue.

In a way it was amazing we hadn't accidentally run across one another before I returned to Hong Kong for the TransPac deal. But we were part of one another's early lives, and that's where we had stayed. Jacqueline was part of my childhood, a part, however indirectly, of those terrible lessons, and I had to set a course on the sea of life that would help me find healing from someone with enough love and enough courage, and perhaps most importantly, with a different past who had other lessons I could learn. When I found that person, I knew it, because I loved her— or I was learning to love her. I was trying to learn.

And something else: at some point, life almost imperceptibly passes into memory, sometimes even when you're still in the middle of the experience. And our memories are like flaming pyres in the night, inextinguishable, burning soundlessly on a vast plain. It's our mistake if we choose to navigate by them through the darkness of our lives.

I wasn't going to make that mistake. What had happened between us in Hong Kong was meaningless. She was loyal to her brother, and probably bored. I was tired and stressed, and looking for a way to make amends for what was fundamentally a trivial incident that Sebastian and I should have forgotten decades ago.

The truth was I had never loved Jacqueline. I knew that now.

That's what I told myself.

Chapter Thirty-Six

"**Give me The Phone,**" I said when I walked into Houghton's office.

He was drawn but composed, and his expression didn't change when he heard what I said. "Fuck off."

"I'm not going to ask again," I said. The Phone was an untraceable mobile phone. It could only be used once. Every major Coldstream office around the world had one, under the direct control of the managing director or senior country officer. They were part of the emergency management protocols, along with secure, expedited access, in most jurisdictions, to local lawyers, cash, and weapons.

"Are you going to call Walmsley?"

"Why would I call Walmsley on The Phone?"

Houghton considered this. He looked ill this morning.

"Okay," he said. "But I want to hear the phone call."

"No problem," I said. "I want you to hear it."

Houghton stood up and walked over to where a safe was hidden in the wall, and within a few minutes the phone, a nondescript Samsung, was in my hand.

I dialed, hung up, dialed again and hung up, and then dialed one more time and let it go through to Winston.

"Yes?" he answered nervously.

"My friend Craig Chin reported to you that the identities we discussed were personal associates of Mr. Richard Houghton, did he not?"

I spoke formally so that Houghton, who had no idea who I was talking to, wouldn't guess it was Winston.

"That's right," Winston said.

"Thanks, that's all," I said.

Craig hadn't known how to interpret the information he had learned because he didn't understand investment banking. He'd been a bit vague on details anyway: for example, he'd thought Jacqueline was living in Seattle when she was living in San Francisco. Perhaps inevitably, he garbled the market information he'd overheard.

He'd risked his life to warn me about the wrong guy. I took out the SIM card and broke it into little pieces so there would be no record of the telephone number I had dialed and put the phone on Houghton's desk. "For the trash compactor," I said.

It wasn't Sebastian Nin.

Houghton's face was very pale.

"So it was you who had my friend Craig killed," I said. "He knew the men who were the unacceptable investors in the short-term unsecured debt of TransPac, and he knew from your wife that three happened to be close friends of yours. After our meeting with Tang, I went back and looked at the balance sheet of TransPac, and I saw that over a quarter billion in short-term securities was repaid yesterday to the very entities Tang asked about. That was the majority of the cash TransPac had left, even after the bond prepayment program I dreamed up."

"So?" Houghton said impassively.

"When I arrived here, you wanted that deal done for lots of reasons, but one of those reasons was because you knew that three of your most dangerous friends had money at risk through their disguised investments in TransPac. You wanted me to close the acquisition so Coldstream would fund any shortfall and protect your friends. You had Craig killed to make sure it happened. You probably knew my first thought would be that Sebastian was behind it, but he had nothing to do with those investments and nothing to do with Craig's murder.

"When TransPac went south a couple days ago, you suddenly realized your life was at risk. I'm sure you've done lots of good things for one another over the years, and they have every interest in cultivating an influential *gweilo* friend like you, but a quarter of a billion dollars is a lot of money."

"That's when you started pushing me hard and threatened to destroy me. But I solved your problem: my idea got more than enough cash in the door to repay your friends. I'm sure the HKMA is going to have a look at those transfers and will probably try to claw them back, but that's going to be tough. The banks are sure as hell not going to tell your friends they have to cough it up. They might just write it off publicly as losses on the collapse of TransPac and move on. I'm sure that money is in the Cayman Islands or who knows where already."

"Maybe you put the hit on Pelham too. But my bet is that one of your friends did that independently—just to encourage anybody else thinking of bad-mouthing TransPac to keep their mouths shut. Or maybe it was Zhu at Three Dragons, I don't know."

"You're mad," said Houghton.

"No, I'm not."

"You can't prove any of this," he said.

"Well, that's different," I said. "You're probably right about that. I can demonstrate the transfers took place, and to whom, and when—and with some investigative work I can probably create the causal link. The murders? I'm not a cop."

"Nothing you described is illegal," Houghton said. "Short-term paper matured and was paid out instead of rolled over. That's normal business."

"Not when it happened yesterday, it wasn't," I said. "There was nothing normal about yesterday."

"I'll ignore the crazy stuff you said about the killings," Houghton said. "I can see why they hit you hard. Especially your friend. But they had nothing to do with me."

"Each piece of the financial moves looks legal," I agreed. "But the pattern is ugly, immoral, and illegal—and people were killed to try and get this deal closed."

"You've cracked under stress," Houghton said coolly. "What you need is sleep. And you can apologize to me when your brain functions normally again. We're colleagues. I'm not going to hold this against you."

I smiled. "A lot of things will work out fine for you if you're voted into Walmsley's seat next year. Your banking friends here could take an eye-watering hit. Your dangerous friends must know how close you came to losing their hard-earned cash. They've all got a stake in seeing you continue to prosper—so that you'll be in a position to make them whole again after your fuckups this week."

"If you make any of these defamatory allegations before, during or after the partnership voting, I'll sue you for everything you're worth," Houghton said.

It was true that I would need the full investigative powers of at least two jurisdictions at my disposal to begin to establish the facts what I now knew to be true. But markets were in a full-fledged global financial crisis. I doubted even Walmsley would give me internal resources—how could I make my case to the Fed or the HKMA? What chance did I have of convincing a DA to investigate? I had discovered a truth nobody wanted to know about. I would never be given the time or the resources to prove it.

Houghton smiled.

I knew what he was thinking: I was just an M & A guy.

"Well, you won't have my vote," I said.

I knew where this was going. Houghton would spend the next year pretending he was my best friend and biggest supporter among the partners, while secretly trying to force me out of Coldstream.

I stood up. "You better hope I live a long, healthy life, Rick—because my lawyers are going to have a full sworn deposition from me with all the data from this week, and in the event of my death, I'll leave instructions to open the material and make it available to a wide variety of regulatory officials and press outlets. Even if I die of cancer, or a ski accident, or an eagle drops a turtle on my head—no matter what the cause—the minute my body is cold you can kiss your reputation goodbye, and maybe your liberty."

Houghton laughed. "Get some sleep, Dusty."

On my way back to the empty War Room, I called my wife to tell her I was coming home. I told her I had lots to tell her but that I would save it for when I got back.

"Like what?" she said, sounding bored.

"Oh, I promise to tell you everything," I said. "But for starters, I'm going to ask Walmsley if I can open an office in Sydney for Coldstream Holdings."

"Really?" she cried.

"Really."

"Finally."

It would put me in AsiaPac, Houghton's sphere of influence, but I had a feeling I needed to go to ground, and Sydney was about as far away from Coldstream New York as I could get without starting to get closer again. And maybe in Sydney I could somehow continue to pursue justice for Craig, and Pelham. I wasn't sure how, but doing anything from New York seemed pointless.

I spent the rest of my afternoon dictating a detailed sworn deposition and then getting it notarized and emailed to my lawyers with full confidential instructions.

I didn't see Sebastian again before I left Hong Kong. He was okay medically as it turned out. He ended up in hospital for a couple of days, and that way he missed the bankruptcy of TransPac and the physical takeover by the Monetary Authority. It wasn't the stuff in the drink that would have done the damage, it was what he was likely to have organized for me once I was unconscious.

Jacqueline and her daughter Anaïs were gone, on their way back to San Francisco. At least that's what her mother said when I rang.

The next morning I caught a flight back to New York. As utterly exhausted as I felt, it was such a relief to know I didn't love Jacqueline Nin and never had. Her beauty, her mind, the way our souls had shaped one another—none of it meant anything.

Once I boarded the flight and settled into my seat, I found myself staring out the porthole at the baggage handling machines whirling around on the tarmac in the pouring rain. Just as they had done yesterday and would do tomorrow, and tomorrow, and the tomorrow after that.

Requiescat in pace, Craig, I thought.

The 747 pushed back from the gate and taxied out onto the runway. Then I felt its great stately turn and the sudden roar of the engines. The vast interior shuddered as the aircraft accelerated, sweeping away the events of the last week as it rumbled down the runway and hurtled me toward the rest of my life. I felt it heave up onto the rushing wind and lift off, bearing me back to my wife and children.

Made in the USA
Las Vegas, NV
27 November 2021

35419273R10151